BLIND WOMAN'S BUFF

BLIND WOMAN'S BUFF

Reinhard Tenberg

YOUCAXTON
PUBLICATIONS

ISBN 978-1-914424-71-7
Printed and bound in Great Britain.
Published by Reinhard Tenberg 2022
YouCaxton Publications

The only thing worse than being blind is having sight but no vision.

Helen Keller

Perhaps only in a world of the blind will things be what they truly are.

José Saramago

Chapter 1

Jenny

'Roll! Come on, Paul, *roll!*' she shouts to her cameraman.

I watch the video clip for the first time. The top right-hand corner displays the date and time stamp of the recording: 12 September 2012, 11.20 a.m. There she stands, my sister Hannah, tall and slim, tatty black jacket, skinny jeans and hiking boots. Clutching her notebook and pen with one hand, the other shielding her face with a scarf from the whirled-up sand. A helicopter has just taken off, throwing up the dust and obscuring the view like a desert sandstorm. Paul keeps on rolling, not sure which direction to point his camera. The sandy haze clears slowly, revealing the Syrian ghost town of Haswiyeh. The camera pans across to Hannah as she steps away from the pick-up truck.

'We're trying to reach the women and children who've been abandoned here for weeks,' she narrates to camera, walking briskly towards the ruins.

All seems calm. Not a sound.

In the far distance, a small figure melts into the picture. Is he approaching her? A voice from the truck shouts. 'Wait, Hannah, for God's sake. We need to check for IEDs first.' The camera zooms in on the distant figure, a boy no older than 13, maybe 14.

'What the fuck …? Come back – now!' the man in the truck yells loudly. 'He's wearing a suicide belt. Prepare to fire!'

Hannah and her cameraman move on steadily. Judging by the sound track, they're now out of earshot. The boy is moving towards them. A second figure, clutching her hijab, runs frantically from the opposite direction, towards the boy, desperate to catch up.

'Ahmed. Ahmed! Come back … come back! You don't have to do this,' she shouts.

When Hannah realises what is happening, she turns round, waves her arms about frantically, trying to signal that her colleagues should hold fire. The woman has caught up with the child and flings her arms around him.

'No shoot, please – we get vest off him,' she pleads to Hannah, who is now getting closer. But, as the first shot from the truck rings out and hits the boy's shoulder, he presses the red button. The explosion violently jolts the camera, which falls to the ground and lands on the sand at an angle, still filming. I catch a glimpse of Paul kneeling over Hannah. He is holding his hand over his right ear in agony. And, then, another shout above the noise of the falling debris.

'You OK? You alright? Hannah … Paul? We're coming to get you out.' The last bit of the film turns fuzzy, then ends abruptly.

I turn off the video clip Paul sent me and push back in my armchair, my feet settling into the footrest. I reach out for my second glass of red, hand slightly shaky. I'm staring past my slippers towards the end of the room to a partial view of the recessed bookshelves cluttered with stacks of old *Observers*. Next to it, by the sash window, a small lithograph of *The Two Sisters* by Georges Lemmen, bought for me by Mum in an antique shop while visiting Bruges. Probably a fake. It depicts sisters Jenny and Berthe Serruys, with penetrating gazes and a commanding presence, yet it possesses little of the usual sentimentality of children's portraits. Although they are wearing identical dresses, it seems they have little else in common and are preoccupied by their own thoughts. I used to call Hannah 'Berthe', after one of them, which she hated (of course!).

I often wish we were closer. I always followed in my big sister's footsteps, envied her, admired her. But, even as a child, Hannah would hardly ever trust me with her secrets. Perhaps the three-year age gap was too big for her to consider me an equal. In some ways we were polar opposites. She would argue with Dad, put up a fight, but I would obey. I so much wanted to be like her: daring, rebellious, unconventional. She thought I was our mum's favourite and could never put a foot wrong – the 'goody-goody girl', as she called me, the one with a blonde ponytail and a good work ethic. Admittedly, I did work much harder at school than she did, but she was the clever one, sailing through with minimum effort and obtaining top marks in all subjects.

A few years ago, I gave up trying to compete with her professionally, and became more cautious on foreign journalist assignments. I had Mum's warnings ringing in my ears: 'Be careful – don't put yourself in unnecessary danger when you're abroad.' However, if there ever was any hostility from outside, Hannah and I would stick together and form a solid wall of defence. Today, there's still an understanding that our relationship is secure, that we will be there for one another whatever. And that's what matters most.

*****

North Wing, St Thomas' Hospital, London. A male nurse accompanies me to Bay 8 on the ward. I gulp when I see Hannah. Both eyes are covered by a bandage. She is wearing an oxygen mask and is attached to a variety of tubes. As I walk in, she stirs.

'Can someone take this bloody bandage off my eyes, please. It really hurts … Where am I?'

'Hey, Han. It's me. Jen.' I squeeze her hand gently, lean forward and give her a peck on the cheek. 'You were injured, but you're safe now. You're in hospital, in London.'

She turns her head in my direction, rather dazed, then asks in a panicky voice, 'Where's Paul? Is he alright?'

'Yes, he's fine. He'll come and see you as soon as he can.'

'What's this tube sticking out of my chest? And what's wrong with my eyes?'

'The doctor said you've got a punctured lung. They're going to do a CT scan to find out what's causing the problem with your eyes.'

'How bad is it? Tell me, Jen. And don't lie to me.'

'They really don't know yet. You'll be OK. Can I ask you something? Why did you go back into Haswiyeh when all the foreign journalists had left?'

'Did Paul save the film?' She coughs and cradles her ribcage. 'Shit, that hurts. Have they broadcast it?'

'Yes, it was the lead story on the *Channel 4 News*, obviously heavily edited. I think your boss wants a word with you. Why on earth didn't you turn back when he asked you to?'

'Oh, Eric – he's such a wuss. I just told him we were going back in, explained that the others had all gone, it was just Paul and me.' Then she mimicked with a wry smile, *Sorry Eric, poor connection, got to go.*

At the end of our conversation, she adopts her usual nonchalant tone. 'You know, Jen, if your pictures aren't close enough, you're not good enough.' No regrets there, then.

I clench my fists, I can hardly restrain myself. Surely we have to ask ourselves whether the level of risk is worth the story. I often wonder whether she is just reckless or I'm simply not brave enough. I had good reasons for not going to Syria. I'd finished my report on Syrian refugees in Beirut and my *Observer* editor felt it was high time I got out, so I took his advice and flew back to London.

Two days later, we are all shocked when we hear the CT scan results. The explosion has caused haemorrhaging and a blood clot has formed behind Hannah's eyes. She has, at least temporarily, lost her sight. The surgeon explains that she needs to recover from the traumatic pneumothorax – the lung puncture – before he can operate on her eyes. Four to six weeks is his prognosis. This news, somewhat inevitably, is met with a long burst of expletives from Hannah.

I'm devastated. I need to talk to friends Cathy and Emily.

The next day, we meet in a café not far from the hospital – a stripped-pine and sugar-free carrot cake type of place, busy and full of yummy mummies around lunchtime, and it doesn't have any newspapers.

They have managed to grab a small table in the far corner.

'So, how's she doing?' Emily pulls up a chair for me. She frowns, eyebrows angled upwards in expectation. Cathy puts down her coffee cup and leans forward.

'D'you know, I'm not sure she feels sorry for herself or has any regrets. She's just fuming she can't have the eye operation straight away. All she cared about when she woke up was if Paul was OK and had saved the film, and whether it had been broadcast. She even asked me not to tell Mum and Dad she's in hospital, as it would spoil their Mediterranean cruise!'

'My God! That's so weird. She must be in so much pain, and all she's thinking about is whether the report went live. What are the chances of her regaining her sight?' Emily asks.

'Jen, I'm so sorry,' Cathy butts in. 'That's really awful. How are *you* coping with it all?'

'I don't know how I feel. Angry, sad, fed up with her. And yet somehow strangely proud of her, what she has achieved, the women and children she has saved through her news story. I feel anxious for her and Rob's future, though. We don't know yet, but what if she *does* lose her eyesight?'

'Well, it would be the end of her career,' Emily gasps. 'D'you think Rob would look after her?'

'I should very much think so. He's always stuck by her. I'm sure he loves her. Listen, do you think I should phone our parents?'

6

They both just look at each other, shrugging their shoulders.

'By the way, I forgot to tell you. Do you know what she called her boss? "A wuss"! We all giggle at that. 'Apparently, he asked her why all the male journalists had left. She just said, "Well, Eric, that's men for you. They don't make them like they used to."'

'Hey, that's our girl!' Cathy shouts. We all applaud.

Rob, Hannah's fiancé, and I have become regular visitors at the hospital. One morning, when he and I bump into each other on Hannah's ward, he asks me for a private chat. I sense a certain urgency in his tone. We arrange to meet for coffee in our lunch break near my work in the Frontline Club in Paddington, favourite hangout of journalists and human rights activists.

'How's she coping, d'you think?' I begin.

'I'd say extremely badly. She can't wait to be discharged, and is pestering the surgeon to operate on her eyes now. She's only been in there a fortnight, for heaven's sake. What's even more worrying is that she's not looking forward to coming home. I know things haven't always been great between us, but ...' He leans back in his chair, folds his arms across his chest.

'Why wouldn't she want to come home?'

'Well, you know, she's fiercely independent. She hates not being in control. I sometimes don't see her for weeks when she's on one of her assignments abroad. I can't even talk to her on the phone. She always tells me it's too dangerous to even switch on her mobile or satellite phone. She claims it would allow the foreign security services to pinpoint her location, and that makes me feel even more on edge.'

'She's right about that, Rob, but I know how you feel. She has this urge to get the story out, no matter how dangerous the situation. I don't get it, either, this devil-may-care attitude to life, this tightrope she treads between bravery and bravado, but it's what she's like. Always has been.'

He nods, unfolds his arms. We pause, then both take a sip of our coffees. His expression turns from worried to sad, his eyes are welling up, his voice cracking a little.

'We were going to get married, for fuck's sake. Have a family, have children, lead a normal life. I told her many times, "You're pushing it, Hannah. Your luck's going to run out one day." I love her, Jen, but she can't keep doing this to me.'

I rest a consolatory hand on his. We sit for a while looking glum, just watching the people around us chatting away and laughing.

'You two can still have a family. Perhaps this will change her.'

'Yeah? And what if she doesn't get her eyesight back? She'll never be able to see her own child!'

'We don't know that. Let's not think about worst-case scenarios. Just wait and see. She might be OK after the op ... I'm so sorry, but I've got to go. Ring me later if you want – any time. I mean it.'

The sky is just one large grey flannel when I leave the Frontline Club – autumn beckons, and it's starting to rain.

I love the rain; it heightens the senses with steady drops of unspecified yearnings.

Do I share my big sister's feelings? We both love the independence and recognition our careers give us, but at the same time I long for security and the stability of family life, if there is such a thing. And deep down I think she does, too. She only drops her guard when she's had a bit too much to drink. Sometimes I feel being away from home for longer spells of time has taken its toll on my relationship with Hamish, too, though he rarely complains. Well, he does occasionally – when I stay out late with the girls and return home a bit worse for wear. Emily, Cathy and I usually meet up on the first Friday of the month for a girls' night out, to put the world to rights. Hannah sometimes joins us, and drinks us under the table.

'She'll never be able to see her own child!' Rob's words linger in my mind as I take the tube back home. How will she do her job? *Any* job? I bombard Hamish with my questions when I get back.

'So, you're planning for the worst possible scenario? Maybe we ought to see how the operation goes.'

'I know. I just can't help thinking about it. Didn't you have a partially sighted colleague at work once? How did he cope?'

'Erm … Oh, yes. Rupert. He's still there. Great guy. He does absolutely fine. He's got lots of gadgets. A large monitor with a screen reader. He dictates stuff into his smartphone and uses voice-to-text software, I think. Oh, and he makes his own coffee, using a liquid indicator. It just hooks on to his mug and pings when it's full!

Quite ingenious. Do you think I should get one for my Glenfiddich?'

'Shut up! Seriously, so you think she could actually—?'

'Of course she can carry on working as a journalist, but travelling to and reporting from war zones might be a wee bit tricky.'

'God, she'd hate being stuck in an office. She barely spends any time hot-desking at Channel 4 HQ – the "opaque glass cage", as she calls it. Can you imagine Hannah being at Eric's beck and call all day?'

'She'll have to get over her technophobia if she wants to stay independent. Have you seen her mobile? Some ancient Nokia brick from the previous century.'

I laugh. It reminds me of the time Hannah and I were mugged on our way home after a night out. They cleared out our handbags, but left Hannah's phone. There was a strong hint of smug self-satisfaction in her voice when she said, 'You see ...'

I stop short of Googling 'assistive technology for the blind' that evening and go to bed early, but still mulling over the what-ifs. How will she make notes? On telly, you never saw her without her pen and notebook. My big sister, the famous war correspondent! The other thing she's good at is writing dairies. Always has been. Well, until her accident. There were whole stacks of them in her flat, all incredibly detailed. I used to take the occasional peek when we were kids, wanting to know what she was up to. She must have been 13, 14, when she wrote about changing into a miniskirt in the park before getting on the school bus. She noted down exactly what she was wearing, which girl looked at which boy, which boy looked at her or returned her smile. Aged 16, the diary became a lot more intimate. Some nights she would abseil from the tree in front of her bedroom window, escape to have sex with her boyfriend and go skinny-dipping in his parents' pool. All noted down in precise salacious detail. I don't think our parents had a clue. How I envied my older rebel sister! Did she ever suspect me of reading her diaries?

What if? She won't be writing any more notebooks or diaries, and she'll be useless with a smartphone, screen reader or other helpful gadgets. In my mind, images float past of Hannah wearing dark sunglasses, hiding her wounded eyes, walking with a cane and wearing a high-vis armband saying 'Partially Sighted'. I'm still tossing and turning in bed when Hamish puts his arm round me and reassures me, 'It'll be alright, love. She's alive, and that's all that matters.'

On Sunday afternoon, I visit Hannah again. I've bought a bunch of heavily scented lilies in an attempt to disguise the all-pervading antiseptic smell, which she hates. It probably triggers memories of previous hospital confinements. Paul has been in touch with her over the phone, but is now sitting at her bedside chatting animatedly. I'm so pleased to see Hannah with a smile on her face, listening intently to his iPhone propped up on her bedside table.

'Hi, Jen. Good to see you.' Paul pauses the video on the phone for a moment and gives me a hug. 'Come and join us. I'm playing Hannah a recording of our Haswiyeh report. As shown on Channel 4 – pretty much unabridged.'

'Have you got a new perfume?' Hannah asks, when I kiss her on the cheek. 'It smells awful.'

I put the flowers to one side and sit down next to Paul. 'You OK?' I point to his heavily strapped-up calf.

'You'll have to talk a bit louder, I'm afraid. Perforated eardrum, from the pressure of the explosion.' I gesture to his leg again.

'Oh, *that*! A bit of shrapnel – ripped through my inner thigh, slashed the tendons and tore out a chunk of muscle. They stitched me together nicely, though, in Guy's up the road.'

Without further ado, he switches the video back on, adding a running commentary, pausing and describing each frame in great detail. Hannah sits up, listening intently, her head slightly inclined towards the phone.

'Look,' he says. 'I even got you dodging the bullets, running across to the hospital.'

'Did they edit out any scenes in the hospital?'

'None. They also broadcast your face-to-face interview with the surgeon, so none of Assad's friends could argue these were unconfirmed clips filmed by the Free Syrian Army. Our footage caused outrage amongst NATO allies. And you'll be pleased to know Eric gave the BBC permission to show the footage in their *Ten O'Clock News*, too. Well, I guess you know the rest: the ceasefire came two days later. We saved a lot of lives, mate!'

Hannah sinks back into her propped-up pillow and sighs.

'Paul, we've done some weird stuff together over the last few years, but this was the most dangerous fucking thing

I've ever done in my life.' With a false note of serenity, she added, 'Looking back on it, I'd say it was worth it.'

'Well, things could have been worse, Han. You could have been kidnapped for a ransom by the Jihadists, with nobody wanting to buy you back.' Hannah chokes to keep her laughter in check. You can sense the tremendous camaraderie between them. Years of exposure to the most dangerous situations have consolidated their bond.

I still don't understand why they wanted to go into Haswiyeh for a second time, when they'd already shot all the important footage several days before. The juvenile suicide bomber and the explosion only found their way into the news as a minor footnote at the end: 'Despite their injuries, Hannah Tring and her cameraman managed to escape from the besieged town.'

I'm not sure whether it is Paul's visit that causes havoc with her sleeping patterns, or the post-traumatic stress of recent events. Unable to fall asleep, she requests sleeping tablets every night. And during the day she often drifts off, her subconscious rerunning the days and weeks before the accident. I once witnessed her waking up in a cold sweat from one of her nightmares, and encouraged her to talk about it.

In one of her dreams, she's crawling through a tunnel, the secret lifeline to Haswiyeh, desperate to reach the starving women and children. Images of Paul and FSA fighters appear, dragging her, semi-conscious, out of the tunnel. The next moment she's running across the road to the hospital, dodging snipers and artillery shells. Then there are traumatised women carrying the bandaged and blood-soaked bodies of children on to the makeshift hospital ward.

She curls up in a ball of fear and stops talking.

'What happened next?' I encourage her to continue.

She mumbles anxiously, 'The boy and his mother!' She holds her breath and covers her ears with both hands.

I stroke her head, to comfort her. We hug in silence. I let her head fall gently back on to the pillow. I imagine tens of camera frames flickering constantly in front of her closed eyes. In her mind, she's probably still crisscrossing the road, dodging bullets, with shells impacting a few metres behind her. She's back in her haunted world, but now fast asleep.

Chapter 2

Jenny

The first few weeks passed like drips from a leaking pipe. Waiting for the operation with no set date in mind was torture for Hannah, and stressful for the rest of us, to put it mildly. She just wanted it over and done with, regardless of the risk. Every day, if the rehab assistant was available, she'd pace the corridor slowly. One hand placed in his hand, she looked like a wounded animal, face grey with fatigue and concern.

Mum and Dad's well-meaning words and get well wishes had fallen on deaf ears, as expected. Dad's problem-solving 'We'll get this sorted, love' didn't help at all. Nor did Mum's slightly patronising, empathic 'I know how you feel, darling' connect with her pain and frustration. Did they expect Hannah to be grateful that they'd broken off their holiday early to come and see her? She didn't even respond to Mum's offer for her to come home after the operation and recuperate in the care of her motherly bosom.

You can't choose your parents, but given half a chance we may have chosen differently. I mean, Mum's alright. She's kind. Buxom. A bit mumsy, although she recently changed her hairstyle to something a bit more glamorous. Always encouraged us to do well at school, clean our teeth and stay away from boys – 'until you're old enough', by which she meant, 'at least 18'. When we pressured her to talk about her own 'experience', she claimed she'd found the right man in her early twenties: Dad, the wealthy farmer and landowner. But, these days, especially after a glass or two of ginger wine, she'd confess that she *had* missed out. 'If I had my time again, I'd have plenty of lovers before tying the knot.' Why, then, did she always make such a fuss when we changed boyfriends – frequently, in Hannah's case – or dared to ask if they could stay the night? Little did she know about Hannah's nightly sexual escapades in our neighbour's pool. Until recently, Mum wasn't even aware that Hannah worked for Channel 4 as a *war* correspondent. They only watch *BBC News*. All she knew was that we both worked as journalists in London.

She's definitely more cultured than Dad. She must have been in her forties – we were still at school – when she started an Open University art history course. I'm not sure about Hannah, but she certainly gained *my* respect for breaking out of her traditional mould and becoming a mature student. Became quite an art expert, our mum. She took us to art galleries and exhibitions, talking knowledgeably about paintings and their historical settings. Her favourites were the fifteenth- and sixteenth-century artists: da Vinci, Michelangelo, Botticelli, Caravaggio, El Greco and Bruegel.

A copy of Bruegel's *Winter Landscape with Skaters and a Bird Trap*, smaller than many of his landscapes, used to hang above the piano in our living room. It was printed on canvas and, to the untrained eye, looked just like the real thing. I was disappointed when she replaced it last year with a Bruegel I didn't like. I can't even remember its title; something about blind beggars holding on to each other's walking sticks, falling over one another. Why would you want to hang that up in your living room?

Dad's not interested in art, except for buying the odd painting as an investment, hoping to sell it on for a profit at a local auction. In his snug – the only place he's allowed to put up his own pictures – the walls are plastered with prints of racehorses, dogs and hunting scenes, the kind you'd find in pubs or in small seaside town exhibitions. For me, he's been an absent father for most of my childhood. Always out and about in the fields and woods with his dogs, hunting and shooting, and returning from his jolly chase mud-splashed and pink-faced. The dogs would retrieve the odd pheasant or guinea fowl and proudly carry the prey home. When I think of Dad, I see him in his brown tweed jacket with leather elbow patches, corduroy trousers and green wellies, making it clear to any visitor that he's a country landowner. He would usually carry a gun, properly broken, in the crook of his arm. Remember Mr McGregor in *Peter Rabbit*? Imagine him without the white beard and a bit taller – that's Dad.

I recall visitors wincing when they shook his hand; he has the grip of a gamekeeper accustomed to wringing the necks of wounded game birds. He almost sees eye-to-eye with Angus and Roy, our two Irish wolfhounds, who measure about seven feet when they stand on their hind legs. That's how tall he is. Those dogs can put the fear of God into the heart of any visitor, but we all (except Mother) adore the shaggy creatures, even when they're wet and smelly.

Hannah loved and feared Dad in equal measure. She relished being able to outrun him, aged 15, chasing the dogs round the muddy farmyard. Yet, much as she wanted to defy and confront him, she also craved his approval (and still does). To me it seemed like an all-consuming yearning for his affection that engulfed her like a slow, devastating bushfire. She wanted to be his apprentice, learn to shoot and hunt, show him a girl could be just as fearless and good with a gun as a man. Today, if he said, 'Don't you think that's a man's job?' she would retort, 'Anything you say I can't do, I'll show you I can do better than any man.'

Han and I managed to pull away from our parents' country life 'idyll' and their gender stereotypes. We've forged a different life for ourselves, rejecting those traditional roles. While Mum realises that Hannah is unlikely to settle for a conventional life, she still hopes that, one day, *I* will embrace family life and have children. Dad's probably not too fussed about having grandchildren, as long as he has his dogs – his two 'boys'. Like Mum, he doesn't approve of us being single in our late twenties. Hannah and he argue a lot about her 'unsteady' lifestyle, her constant money problems – she's broke most of the time. And that's when she starts drinking again.

'I'm happy to be single, Dad,' I recall her saying. 'Everything I own fits into a suitcase, so if need be I could move tomorrow, wherever I feel like going. Can *you*?'

'That's hardly something to be proud of. Everyone needs money and a home. You can't just whizz around the world for the rest of your life.'

Yet, after every row, every standoff, they seemed to have this curious tacit understanding that they'd acknowledge each other's strength and respect. A temporary ceasefire, at least, would ensue.

However, now she's seriously wounded, Dad's ready to slip into the role of the benign patriarch, become her helper and best friend, and do his utmost to get her back on her feet. He wanted to be at her bedside before the operation, be there when the bandages were coming off, but Hannah declined. She only wanted Rob and I to be there before she went 'under the knife', as she described it.

'My God, look at that sky!' Rob comments, as we approach the hospital. 'Those dark clouds are going to burst any time now, and we're driving right into it.'

Then, sure enough, the skies do open. Small translucent ice pellets are hammering against the windscreen – unusual for mid-October. Bright and sparkly against the gloomy sky, they fall on and on, merciless and unstoppable, bouncing off or sliding down the glass, before being washed away by the wipers. We eventually find a parking space in a side street, since the hospital car park was full.

No umbrella. So we arrive completely drenched, leaving a trail of water on the ward's corridor. Hearing our footsteps, Hannah sits up in bed.

'Who is it? Is it time?' Her voice sounds anxious.

'It's me, Hannah, and I've brought Jen along. You OK?' He bends over to give her a kiss.

'Eurghh – you're dripping wet!'

'We're fine; just a bit damp. Got caught out by the hail.'

'How are you feeling?' I ask. 'You don't need to worry – you'll be fine. You're in very good hands here.'

'What's the time? They said they'd come for me around four.'

'Not long now. They'll be here soon.' I put a calming hand on hers. I'm glad she can't see my smudged mascara. Silence. It's one of those moments when nobody wants to make small talk, and yet you try, disguising the fact that you're in a state of inner turmoil and fear. You wish you could put the clock forward, wipe away anxious tears, jump straight to a successful post-op outcome. Rob, silent, is nervously perching on the edge of his chair, holding her hand and looking glum. Not much help there, then.

'What happened to the lovely lilies I gave you?'

'One of the nurses took them away soon after you left. Infection control – the rule's been in place for a while, you know. But heavily scented flowers can also give you nausea.'

Keep calm, don't rise to the bait. Not while she's in hospital. I hear my inner voice.

Another embarrassing silence. Finally, the matron, recognisable by her black uniform, approaches with long, energetic strides. She gives us a friendly look through heavy black-rimmed glasses.

'Hello, my name is Emma. You're family?' Before we can even nod, she draws the curtains round Hannah's bed for privacy. Rob and I move over to one side.

'I just need to ask you a few questions, Hannah. Then the anaesthetist will come and talk to you before you go into theatre. Is that alright?' Her pen is poised over the clipboard, ready to tick off each question.

'Can you confirm your name, your address and your date of birth?'

Hannah mumbles the requested information in a low voice, keen not to be overheard by the other patients in the room.

'Do you have any allergies? Are you diabetic? Do you smoke?' The matron talks and ticks quickly, three thoughts in a sentence. More health questions.

Apart from the smoking, she seems relieved that she can tick all the 'Nos' – otherwise, it would mean filling in more details in the boxes below.

'Can you confirm the information on these wristbands is correct?' she asks routinely.

'No, I bloody well can't. I'm not wearing my reading glasses,' Hannah replies sarcastically.

'I'm sorry. That's all correct,' I chip in, having checked the labels on both wrists. I am uncertain which of the two women's sentences I should be apologising for.

'There is even a barcode on the label,' Rob grins. 'I can scan it on my smartphone, see how much we can claim on our life insurance.'

The matron frowns at him disapprovingly. Hannah responds with a false smile. Bad joke. Shortly afterwards, Rob and I have to wait outside the drawn curtain while the anaesthetist discusses local versus general anaesthetics with Hannah. He speaks calmly, with a slight foreign accent that is difficult to place. 'Knock me out, then,' says Hannah at the end of their conversation.

A young nurse with a ponytail – she can hardly be older than 20 – brings Hannah a flowery gown. It looks like it's been taken out of Grandma's wardrobe, and the nurse helps her to slip it on. She consults a piece of paper on her clipboard, asks the same questions the matron ticked off before, including whether Hannah can still remember her name and address and, of course, her date of birth.

'After the procedure, you might come back here or go to a different ward.'

I pick up on the word 'procedure', a cunning euphemism for 'complicated eye operation'.

This time it's *my* mind that plays 'worst-case scenario'. By 'go to a different ward', she means that, if things go wrong or there are unexpected complications, Han will be wheeled semi-conscious to ICU, and then ...

The nurse draws back the curtain to allow the porter to push another bed on wheels next to Hannah's. When she guides her to the new bed, the gown opens at the back. Rob and I share a conspicuous smile.

We're just about to wish her good luck when she turns her head in our direction, as if narrating to camera: 'And in I go! It's like diving from a ten-metre board. When the moment comes, you don't hesitate. How do you do it? You just jump.'

When we leave, there's a noticeable change in the weather. The rain has stopped and the sky shows large rafters of cloud, set against small patches of azure, almost as if deliberately spaced. An orderly pattern that I've never seen before. A display of hope and stability, maybe?

'Would you like to come for dinner tonight? Hamish is cooking,' I ask as we turn into our street. Rob hesitates.

'I don't think I—'

'No, he's a good cook. Creates his own dishes. Mind you, he puts ginger in almost everything.'

'It's not that. It's just … I don't think I'll be very good company tonight.'

'Don't worry. It'll take your mind off Hannah. Look, it's almost six o'clock – you might as well come in now.'

We settle down to a tasty lasagne with home-made béchamel sauce and a decent bottle of red. Hamish bursts out laughing when we tell him that Hannah went into theatre narrating to camera. 'That's vintage Hannah style!' Afterwards, as I hoped, the topic of conversation shifts away from Hannah, at least for a while.

'And how's work at the Home Office, Rob?' Hamish tries to introduce an uncontroversial topic.

'Foreign Office, European Desk. I moved a year ago.'

'I'm sorry, I completely forgot. Was that a promotion?'

'Well, it's a different job altogether. I deal with Anglo-German relations, mainly trade and inward investment, liaising with the British Consulate General in Düsseldorf.'

'Wow! Any travel involved?'

'Some, but not nearly as much as our two ladies, whizzing around the world for weeks on the trot.'

There is that accusatory tone again. I know it so well from Hamish. It often culminates in a lengthy row. *Thanks for reminding us, Rob.* I decide to keep schtum, allow the men to have their chinwag, to let off steam. They're soon talking shop again. When asked about *his* job, as a rule Hamish states monosyllabically that he works in IT security. Normally, that's sufficient information to stifle any further enquiries. Most people don't want terminology thrust at them – 'phishing', 'malware', 'spoofing' or 'botnets' – terms they don't understand or which make them feel ignorant. But, a little out of character, or perhaps he was trying to distract Rob, Hamish reveals in some detail what his job entails.

'Most of my work revolves around penetration testing, which means that I will do my utmost to find a way into an organisation's IT system or network, expose vulnerabilities in their IT security and suggest ways to improve it. It pays well, but sadly there's very little travel involved.'

'So, in other words, you're a hacker!'

'A different kind of hacker,' he hastens to add. 'The job description is actually "white hat" hacker – those are the good guys.'

'The first time Hamish told me this, I thought it was one of his jokes. Last year, I bought him a white trilby on holiday, so now he even looks the part. More wine, anybody?'

'Talking about jobs …' Rob picks up on the thread. 'Last week, I was offered a year's secondment at the Consulate in Düsseldorf. It would be a great career move. Under normal circumstances Hannah would probably encourage me to go. But now… perhaps I should just turn it down. Obviously, I haven't told her about it.'

'Neither *should* you, under the circumstances,' I say protectively.

What follows is a long pause, everyone thinking about Hannah again.

'Do you know what worries me most?' Rob breaks the silence. 'That Hannah will go back to her old job as if nothing has happened – providing the op is successful. Eric rang the other day, wanting to know how she is. Trying to play the good guy, he announced proudly that he had a couple of "soft jobs" lined up for her. He wittered on about

24

offering Hannah the chance to travel to The Hague for an interview. I was really pissed off. Told him to go and visit her in hospital if he wants to find out how she is. Then I just hung up.'

I hold my breath. I know exactly what he's talking about. Hannah's boss rang me too, desperately pleading for me to step in for Hannah, 'just on this one occasion', to interview the head of the Organisation for the Prohibition of Chemical Weapons. Facing the prospect of US military intervention, President Assad agreed to the complete removal and destruction of Syria's chemical weapons arsenal. I was supposed to find out how the negotiations went in The Hague. Since Eric had cleared it with my boss, I couldn't see why I shouldn't go. However, I haven't told Hamish, and I'm now wondering whether he might cotton on that I could be filling in for Hannah.

'You're right, Rob. She *will* want to go back to her job if she can. She adores it, loves the kudos and excitement. Following in the footsteps of foreign correspondents like Martha Gellhorn and Kate Adie is her dream. She wants to prove herself in what was once a male-dominated territory. And she's bloody good at it.'

'I know.' Rob nods, acquiescent if a little disappointed, running a nervous hand through his hair and flicking it to one side. 'I just wish, we could spend more time together. Her job always comes first. How do you think I feel when she's in a bloody war zone and I can't even contact her?'

Hamish puts a friendly hand on his shoulder, then opens another bottle and tops up our glasses.

'I just wish ...' His sentence trails away.

'You're not going to change her,' I reply. 'She's a risk taker, always has thrown caution to the wind – unlike me. She's always been like that. Did she ever tell you about the time when she almost lost an eye as a teenager?'

'Nooooo! I never knew that. What happened?'

So I tell them the story. We had 'borrowed' a shotgun from Dad's collection while he was away on business. Han and I, aged 13 and 10, went on a secret hunt. We lied to Mum that we were 'just taking the dogs for a walk'. I hid the box of cartridges in my pocket, Hannah smuggled the gun out of the house in a slip bag. She assured me that Dad had shown her how to work a gun. It was now my turn to become her apprentice. We lay low for a while and waited for something to aim at. I was peering through the scope, left eye closed, cheek against the side of the gun, my index finger hooked loosely around the trigger, ready to fire. When a pheasant ran past, I pulled the trigger, but nothing happened. Hannah thought the cartridge had got stuck and looked into the barrel. Suddenly, a shot rang out from the adjacent field, which made me jump and drop the gun, releasing the bullet. Hannah turned her face away just in time, the bullet narrowly avoiding her eye. It grazed her left temple, though. I felt absolutely awful and cried my eyes out. I could have killed her, and all she said was, 'I'm fine. I'm not a bit hurt.' Our parents never found out.

'Well, that's really cheered me up. Thanks, Jen. I'd better make tracks before I hear any *more* depressing revelations about her near-death experiences.'

What follows is more or less predictable. Hamish twigs that I have agreed to go to The Hague instead of Hannah, accusing me of being completely insensitive at a time when she was fighting to regain her eyesight. I am annoyed. There is no conspiracy to take over her job; Eric has simply asked me to help out and I'm happy to oblige. What's wrong with that?

At this point, Hamish picks up his inquisitorial tone, wanting more details about dates and the duration of my assignment.

'So Rob and I will look after your sister while you're away. Great! That's sisterly love for you.' He's taking a different tack now, trying to make me feel guilty. Then he has a go at me for being insensitive towards Rob. I should have been more understanding and positive about the good news of his secondment, apparently.

'Oh, for heaven's sake, Hamish!' I say in a harsh tone. 'This is no time for Rob to consider being away from Hannah for a year. What if she doesn't—? She may not be able to live on her own.'

'Perhaps *we* could show some compassion and help out. After all, Rob would only be an hour's flight away.'

He keeps shaking his head. We argue for another hour. But at last he gives up.

'I guess there's nothing more to say. You always get your way. So, go and chalk up one more victory. But don't tell your sister that you're standing in for her.'

Chapter 3

Hannah

'How are you feeling? My name is Melanie. I'll be looking after you while you're in the recovery room. Can you tell me your name and date of birth ... ?' A friendly female voice asks. I've just come round from the general anaesthetic.

'Is there anything I can get you?' I try opening my eyes and realise they *are* already open. Although all I can see is a foggy, milky blur with dots. It's like looking at a pegboard: one dot after another, after another! Plus, strange geometric figures are dancing in my mind. The nurse says these are caused by my brain trying to see.

'I can't see you,' I say loudly, as if it's her fault. *What's happening to me?* My eyes seem to be moving rapidly, as though trying to keep hold of the final image they captured – the explosion. My heart's pounding. I'm scared. I wave my hand in front of my eyes. Nothing. I panic. Now I'm shouting.

'Nothing – just these bloody dots. I can't see,' I repeat desperately.

'Hannah, calm down. Listen to me. Your eyes need rest.' She places a comforting hand on my shoulder. 'We're taking you back to the ward now. The surgeon will be round to see you very soon to discuss how the operation went.'

My bed then starts to move. I hear a male voice – must be another porter. The footsteps accelerate while the wheels under my bed spin, faster and faster, out of control. My hands grab the bedframe. I'm holding on for dear life; my world's spinning out of control. *Press the reset button! Do it now*, I tell myself.

'Stop!' I shout.

'You OK?' There's that friendly voice again. She speaks calmly and pulls a chair towards my bed. I feel drowsy and confused.

'My head hurts, behind my eyes.'

'That's quite common after an operation like yours. I'll fetch you some ibuprofen. Would you like a cup of tea or coffee?'

'Just some water. My throat feels really sore.'

While she pours me a cup of water, the nurse tells me I'll need to stay in hospital for at least another day, so they can monitor my recovery and make sure it is safe for me to go home. She talks me through my medication, and explains that Rob and my sister will be coming to take me home as soon as possible.

I sit up in bed, sipping water from the plastic cup, trying to remember what the surgeon looked like when I first met him. I recall a stout, bald-headed man with a slightly harassed manner, but then I *did* pester him to operate as soon as possible.

'Hello, Hannah. I'm Doctor Yannis, your surgeon. I'm afraid you may not get your sight back for a while,' he begins, with barely any preamble. His account is brief but full: no circumlocutions, no superfluous words, and all expressed with a clinical dryness that, taking my situation into account, frankly took me by surprise. There were a few words about the successful removal of the blood clot, with a few medical terms thrown in for good measure, ending in an unconvincing flicker of optimism. 'We'll need to do another examination in a fortnight, to assess the outcome of the operation. Don't lose hope. Any questions for me?'

I don't. I turn my head in his direction, imagining a lopsided smile on his face as he mentioned the word 'hope'. My instinct tells me there is none. End of.

There are a few moments of silence as Rob and Hannah digest the news the next day. I can easily sense their mood. I feel their arms around me, consolatory kisses, all trying to overcome my slightly stiff resistance. I can feel Rob's tears on my face. I think he suspected it from the start, but to have it irrevocably presented in words, despite the surgeon's lukewarm encouragement, gives you pause for thought. Then more desperate pleas from Rob and Jen not to give up, mixed with offers of help and support with adapting to 'the new situation'.

I wonder how Dad would have reacted to Doctor Yannis's words? Something like 'We appreciate your honesty, doctor, but I hope you won't feel offended that we intend to consult other specialists in your field.' Will we? Should we?

It doesn't take long for us to run out of words – all three inwardly contemplating my future.

'How do I look?' I break the silence.

'Your eyes look pretty normal,' Jen answers. She seems relieved to return to an uncontentious topic.

'A little red, but your irises and pupils look fine. No one would suspect that—'

'That I'm blind. Just say it! We all need to get used to the fact, don't you think?' I wait in vain for a response, so I simply add, 'I've been discharged. You can take me back now.'

On our way home. I remember sitting in the back of Dad's Land Rover, eyes closed, hearing cars travelling in the opposite direction, deafening motorbikes whizzing past and the siren of an ambulance as it overtakes us. Now I'm listening out for those strangely reassuring childhood sounds. I always felt safe in Dad's car. We stop after a while and drop Jen off at her place.

'I'll see you soon, Han. Take care. Love you!'

'Where are we now?' I try to suppress the sense of panic that's welling up inside me.

'Calm down, I've got you. Almost home.' He takes my left arm and puts it on his shoulder as we climb, at a snail's pace, up the flight of stairs leading to our flat. He talks me through every movement, points out obstacles that might impede our way, steers me round something. 'Careful, the Murrays have left their pram in the hallway. Nearly there … just three more steps.'

We stop. I hear the door key turn twice. Then the click of the light switch. But nothing happens; there *is* no light. He takes my hand and guides me to the sofa. I'm back home. It's as if someone has fiddled with the TV: the sound's still on, but the screen's gone blank.

'What can I get you, love?' Rob asks.

'A decent coffee – strong and black, please. That instant muck they give you in hospital is undrinkable.' (Mind you,

31

when Paul and I are on the road, we don't even think about it; we drink that stuff all the time.) The coffee machine is whirring. Rob will soon see the display saying, *Heating up, please wait*. A couple of bleeps later, I hear the most welcome grinding sound of fresh coffee beans.

'Smells so good.' I thank him as he carefully steers the mug into my outstretched hands.

'So glad to have you back, my love.' His voice sounds tender and a bit tearful. 'I've taken a couple of days off to help you settle in,' he says, as he sits down next to me. 'I've also tidied up a bit, so you can find things where they used to be.'

I sink back into the sofa. *Nothing's* going to be like it used to be. My world no longer exists. Extinguished by the press of a red button on a suicide belt. Two lives tragically erased in front of my eyes, an image that will haunt me forever. It could have been me, as well. Should have been. Rob would be better off without me. I'll just be a bloody burden for the rest of my life. From now on, he'll take pity on me, watch me struggle silently, the beetle that has fallen onto its back and cannot turn itself the right way up. He puts my empty mug on the coffee table. I feel his arm around my shoulders and cuddle up to him. I sob – short deep breaths, because my ribcage still hurts.

'Nothing's going to be like it used to be, Rob. What use will I be to you now, to anybody?'

'Look, we don't know what the future holds. Let's wait and see. You mustn't give up. Your eyes may well recover … but you have to be patient.'

'What? Just sit around, doing nothing, seeing nothing? I need to work, I want to write. I'm a journalist, for fuck's sake.'

'Alright. Calm down. Look, you've only just come out of hospital. You need time to recover and adapt to the new situation. I'm here to help you and show you how—'

'Show me? How can you? I can't see a thing!' His slightly patronising tone puts my back up even further.

'Wait. Back in a minute,' he says and rushes into the study. My chest feels sore when I stand up and stretch. My shoulders and neck click – they probably always do, I just never hear them normally. I put out my feelers and manage to stagger towards the bathroom. On my way, I knock over a vase in the hallway, which comes crashing down. Rob rushes back and takes my arm. He steers me round the broken glass.

'You OK? Never liked that vase, anyway. Come and sit down. Here, hold out your hand. You may want to use this.'

'What is it? Feels like a small remote control.'

'It's a voice recorder. Hold it like your mobile. Now, search with your thumb for the round dial in the middle, and press the button to switch it on. It beeps. On the right of the dial is a *Record* button; left is *Stop*. Press the middle to play your recording back. Bottom left is the *Erase* button. *Rewind* and *Forward* is on—'

'Hey, not so quickly! Go through that again.'

After a bit of trial and error, I manage to record some gibberish and replay it. We laugh. Apparently, a partially sighted colleague at Hamish's work showed Rob how to convert a recording into text. It all sounds pretty complicated. I don't think I can work like that. I'm used to plain pencil and paper, and it was only with Paul's help that I managed to file and send my reports on a laptop!

'It'll do to start with,' Rob concludes. 'But it's a lot easier on a smartphone. We'll get you one.'

I want to keep my old Nokia, I object to myself, but I'm too tired to start an argument. I know he means well, and I'm very glad he's given into my plea for a glass of red, even though I am starting my medication tonight. I know it sounds strange: I want him to be near me, but at the same time I'm dreading it. I hate being at his mercy. All the same, I cuddle up to him in bed and warm my cold feet on his calves.

'When you were in hospital, I spotted a poetry anthology on your bedside table which I hadn't seen before. So you read poetry now?'

'And? Did you like it?'

He hesitates, as if considering the question for the first time. 'Yeah. I mean, there are a few poems I really like. But this one you marked is particularly poignant. Can I read it to you? It's a bit sad.'

'Go ahead.'

One Day
There's no light, no voice
In the dark vault
Of our silent mutters
No life left, no road ahead, except
The winding path to yesterday's tomorrow,
The dejà vus and groundhog days.
But one day, my love,
I'll put fresh flowers in your vase
and light a new candle.

I can't hold back my tears any longer. I didn't think this 'one day' would ever come. We curl up and spoon. Rob soon breathes regularly and deeply, while I lie awake for hours, tossing and turning.

My mind travels back to the safe house near Haswiyeh. I'm with Paul in one of the bombed-out houses, waiting for a lift. A soldier from the Free Syrian Army drives us to the tunnel, the only way left to get to the trapped women and children nearby. We crawl for ages through the hot tunnel, filled with diesel fumes. With every sip of warm tea from my flask, my determination to move is crumbling. I'm exhausted. 'We're almost there,' I hear Paul's voice fading away ... eventually I doze off.

'Nooo!' I shout out, waking us both up in the middle of the night.

'It's OK ... You're safe. It's just a dream ...' Rob holds my head, strokes my hair. 'Do you want to tell me about it?'

'It's the same dream I had in hospital. I'm at my parents' house ... '

'Go on!'

There's distressed warbling from the garden. I rush out to the greenhouse, trying to help several trapped birds to escape out of the window. But it's jarred and won't open. Their wings beat frantically against the glass. Suddenly, more and more appear from nowhere with their young, following the flock instinct. Then there is an explosion, shattering the glass. Some birds escape; others fall dead to the ground. I wake up when I hear the blast. So weird. I don't know what it means.'

A few moments later, my heart rate is back to normal. I turn over and go back to sleep, in foetal position.

The next morning, as we sit at opposite ends of the breakfast table, I feel how much the balance of power in this uneasy alliance has shifted. I'm not in charge any more, no longer 'wearing the trousers', as Jen has described our relationship. Rob hands me a ready-mixed bowl of muesli and fruit, with a spoon stuck in it, and asks whether I want to go for a walk later. I decline. His speech is persuasive and yet somehow elliptical, with long silences. It's like he's struggling to shape his thoughts, so he doesn't sound too disappointed about our 'new normal'.

'You may wish to have some additional help,' he suggests, 'a few hours a day, when I have to go back to work.' Subtext: *You're not able to cope on your own, dear.* In the spaces between his words I hear the screaming of artillery shells. I see a young mother in her early twenties being gunned down by a sniper in the so-called death strip, where women run towards the shop to buy food for their children.

I look at him uncomprehendingly. We're worlds apart. We sip our coffees. The kitchen clock ticks away, unstoppable, every second, to fill the quiet void. I feel overwhelmed by his perpetual preoccupation and anxiety, his desire to organise everything for me. I hear Dad in the background: 'We'll get this sorted, love.' What is it with men? They always think they have to solve our problems.

A week later. Rob's working from home today. I spend the morning listening to Radio 4. Missed the news again.

It's *Woman's Hour*, the female perspective on balancing children and work. *Not yet, thank you very much.*

Anyway, how would I cope with a child *now*? I can't begin to imagine. I can't even move around the flat without constantly bumping into things. I crash into chair legs, half-open doors or stumble over carpets, rugs and bathmats. I should really start using the cane they gave me in hospital. The nurse did a little practice walk with me and showed me how to use it. You move it along the floor from side to side, feeling your way like an insect with his proboscis. However, it doesn't make me feel any more secure. I'm used to walking and feeling my way along walls, dodging snipers.

I'm in the kitchen. I fill the kettle. When the water boils, it clicks and turns itself off. I try to visualise where everything is, or is supposed to be; what's on the shelves in front of me and what sits where on the worktop. I open the cupboard over the microwave and find the tea caddy in its usual place on the lower shelf. I'm still holding the empty mug in my left hand, reluctant to put it down somewhere and then not be able to find it again. Aiming the boiling water into the mug is a challenge. I rest the kettle's spout on the mug and start pouring. *But how do I know when it's full?* I don't, and I overshoot, luckily without burning myself. I wait for the tea to draw, then fish out the bag. *Milk! How do I do that without spilling it? Think!* I'm glad no one's watching. Rob's gone into his study to work. I take a swig of milk from the bottle, put it back in the fridge and empty my mouth into my mug. Mission accomplished. I've made my first cup of tea!

Rob sneaks in and sees the mug on the table next to my chair.

'Did you make yourself some tea? That's amazing, but you should have asked me.'

'I can make you a cuppa, too,' I respond defiantly. 'Milk, no sugar?' I grin.

Other things are not so easy to accomplish, but I'm slowly getting there. For example, bathroom routines. I've given up putting on make-up, though I still stand in front of where I think the mirror is, brush my short hair, feeling and patting down the unruly bits. Brushing my teeth is OK, but getting the right amount of toothpaste on the brush is a bit tricky. *Think laterally!* I squeeze a bit on my finger, rub it onto my teeth and then brush. Perfect.

Other vital daily routines: making coffee. Hands stretched out, fingertips turning into feelers, I bumble my way into the kitchen. I can't operate the coffee machine, as it's all touchscreen, so I use the small cafetière instead. And, what's even better, now I hook a little liquid indicator into the jug that bleeps when it's full, so no more spillages. Rob bought it for me the other day. He's gone back to work. I feel safe but claustrophobic in the flat. Loneliness tastes bitter on my tongue.

I haven't called anyone for two weeks, nor have I dared to leave my rabbit hole without Rob. I want to phone my friends, meet up with long-lost contacts, but I can't bear to hear myself explain what has happened, as it will make it irreversibly real. More hospital visits, more tests, more doctors and more mysteries, but no answers. At this point, HR put me on disability allowance.

Jen calls me every day for a chat. She's my lifeline to the outside world. I tell her about my EMDR therapy, which apparently stands for 'Eye Movement Desensitisation and Reprocessing'. At first, I thought it was some kind of therapy for my eyes. It turns out it's a treatment for trauma and post-traumatic stress. So this shrink turns up twice a week now, and encourages me to talk about Syria and similar assignments I've been involved in. The idea is that I visualise a traumatic event that haunts me. He gives me some stimuli, makes some repetitive noises, which I'm supposed to follow with my eyes. I then need to let my mind go blank and tell him what images spring to mind. He seems a nice chap.

'What does he look—? Sorry, Han.'

'It's alright. I wish I knew. He's very articulate and has a quiet, gentle voice. Depending on my mood, I make him look like an Action Man with rolled-up sleeves and chiselled features. On other visits, he's a big, ragged-looking nosy parker. We talk a lot about coping skills, relaxation techniques and dreams. He must have seen the voice recorder on the coffee table, because, like Rob, he's keen for me to record how I am feeling. I told him I haven't quite mastered the technology yet. I did make a few recordings, but they're my oral diary, and that's private. I'll have to keep it in a safe place!'

Jen updates me briefly about her work – a visit to The Hague. She's interviewing some bigwig from the OPCW about the destruction of Assad's chemical weapons arsenal. Unusually for her, she doesn't go into much detail and quickly changes the subject. She wants to know how Rob and I are coping with the situation, and whether I want to go out for a bite to eat at the weekend.

'How can I?' I say. 'I'd hate the feeling that everybody is staring – or even laughing – at me, making a fool of myself, spilling my food. Rob's tried to take me out a few times, but I always dig my heels in.'

'Hey, I've got an idea. Why don't you two go and eat at Dans le Noir? It's a restaurant in Clerkenwell for blind and partially sighted people. Mind you, other people go there for the sensory experience.'

'How would that make me feel any better?'

'It's pitch-black – you eat in the dark. You'd be on equal terms with the other customers, and Rob. And it would help him understand how difficult things are for you – *and* how incredibly well you're managing.'

A bit of nagging, and Rob reluctantly has agreed to take me.

'Where are we now?' I ask, as the tube train stops again.

'This is us – Farringdon,' he says and takes my arm. 'Large step forward onto the platform. Good. Hold onto me.'

We're in the tube station now. Another train seems to be pulling in from the platform opposite. As it gets closer, it makes a rumbling sound. The brakes hiss and screech when it slows down to a stop and the doors open with the usual beeps. I detect a variety of smells wafting past me – perfume, smelly food and sweat. Rob takes my hand and pushes my bum through the barrier when it opens.

40

I don't know how long it takes us to walk to the restaurant. *Are we still on time?* I tilt my head to the left to check the time – a mechanical gesture. I'm not sure why I'm still wearing a watch. Rob describes the blacked-out windows of Dans le Noir. Apparently, the reception is lit, so we can stash our coats, bags and phones in the lockers. Then, we're lined up with a few other guests. Our blind waiter makes sure everyone has their left hand on the right shoulder of the stranger in front, before guiding us, conga-style, into the restaurant. The waiter steers each one of us to our seats. He lets us feel the position of the knives and forks and tumblers.

'Drinking from a wine glass in the dark is just asking for trouble,' he laughs.

'I feel strangely vulnerable,' Rob says, as we settle down to our meal. He's gone for the meat; I've chosen the veggie option. What's in front of me smells delicious – definitely goat's cheese! I use my fingers to feel what else is on my plate: asparagus, Parmesan-encrusted parsnips, possibly some beetroot, and some sort of vegetable mousse, along with breadsticks.

'Apart from the steak, I have no idea what I'm eating and how much food I've already spilled,' he says in a toneless voice, while chewing. 'I bet I've made a right mess. Half my meal's probably slipped off the plate!'

We drink and laugh, and talk about old times, when we used to go out for romantic walks by the Thames, strolling along Victoria Embankment at night – the lights of the Festival Hall twinkling across the water in the warm summer breeze. We talked, we flirted, we saw the best in one another, sealing our unspoken affection with gentle kisses (with a little prompting from me).

It was Jen who had introduced me to this 'career diplomat' from the Home Office two years ago. 'You have lots in common,' the self-appointed match-maker made her case. 'Rob's interested in politics and foreign affairs – he really knows his stuff – you'll have lots to talk about ... and he might bring some order into your chaotic lifestyle.' Thanks, Jen. She set us up for a chamber concert in St Martin-in-the-Fields, pretending she wasn't able to go. I was late as usual, but he didn't seem to mind. As I entered the lobby, I could see him sitting near the bar with quiet confidence, pint in hand and looking pretty laid-back. His head turned whenever a single female went past him. We had little time to chat before the concert.

But Jen was right, we had lots to talk about when we went for a drink afterwards. I can't remember how we managed to stagger into one of the most controversial topics in foreign affairs – the Israeli–Palestine conflict. He argued that the Israelis would never agree a peace treaty with terrorists (PLO or Hamas), whereas I put the case for freedom fighters in their occupied homeland. There was no common ground. In the end, we found some less contentious topics to talk about, and I did like his criticism of Theresa May's hostile attitude towards immigrants.

Towards the end of the meal, once we have exhausted all the safer topics – his work, my chats with Jen – there is a deceptively calm silence. It's as if our appetites have suddenly gone. The desserts and the second bottle of wine remain untouched. The silence then becomes oppressive.

Unspoken mutual recrimination troubles us. Still on *my* mind is his constant *I can do this, I can do that for you.* On his, I presume, the pent-up feeling and recrimination: *Why on earth does she take these risks?* I want to say: *I know, Rob. No story is worth dying for, but there are stories worth taking risks for. This report was one of them. These stories really matter. They save lives. They have to be told.* Instead, I say sarcastically, 'How was it for you?'

'Honest answer?' he says. 'Terrible. Half the time I didn't know what I was eating. I mean, don't get me wrong, the food tasted good. It's just ... I want to see what I'm eating.'

'Quite. We normally eat with our eyes. Remember when we used to take photos of all those yummy, beautifully arranged dishes?'

'I'm so sorry, darling. I'll try to be your eyes in future. Help you see what's on your plate or describe things to you when we're out for a walk. It might make life a little easier.'

Chapter 4

Hannah

I'm breathing in the cold November air from the half-open window. My lungs are almost fully mended now, so I'm able to breathe normally. It must be late morning, I guess, but it hardly matters, as one day is pretty much like another. I 'read' the *Guardian* and *The Times*, downloaded from the RNIB's Newsagent. I'm gradually getting the hang of all this new tech stuff. However, it's really frustrating when I can't get back to where I was, because I somehow managed to press the wrong key. What's much worse, though, is that I feel lethargic and sleepy during the day. Probably because I've become a bloody insomniac.

It's the afternoons I can't cope with. A terrible listlessness sets in after the *One o'Clock News* ... once you've read all the papers, listened to every news story, done a few household chores, not to mention the umpteen cups of tea and coffee. It's at that point, late afternoon, that I start listening out for Rob. Why do I resent this waiting for the key to turn in the lock, the sudden attention to footsteps passing through the corridor – poised – holding my breath? As he comes to greet me, I sense his nearness even before I hear his steps on the creaking floorboards. I know what his first questions will be. He'll ask how I've been, what kind of day I've had, whether there's anything he can get me. Once he's back, I sense that he steps daintily around me like a ballet dancer, so I don't bump into him. I still don't have much spatial awareness: I hit all kinds of objects and swear when I stub my feet on chairs and table legs. Sometimes I just want to yell out loud: *Why am I in this cage, like the trapped birds in my dream? I want to smash the window and jump out.* His footsteps are coming towards me again.

'I've bought you a brilliant present.' He bursts into the kitchen with boyish enthusiasm, just as I start chopping the vegetables for our evening meal. He gently takes the large knife out of my hand and leads me to the living-room sofa. I dread to think ...

'The very latest iPhone 5,' he trumpets, like a double-glazing salesman. 'It's just come onto the market. So you won't need that old-fashioned voice recorder any more. If you talk into the phone, your notes appear on your screen straight away. Then you can tell it to read it back to you for editing. It'll read anything – web pages, eBooks, the lot. It's fantastic!'

You can use VoiceOver to dictate your reports and they'll appear on your screen straight away. Use spoken commands to have it read back for editing. In fact, it'll also read internet pages out loud. And eBooks, audiobooks – it's really good! *Everything* works with spoken commands!'

'Do you seriously want me to go back to work as a blind journalist?'

'It's too early to consider it at the moment, but maybe in a few months' time? Entirely up to you.'

'Sitting in an open-plan office, with everyone staring at me? And Eric breathing down my neck, "helping" me, telling me what to do? No thanks.'

'All I'm trying to say is that the technology *does* allow you to work. Look at Gary O'Donoghue. He's the BBC News' chief North America political correspondent, in Washington.'

'I know. He's very good, but then he's always been blind and has never known anything else. Look ... can we just get on with dinner now? I'm starving.'

'Can I just show you a couple of voice commands. It's so—'

'Not now. I'm going back to the kitchen.'

I leave him standing there, all forlorn, with his new toy. Only later do I find out that he's upgraded his own iPhone at the same time.

'Come along,' I shout. 'You can fry the chicken for me, but make sure it's cooked through.'

'You've dropped a carrot. It tried to escape from you by rolling off the table,' he says jokingly, and puts it back next to my hand on the chopping board. It gets executed on the spot! I carry on slicing the vegetables more vigorously than necessary, making excruciatingly loud chopping noises.

After dinner, he asks me for my Nokia, so he can copy all my contacts onto the new gadget. I agree grudgingly. He spends the rest of the evening setting up and talking to the smartphone rather than me. I have to admit, reluctantly, that most of the time his spoken commands do actually work.

'What was the name of the blind Home Secretary under Tony Blair?' he asks, and gets an immediate response from the phone: 'I found this on the Web.' Rob instructs the phone: 'Read David Blunkett's Wikipedia page.' It starts reading his entire biography. I'm impressed, but I'm not going to let on. Then Rob tries to humour me.

'Siri! Tell my fiancée that she's still lovely, even when she's sulking.'

'What is your fiancée's name?' the phone responds.

'OK, OK. You win! You can show me tomorrow.'

Moments later, as if to celebrate his victory, Rob comes back and puts a glass of bubbly in my hand. I take a cautious sip.

'That's real champagne! Have we got something to celebrate? I haven't forgotten your birthday, have I?' *No, that's not until the end of December.* 'Another surprise? Not another gadget, I hope.'

'Well, it's not exactly worth celebrating. It's got to do with my job. You see, while you were in hospital I was ... well, I had an offer—'

'Come on! Stop dithering and tell me what's up.'

It turns out he's been offered a year's secondment in Germany and, although he's pleased about it, he says he can't possibly accept because of my 'situation'. *So why the champagne, if he's already turned it down?* He hasn't. He just wants to sound me out, involve me in the decision-making. How very decent of him! He snuggles up to me on the sofa and wraps his invisible tentacles silently around me. First he buys me an expensive present to help me cope on my own, then he drops the bombshell, doused in champagne. *Nice work, Rob!*

'You must accept. It'll be good for your career,' I assure him in a toneless voice. He struggles with counterarguments, exaggerating the 'I can't possibly leave you on your own while you're still adjusting to the new situation.' In the same breath, he mentions that he'd qualify for a free flight home every month. And the secondment wouldn't start until January, by which time ...

'No, you really must go,' I insist and congratulate him on his achievement. 'Cheers! And ... well done!' I empty my glass in one.

'You could always live with your parents for a while. They'd love it, especially your dad.'

Quite! The return of the prodigal daughter, blind and destitute, having squandered her fame and fortune in a silly accident in the desert. That would be fun indeed!

'I'm off to bed.'

I'm tired, as usual, but determined not to let the worry whittle away at me, as the muscles in my legs begin to relax and twitch. And yet I lie awake, going over the different parts of our conversation, hearing Rob's voice saying, 'It'll only be for one year.' *He* was the one who complained when I was away on international assignments for a mere week or two. Now the table's turned in his favour – completely.

It's no good, I can't sleep. So I get up quietly, mindful not to wake him. I retrieve my voice recorder from its hiding place under the kitchen sink. My recordings are a strange mixture of diary entries and, occasionally, what proper writers would probably call stream of consciousness. Or is it interior monologue? I can never tell the difference – just recording thoughts and memories as they come to me. Tonight I'm too exhausted to give the recording any structure, so I merely press the button and start speaking in a quiet voice.

Today is the fourth of November 2012. 'You could always live with your parents for a while.' Rob's words echo in my mind. Imagine coming home after all these years! Living with your parents, at my age …

God, no. It would be like Jane and Stephen Hawking's story. Mum transforming herself into a reluctant carer out of Christian duty. Then, after a while, finding that she's had enough of my mood swings and PTSD, wanting her life back. And rightly so.

And you, Dad. We'd just laze around in your snug, sipping tea and coffee, playing backgammon, reminiscing about our hunting and shooting adventures. I'm useless with a gun now, Dad.

I hope it's alright to sit in your chair. I miss you. I wanted to make you proud of me, and – for a little while, at least – I think I did. I felt it when you said, 'Saw you on telly today, my famous reporter.'

Do you know the last thing I 'see' these days when I lie in bed at night? That little plastic Jesus Mum gave me when I stopped going to church with her. You know, the kind they have in taxis, which are supposed to prevent accidents. Well, it didn't work, Mother! Also, the arms have come off the crucifix and are just dangling by Jesus's side. He probably looks more relaxed that way. I can't put them back on now, anyway. It would feel like I was pinning the tail on the donkey!

I think I'll sneak back into bed now before Rob wakes up.

'It's going to be a nice day,' Rob says as he kisses me goodbye. 'You were fast asleep. I didn't want to wake you, but I made you breakfast. I'll do the shopping on my way home. Text me if you want anything from the shops. Your iPhone is on the kitchen table. Have a great day!'

There they are again, those familiar phrases: 'I've done this ...', 'I'll do that for you ...' How much longer?

I've made up my mind. From now on, I'll show him what I can do. For a start, I'm going to venture out on my own today. First time! Sunny Hill Park, close to our first-floor flat, is familiar territory – I used to go there for a run before work, almost every day. Although it's fairly small, I managed to run four miles on the tarmacked paths, alongside numerous dog walkers.

Here we go!

I'm wearing a black (or is it the pink?) gilet, sunglasses ... And I'm taking my cane – that's a must! Stairs are no longer a problem. Then, through the gate, my cane finds the end of the pavement and I stop at the kerb, listening out for cars. All clear. I step into the narrow road and walk across swiftly. The little ball at the end of my cane hits the kerb on the other side of the road. Step up and onto the pavement. Phew! I sweep the cane from side to side until it hits the metal fence surrounding the park. Left turn. Walking slowly, I run the cane along the fence's metal bars, playing them like a xylophone. Last bar – I've reached the open gate. Now for a bit of Mind Mapping. *Remember your run!* I need to follow the tarmacked path straight ahead up the hill to the T-junction where I turn left, towards the green. In about a mile, there should be a bench overlooking the playground where I can sit down for a while and listen to the joyful sound of children's voices. *Keep walking.* I can hear children singing 'Happy Birthday'. I wonder whether

I've already gone past the playground. I stop to catch my breath. I've become so unfit.

I hear a panting dog nearby, so I turn my head and ask the owner, 'Excuse me, do you know where the bench is – the one that looks onto the playground?'

'You've just gone past it, dear,' says an elderly female voice. Her dog starts barking at me, and I freeze. 'If you turn around, it's about a hundred yards on your right.'

The air feels crisp and earthy, with a distinct smell of rotting leaves and smoky bonfires. The clouds seem to be lifting, because suddenly I can feel the sun on my face – it's as if tiny beams of light are piercing through the narrowly angled slats of a blind. I've reached the bench and, sure enough, I can now hear the happy children's voices, muted slightly by traffic noise from the main road. I sit down, allowing the autumn sun to caress my pale face.

Footsteps. They're slowing down, and then they stop right in front of me. I feel vulnerable and fold my arms defensively across my chest. A male voice, huffing and puffing, addresses me.

'Sorry. Do you mind if I sit down for a minute? It's that hill at the end of the path that always gets me.' *Aah – a jogger.* I'm relieved.

'I know. I used to run this track fairly regularly, but now …' I raise my cane a fraction.

'What happened … If I may ask?' He's still breathing heavily.

'An explosion. A boy blew himself up right in front of me.'

'What – a suicide bomber? That's terrible. Where?' He's keen to know more. When I tell him that I work

51

for Channel 4 News and was reporting from a Syrian war zone, it suddenly clicks.

'I thought I recognised you. God, you're not that famous reporter …?' He struggles to remember my name. 'I'm sure I've seen you on the seven o'clock news. You are, aren't you?'

The kids in the playground start screaming at the top of their voices.

'What are they doing?' I ask.

'It looks like a birthday party. They're playing a game on the lawn just outside the playground.'

'So what's all the screaming about?'

'Well, there's a girl in the middle. She's blindfolded, and she's groping around, trying to catch one of the others. They scream each time she gets close, and tease her, so that she changes direction. What's the game called again?'

'Blind man's buff?'

'Yeah, that's it.'

I think the jogger's standing up now. He makes some stretching noises. The screaming from outside the playground recedes – applause for the winner, perhaps? I lean forward slightly and gather the sounds and memories that take me back to my childhood.

I'm in my parents' garden. It's Jen's seventh birthday and we're playing blind man's buff. I'm 'it' – stretched-out arms, listening out for any teasing voices. My hands hit one of the apple trees when I hear a timid sound from above. Hiding in a tree is against the rules, someone shouts! I recognise the cheeky voice above. It's bloody cousin David. So I pull myself up to one of the lower branches and, guided by voices below – 'Left, right, left again' – I finally catch the little sod and triumphantly pull off the blindfold. Mum has only just realised what's happening as I climb down. She shakes her head in disbelief, whereas Dad raises his eyebrows and nods approvingly. Those memories used to warm me up from the inside, but now they're tearing me apart. I wish I could just rip off the blindfold.

'Wait! I remember …' The jogger starts talking to me again, as I make a move to get up. 'Hannah Tring: foreign correspondent for Channel 4! Am I right? So brave of you to report from those dangerous places. How did you—?'

'Sorry, I really need to get back now.' I'm not in a chatty mood, and I certainly don't want to be interviewed. It's normally *me* asking the questions. As I take my sunglasses off, I can feel his gaze upon me.

'You don't look blind. Your eyes look perfectly normal.'

A comment that I would hear many more times in the months to follow. I want to reply, 'You don't look stupid, but I'm sure you are.' Jen already told me my eyes were in perfect condition, to look at, without any lesions or other visible injuries. And yet, they're still eyes that are totally blind.

'Would you mind if I walked back with you to the park entrance?' he asks.

What I actually fancy is a run.

'How about *jogging* back? I'll just hold onto your arm, if that's OK with you.'

'Sure.' He takes my wrist and hooks it over his arm. We almost seem to run in step and echo each other's breathing.

'I'm impressed,' he comments as we arrive at the gate. 'You're a pretty fast runner. I'm John, by the way. Would you like me to walk you home?'

'Thanks, John, but I can walk the rest on my own.' I'm out of breath, but I'm thrilled. I went for a run – something I haven't done for ages – and proved to myself that I can do something that most people assume a blind person can't do. It feels so good! And John seems a friendly guy; I might meet him again for a run.

As soon as I set foot in the flat, my mobile phone rings.

It's Rob, sounding concerned.

'Hi, it's me. Why didn't you answer your phone? I tried several times. Jen and your dad both rang me at work, saying they couldn't get through to you, either. You've got everyone really worried. Where are you?'

'I'm back home now. I went for a run in the park and forgot to take my phone.'

'*What?*'

'You heard me. I went for a run. I latched onto a friendly jogger. That's all. It was perfectly safe.'

'Well, just stay where you are now. We'll talk about it later.'

I thought he'd read me the riot act when he got home, fearing that we'd have a prolonged argument about health and safety for the blind, but I got away with a mild warning.

He even bought me some roses. 'Don't touch – just smell,' he said. I guess he wanted to butter me up before discussing his travel plans. He needed to go to Düsseldorf to find a suitable flat, in preparation for his secondment. He'd only be away for two nights, he said, and Jen might be able to help out.

'What did Jen want? I only spoke to her yesterday.'

'Something about a concert? You'd better ring her back.'

'And Dad?'

'Not sure what he meant. He rambled on about having done some research and needed to talk to you – "very important and quite a discovery", he said. He wouldn't tell me any more – wants to discuss it with you in person, either here or at their place. We can go and visit them at the weekend if you like.'

'Yeah, OK. What day is it today? I haven't a clue. And when are you off to Düsseldorf?'

'It's Tuesday. We can see your parents on Sunday, if you like. Perhaps you can persuade them to invite us for Sunday roast. I'm going to be away for two days next week – Thursday and Friday, back Saturday morning.'

Two days on my own. That's exciting. What else can I attempt, without constantly having to report back to my 'safety officer'? *Clothes shopping? Not really. Maybe the supermarket. Another run in the park? Finding a jogger to run with me shouldn't present much of a problem – you can literally smell them as they run past you. We'll see.*

Oh, and Jen wants to go to a concert with me next week. She's got tickets for Beethoven's Ninth Symphony – fabulous.

Rob must have put the roses on the coffee table. I can smell them from where I'm sitting on the sofa.

Is there anything positive to be said about blindness? Any heightening of the other senses? Maybe. Or is it just a feeling of going to a darker, lonelier place? I really don't know.

Chapter 5

Jenny

We're on our way to Chalfont St Giles, to visit our parents. Hamish is driving. I let Rob sit in the front, so I can chat and snuggle up to Hannah. Hamish is cracking jokes, teasing Rob for making such a mess with his food at Dans le Noir.

'I heard all about your dinner in the dark. Bit tricky eating with a knife and fork, was it? How, exactly, can you miss your own mouth when you're eating? Got distracted by the waitress?'

'Very funny!'

'Perhaps just order finger food next time.'

'*You* should try it one day,' Hannah butts in defensively. 'I doubt you'd get on any better.'

She's right: we'd all struggle to eat in complete darkness. Even moving around in familiar territory is difficult, and really scary. I tried walking with my eyes closed the other day – didn't get very far. It's a bloody nightmare! Hamish's insensitive remarks have riled me.

'I've got an idea. Why doesn't Hamish eat his lunch blindfolded today? We could watch, just to make sure he doesn't spill anything.'

All of us laugh, except Hamish. He's not amused, but gets the message. I wonder whether Hannah remembers playing blind man's buff in the garden when we were young. Would it bring back good or bad memories for her?

She has her window half open. With her arm stretched out, she directs the fresh air towards her face. She yawns, then turns her head towards me and talks in a bittersweet but unstrained voice.

'You know, Jen, I wonder whether one day I won't be able to remember what our parents' house looks like. Or what Mum and Dad look like ... or any of you. The picture stored in my mind is probably the one when we all got together for Dad's birthday.'

She closes her window and sits back in her seat, her brows furrowed.

'It's similar to when people get shot before your very eyes,' she continues. 'In a split second, their light goes out in front of you – extinguished – once and for all. But that image stays frozen in your mind. It never changes ... However, all of you change over time, and—'

'That's not necessarily a bad thing,' I quip. 'It means I'll always stay young for you.'

'No, you don't understand. It's different with people you know well. I'm worried that, over time, your face, Rob's – and others' – will slip away from my memory and I won't be able to see you any more.'

'Look, Hannah. Look! We're here!' Rob announces in an upbeat voice. We take a sharp left turn, pulling into the long gravel drive. I think he wanted to drown out Hannah's defeatist remarks, unaware of the irony in his sentence.

Our parents live in a large detached Georgian house with red-brick walls, white sash windows and matching window shutters on the inside. In the summer, red and white roses climb up to the first-floor windows. Lush Virginia creeper cover the side of the house. Now they all look as if they've undergone some judicious pruning, because there's no sign of any spent blooms or diseased foliage. *Well done, Mother!*

As soon as Hannah hears the crunching sound of the tyres on the gravel, she undoes her seatbelt and sits bolt upright in the car, listening out for other familiar sounds. I take her arm as she steps out onto the driveway, and walk her towards the house. Rob and Hamish follow, each of them carrying a bottle of wine.

'I'll be your eyes for today if you like,' I'm keen to offer.

'Yes, I'd like that. Is that creepy red ivy still there, strangling everything? And where are the dogs? I can't hear them.'

'I don't know. Dad may have taken them for a walk. And it's not ivy, by the way.'

The house seems to have suffered a little subsidence, cracks have appeared in the brickwork here and there, and the iron handle on the front door looks tarnished, but I don't tell Hannah that. I don't want to spoil her picture of the rural idyll, if there ever was such a thing for her. She does love reminiscing about her childhood, though: roaming the countryside with Dad, accompanying him on his hunting adventures and mysterious forays into the woods.

Angus and Roy announce themselves, barking loudly, as they come bounding round the side of the house. They ignore the men and shoot straight over to us. Well, strictly speaking, they're welcoming Hannah first, jumping up, thrusting their wet snouts into her face. She responds to this enthusiastic welcome by pushing them playfully from side to side and roughing up their coats. Dad comes into view and, seeing that the dogs are still excitedly jumping up and almost pushing us over, he shouts, 'Down, boys!' They instantly become subservient. Hamish and Rob look nervously at each other, wondering whether they should follow suit, but find the gravel a little too hard to kneel on. They endure Dad's uncomfortable iron handshake and manage to force a strained smile. With Dad's permission, they walk over to the barn to look at his vintage car collection, and he shows his affection by greeting his 'girls' with his usual rough bear hugs. Then he takes over from me and leads Hannah into the house.

'They're here – and we're all starving!' he shouts, walking with her towards the kitchen, closely followed by the dogs.

Mum wipes her hands on her apron and greets us with hugs and kisses. She's all red-faced from the heat of the old Aga.

'You look well, my love, despite everything,' she says to Hannah, holding her cheeks gently in both hands. 'Welcome home!'

'Forgot to mention,' she turns round to Dad, 'we'll be seven at lunch. I've invited Noreen to join us. She hasn't seen the girls in ages.

I wish you hadn't, Mum! Noreen, Mum's older sister, is a well-informed gossip who always knows what's best for you. I truly hope she's not going to ask Hannah any embarrassing questions about her sight loss.

Dad just shakes his head in disbelief and sighs. The three of us, dogs trailing behind, disappear into the garden. We all defy the cold breeze and trudge through the brown autumn leaves that have fallen. As the wind tears through them, they take to the air in a merry dance, pirouetting around the trunks of the fruit trees until they come to rest – newly assembled, it seems – in the same place as before.

'How's the garden looking?' Hannah asks. 'Bare and wintry, I guess. Have you had loads of my favourite apples this year?'

'Plenty of Victoria plums and, yes, quite a few apples, as well. Your mother used up all the plums and made tons of jam, but we gave most of the apples away. We didn't see you for months.'

Hannah lets go of Dad's arm and walks to where she thinks the apple trees are, arms stretched out in front. Dad and I direct her from close behind.

'Left a bit ... Straight on now ... You're very close. Stop! That's the one you used to climb.'

Her left hand touches the tree and reaches up to one of its lower branches, then the right hand. She pulls herself up, but as she tries slinging one leg over the branch it breaks. I just about manage to catch her.

'Thanks, Jen,' she says, a bit breathless. 'Do you remember, Dad? We used to play blind man's buff at our parties. I think it must have been at one of Jen's birthdays when cousin David thought he was being clever and hid in the tree.'

'I do remember. You climbed right up, with your blindfold still on and got the little sod in the end. Mum told me off afterwards for being irresponsible, but I thought you did great!' Hannah turns round and smiles. 'Really great,' I echo Dad's voice. We all trudge back to the house.

The doorbell rings. Auntie Noreen has arrived. A tall peroxide blonde, dressed with careful and expensive informality in a purple cashmere jumper with silk scarf round her neck and black trousers. She puts her arms round me as if she's hugging a tree and gives me a disgustingly wet kiss on the cheek. My sleeve does the necessary wiping.

'So how's our poor Hannah?' she enquires. Without even waiting for an answer, she walks straight over to the kitchen and starts chatting to Mum. I leave them to it.

An hour later, everyone's together in the dining room. We're ready to eat. Dad has squeezed a chair for Noreen in between Hannah and me. Great! He raises his glass in a toast 'to the cook' and, turning to Rob and Hamish, says he regrets that there wasn't time to go to the Fox and Hounds for a pre-prandial drink.

It was always Dad who laid down the rules in the house. Sometimes Hannah insisted that she and I should go along with our guests to the pub. Mum never even considered it, as she hates the place. For me – maybe not so much for Hannah, as she loves her drink – it was more the village atmosphere that would entice me to tag along. It's a real picture-postcard village, complete with its twelfth-century parish church and thatched cottages lined with impeccable front gardens. There's a village green with a duck pond, cricket pitch and village pub, which all adds up to a perfect slice of English country life. I love the air of tranquillity and timelessness about the place. It's as if time has stood still for centuries. A very different world to the hustle and bustle of our frenetic London lives, for sure.

The knives and forks are doing the talking during lunch, apart from the odd 'Could you pass me ...?' request.

Everyone is eager to avoid 'the topic'. But it's Hannah who breaks the silence.

'The food smells and tastes delicious, Mum.' The men join in, mumble-chewing 'Hear, hear!'

'Would you like me to help you cut your meat, Hannah?' Noreen asks, half leaning over her plate.

'I'm alright, thanks,' she declines with a lopsided smile on her face, and adds, with a pinch of sarcasm, 'I'm a big girl now, Auntie Noreen.'

'But I thought you can't see any... I mean, your eyes look normal, but—'

'OK, that's quite enough,' Dad interjects, his voice taking on an acrimonious tone.

It seems to do the trick, as we all begin to make small talk like pros. Dad is pleased he can expertly answer all of Rob and Hamish's polite questions about his vintage cars. Mum's chatting away about their cruise and stopover in Naples, where they managed to see an original Bruegel in the Museo di Capodimonte. It only dawns on me later in the afternoon why she put *The Blind Leading the Blind* on the wall instead of our much-loved print of his *Winter Landscape*. I thought that was pretty tasteless, given Hannah's situation. It's actually a pretty convincing reproduction of *The Blind*. I guess it's another picture she can flaunt, to impress her arty friends.

I sense that Noreen is desperate to quiz Hannah about her loss of sight. She's only half listening, and not taking part in our various conversations. From time to time she looks at Hannah with a false smile, unsure whether she would notice her gaze. She puts her knife and fork down on her unfinished plate.

'Do you …?' she begins deliberately. But she's not sure of her ground, and the sentence trails away. Another more confident attempt at eliciting information from her comes to an abrupt end when Dad stands up to what, at first sight, looks as if he's launching into an after-dinner speech. Before he says a word, he adjusts his trousers for all to see. Normally, he'd wear his belt just below his paunch, which Mother always considers to be a sign of depression, but now, with some effort, he has hauled his trousers up to his navel, proclaiming an optimism that his subsequent announcement will justify. He makes eye contact with his audience, smiles, then takes a deep breath.

'Hannah's blindness came as a terrible shock to all of us.' He lowers his voice as he utters the dreaded word, the smile quickly fading from his face. 'But we do have grounds for optimism. This morning, I received confirmation from the Federov clinic in Berlin that Hannah is eligible for a ground-breaking new treatment to restore her vision. Hannah and I will talk about this in more detail after lunch,' he announces.

All eyes are on my sister. She shifts uneasily in her chair, shredding bits of her paper serviette into little pieces, and pushes her plate away.

'Thanks, Dad. Rob told me you'd made some enquiries on my behalf, but I don't want to talk about it now. Perhaps you'd like to tell us all about your recent hernia operation instead?'

'Listen, Hannah! Seriously. All I'm asking is that you take a look at the bumf they sent me, so you can decide for yourself. From what I gather, it's non-surgical, non-invasive. They say that—'

'Your dad is right. You *must* look into it.' Noreen puts her spoke in, her curiosity now thoroughly aroused. 'Doctors can work wonders these days. My friend Emma has just had a heart operation, all done with computers – lapa … technique, or something like that. I can't quite remember.'

Hannah's chair screeches on the parquet floor as she gets up from the table, swiping the gravy boat right into Noreen's lap.

'Don't you get it?' she shouts. 'All of you! I'm fucking blind and I'm getting used to it. So you'd better do the *same*. There *is* no cure.'

Now Noreen screams. 'Oh my god! It's all over my new cashmere jumper. Look at it! You're so clumsy!'

I jump up and rescue the gravy boat from falling to the floor. Hannah tugs my sleeve, then takes my arm, urging me to leave the room. Mum grabs a handful of paper towels, but Noreen is already rushing to the bathroom.

'Dessert, anybody?' Mother announces as if nothing has happened.

Hannah and I leave the table, and make our way to the comfort of the living room.

'That was a bit harsh,' I say. 'Dad means well and would do anything to help you.'

'I'm so fed up, Jen. I've had weeks and weeks of hospital appointments and examinations. I don't want to have any more "ground-breaking" operations and become yet another hospital guinea pig.'

'I get that, but there's no harm in looking at the brochure. Whether we visit the clinic or not, a trip to Berlin – all paid for by Dad – would be amazing. Don't you think? I'll come with you.'

She settles down on the sofa and rests her head on my shoulder, withdraws her hand and clasps mine.

'Bloody Noreen. She did ask for it. Sounds like it must have landed right in her lap!'

We both burst out laughing. From the corner of my eye I can see a Machiavellian smile, a single beam of sunshine lighting up her face.

'What about Berlin?'

'Berlin … Hmm …'. Her smile broadens. 'I met this German reporter in Beirut last year. I think he was working for Deutsche Welle. He was from Berlin, stayed in the same hotel as Paul and I. He was really hot! We spent the evening drinking together.'

'And? Did you?'

'Mind your own business! Nothing much happened, but he did give me his number. You know, one of those overused clichés: "If you're ever in Berlin …"'

'Are you actually *going* to Berlin?' Mum comes in with a tray of tea and coffee, Noreen trailing behind her. They join us, since the menfolk have withdrawn to Dad's snug to watch the test match.

I get the feeling Hannah doesn't want to chat to them, though. She gets up and slowly feels her way to the piano. Pulling the stool slightly forward, she sits down and then lets her right hand glide over the keys until she finds middle C. The left hand does a similar movement until her little finger lands on the C one octave below. She plays a few arpeggios as a warm-up and, after a few minutes, launches straight into the third movement of the *Moonlight Sonata*. It's the stormy final movement, very much more demanding for any player than the first and second, and ever so fast. I listened to her practising this piece many times during her final year at school, but never before has she played it with such ferocity, such unbridled emotion. It sounds as if she's playing out the harmonies and discords of her soul. The music goes right through my spine – so much anger and frustration, but what a rousing performance!

The men have obviously heard her playing and have surfaced from their hideaway. We're now all standing behind Hannah in a semicircle and applaud as she finishes the piece. She doesn't turn around, but from where I stand I can see tears running down her face. She stays seated on the piano stool, upright, stiff, almost frozen, until all except me leave the room. I put a comforting hand on her shoulder and hand her a tissue.

'That was simply amazing, Han; the best I've ever heard you play that piece.'

We sit down for a while and sip at our lukewarm coffees.

The men go back to the cricket, while we stroll round the village to walk off the food excesses. Except for Noreen, who hasn't brought the right shoes and apologises profusely. On our walk, Mum tells us about Dad's plans to earn more money by leasing out some of their land for leisure activities.

'He wants to build what? A scramble track?' Hannah asks, simply out of curiosity.

'Yes,' Mum replies angrily. 'You know, yobs on motorbikes, roaring about in the mud on Saturday afternoons! Money, money – it's all he thinks about. I won't have it. He calls me Lady Maud. From *Blott on the Landscape*.'

'That's unacceptable,' Hannah and I agree, unsure what she's referring to. 'Clearly, we'll have to talk him out of it, Jen.' I remain sceptical about her powers of persuasion. But she promises to have a word with him when we get back from our walk.

'May I ask you both a question?' Mum lets go of our arms and pauses in front of the parish church. 'Have I ever been a bad mother? I mean, did you feel neglected when I did my Open University courses? Your father and Noreen think I should have been there for you when you were still at school, instead of "swanning off" and burying my head in books.'

'Don't be silly. We never wanted any help with homework, and you were there when we needed you. That's what counts.'

'We are both proud of our mum,' I add to Hannah's response. 'Even told our friends at the time that you were studying for a degree at uni. Admittedly, as teenagers we weren't that interested in fifteenth- and sixteenth-century art, but we enjoyed going to museums and art galleries with you later on. Hamish and I still do.'

Hannah pulls my sleeve and shows me her middle finger. I don't think Mum noticed.

'You see, your dad and I have very different interests. I loved looking after you when you were children, but didn't want to be a housewife for the rest of my life.' She puts both her arms around our shoulders, drawing us into a close huddle as though we're her trusted confidantes.

'I've never told you this, but before I met Dad I fell in love with an art student. Mike was unbelievably talented and passionate about all of his art projects; his enthusiasm was infectious and must have rubbed off on me. He even tried to teach me how to draw, but I wasn't any good.'

We unfold from our huddle, link arms again and walk slowly along the green.

'What happened to the relationship?' Hannah is curious to know.

'He emigrated to Australia, a month after an unsuccessful exhibition. He didn't sell a single painting.'

'You must have been devastated,' I say.

'Of course I was. For weeks afterwards, I went to local auctions, hoping to get hold of one of his paintings.'

'So what attracted you to Dad, then?' Hannah asks bluntly.

Mum stops at the threshold of the green, where a cobbled pathway meets the pavement. She cocks her head to one side as though drifting back to the past for a few moments, then grasps a memory and smiles. 'I was bidding for a painting at the local auction, but couldn't afford it. I'd misunderstood the price – thought it was going for £50, instead of £500. So Dad bought it for me. That's how we met! The irony is, it was one of Mike's paintings. But I never told your dad.'

'You married him because he bought you a bloody painting?' Hannah snaps.

'No, silly. That's just how we met. He'd seen me at auctions before and rather fancied me, apparently.'

'Are you saying he was stalking you? It gets worse!'

'Oh, shut up, Hannah. Leave her alone. It's romantic.'

I hold onto Mum with both arms and kiss her on the cheek. 'You and Dad may have different interests, but they do say that opposites attract.'

'What? Like you and Hamish?' Hannah goads me.

'*You* can talk!'

'Come on, girls! We're all, more or less, in happy relationships. We should be grateful for that.'

More or less, I thought. We leave it at that. Maybe Hannah is right. Our parents did argue quite a lot. Dad never wanted Mum to study art history – nor anything else, for that matter. Mum had never been gifted with the self-respect that women our age take for granted. Perhaps it was partly due to our encouragement that she had stood up to Dad when she finally applied for her course. I remember the evening when she proudly announced that she'd enrolled on her chosen course. Dad dismissed art history as frivolous; all he could say was, 'Whatever will you do with a degree like that?'

Out of the blue, on our way back to London, Hannah announces, 'By the way, Dad and I have agreed a year's moratorium on his madcap idea about the scramble track.'

I'm driving, with Hannah by my side. Snowflakes are landing on the windscreen. They fall on and on, effortless and unstoppable, trying to settle. They hold their star shapes for a split second before sliding hopelessly down the glass and being washed away by the wipers.

Hannah is clutching a folder containing documents from the Berlin clinic.

'Wow! How did you manage to persuade Dad?'

'Bit of a trade-off. I agreed to look into this alternative treatment, read all the bumf, if he holds back on his track plans.'

I glance in the rear mirror. Rob is leaning forward, looking over Hannah's shoulder and trying to catch a glimpse of the brochure that's poking out of her folder.

Hamish is slumped on the back seat, fast asleep.

Chapter 6

Hannah

'I'll check the Berlin brochure out for you, do some due diligence when I'm back in the office,' Rob says before getting into bed beside me – half-dressed. He's the kind of civil servant who reads with a pen in his hand, running slowly from line to line, poised to question or annotate in red ink.

Why does he always wear those shorts and T-shirt in bed? I was naked and expected him to take very special care of me. Nothing. Just a standard good night peck on the cheek.

I'm restless again, tossing and turning – no sleeping tablets left. I've just got to sleep when Rob's alarm wakes me. It's Thursday, 6 a.m. I put on my dressing gown and feel my way to the kitchen. He's left me a bowl of cereal in the usual place, spoon stuck in.

A short while later, his taxi to the airport arrives. He's wearing his warm winter coat, all ready to leave. I can feel his overnight case rubbing against my thigh as he gives me a one-armed hug and kisses me goodbye.

'I'll call you from the hotel. I talked to Jen; she's going to look after you while I'm away. Back Saturday morning. Take care, darling, and no more hitching up with joggers. So dangerous!'

I ignore him. He treats me like a bloody child. Deep yoga breath. I'm free now for two whole days! Right. What did I say was on the agenda for today? Early gentle walk in the park, or even a run – if I can find a jogger to latch onto, that is. Then, a bit of food and booze shopping, concert with Jen in the evening. Sounds like a plan.

Hoodie, trainers, sunglasses, cane – that's it. Bum bag instead of handbag, just in case. Locking the flat and front door is still a bit of a fiddle for me. The flat key has a serrated edge, and the other one has a straight edge with lots of grooves, so that's OK. The tricky bit is feeling for the keyhole with my left hand while guiding the key into the lock with the right. But I get there in the end.

I can hear a few cars coming from both directions, so I decide to walk a bit further up the road to the zebra crossing with the traffic light and wait for the bleep. I will no longer know when the light changes to green, of course, but there's also some tactile paving, and that helps me to sense when I'm about to step into the road.

I've just remembered I'm approaching the gate from the other side, so turn right when my cane hits the park fence. As I did last week, I run the cane along its metal bars, playing them like a xylophone, but this time the sound is different: deeper, even a bit sinister. Maybe I'm just imagining it. I turn left through the open gate, walking my normal way towards the playground, when I hear fast footsteps approaching me from the front. Two male voices chat. They sound out of puff and a bit rough. The grip around my cane tightens. I stop for a couple of seconds, hold my breath and listen. *Phew, they've run past me!* I overhear the last few words of their conversation '… think it was her.' I pull the strings tight on my hoodie. It's getting chilly. I reach the bench overlooking the playground and settle down for a few minutes to catch my breath. This time there are no happy noises from the playground – it's too early in the morning. My feet shuffle, crunching the dead leaves underfoot.

As kids we used to collect the prettiest leaves, the ones with vibrant autumn colours, the red-tinted golden ones. Like most children, I sometimes pretended to be blind and, after keeping my eyes closed for a few minutes, came to the conclusion that blindness, though undoubtedly a terrible affliction, might still be bearable if one had held onto enough memory – not just of colours, but also of textures, forms, shapes and surfaces. At least I can remember and visualise what things look and feel like. But I wonder how people who are blind from birth see the world. Just sound, smell, taste and touch to build up images in the mind? I can't imagine.

I'm not sure how much time has passed, but there are fast-approaching footsteps again. They slow down and stop right in front of me. I hear the heavy breathing and freeze, fist clenched around my cane.

'Hannah. I thought I recognised you. Sorry – didn't mean to frighten you. It's John, the jogger. Remember me from last week? And this is my new running mate, Tim. We only met last—'

'It's Tom, not Tim. Hi, mate. You alright?'

'Yes, I'm OK, thanks. I do remember you, John.'

'She's a famous reporter on Channel 4,' he explains to his friend.

'Yeah, I may have seen her on telly. One of those powerful women, eh? And a pretty one at that. Do you want to—?'

'We're done for today,' John interrupts him. 'Fancy a gentle jog back to the gate? She's blind, but she's ever so fast.' He tries to impress his friend. To me: 'Same routine?'

And, without waiting for an answer, he takes my wrist and puts it over his arm like a hooked fish. His friend follows at a steady pace behind us. I wonder whether he's staring at my bottom. I shouldn't have worn such tight leggings. John increases the speed and we're no longer in step. I can only just keep up.

'Would you like to go for a drink tonight?' he puffs.

'No, sorry. I'm going to a concert with my sister. Perhaps another time.'

'Let me help you cross the road. There's quite a bit of traffic. Now – which number are you?' he asks as we cross the road.

'Fifty-nine.' I answer without thinking. 'Don't worry. I'm OK now. Thanks for the jog.'

'Any time. See you. We're almost neighbours.' And, like an echo, his friend adds, 'See you again soon.'

We part in opposite directions – I think. His friend must have gone with him.

I freshen up and change before hitting the supermarket for a stint of assisted food shopping.

I didn't know anything about personal shopping for disabled people before Jen told me. I thought it was only for celebrities. It's really easy, and totally free. I usually ask for Sheila, because she actually tells me which aisle we're in and finds all the special offers. I pass her my mobile with the shopping list. She hands me each item, so I can feel it before it goes into the trolley. It helps me to 'see' what I'm buying.

'Raspberry gin?' she asks. 'That's a bit special, and rather pricey! You sure? And there is *more* booze on the list! Two bottles of red, Shattoe Ley Coin. How do you pronounce that?'

'Château Le Coin – not to worry. I think that must be all. Thanks ever so much, Sheila. Here's my card.'

I like shopping with her. She takes her time with me; we look around together. Very different from shopping with Rob. He just races through the aisles as if stung by a hornet and shoves everything into the basket without showing or consulting me. *I can't see, but I'm not invisible, Rob.* There's no point me being there at all, so now I let him do the weekly shop on his own. Shelf-surfing with Sheila is infinitely more fun!

'*Big Issue! Big Issue!*' a male voice close to me shouts as I leave the supermarket. I turn right to avoid him, feeling my way with the cane. There's a clink of coins.

'Oi, watch where you're goin'!' a female voice shouts at me. Another voice – croaky, male and elderly – comes to my rescue. 'Can you not *see*? The young lady has got a cane, she's blind. She's trying to get past you, loitering on the pavement in your sleeping bag.'

I put down my heavy shopping bag for a moment to apologise.

'Beggars! Shouldn't be allowed. Look at her. Four empty Skol cans. People give them money and they just get drunk. Scum,' he mutters, walking away.

'Fuck off!' the woman on the pavement yells in his direction.

'I'm so sorry I knocked your cup over. Do you mind if I sit down for a moment?' No answer. I feel the edge of a piece of cardboard, move my shopping bag and sit down next to her. 'Are you hungry?'

'I'd love a coffee.' The coins go back in her cup with a clink.

'I've got a bottle of water, and a tuna sandwich.'

'OK, then. Thanks.' I search for the items in my shopping and hand them over. Her breath smells of alcohol and I get a whiff of her musty sleeping bag.

'How long have you been sleeping rough?'

'What happened to *you*, then? Are you really blind or just pretending?'

A passer-by throws a coin into her cup. Then, shortly afterwards, another clink.

'They're all staring at you,' she mumbles, while tucking into the sandwich. 'Feeling pity for a blind beggar, I get that. It's the opposite for me. I'm invisible to them. They just ignore me most of the time. Really drags you down, you know.'

'You drink a fair bit, don't you? I'm not judging. I used to drink loads – the hard stuff, when I was travelling.'

'Where?'

'I used to be a war correspondent before the accident. Lebanon, Afghanistan, Syria … Some young boy blew himself up in front of my eyes.'

'Bloody hell. So that's what happened. What are you going to do now?'

'Get on with life … Listen, you need to find some shelter. You can't sleep outside in winter. Do you want me to—?'

'No, I'll be alright. I've got a friend who lets me crash in his pad. Proper mattress, you know, in a hotel courtyard storage cupboard.'

We chat for a few more minutes before I make my excuses, pick up my shopping and walk back to the flat. By now, she will have seen the cereal bar and hand wipes that 'fell out' of my bag as I left. Homeless in one of the wealthiest cities in the world. And all they get is a penny's worth of abuse and harassment.

Back home, I pour myself a large G&T. I've forgotten where I left my liquid indicator, so instead use my finger to feel when the glass is full, then lick my raspberry-tasting finger – gin with a difference! I follow my liquid lunch with a couple of glasses of the expensive Bordeaux. After a while, I begin to relax. Semi-conscious, my head sinks into the soft sofa cushion. With my hands stretched out, I search for the blanket and tuck myself in.

Unwittingly, my mind drifts off to Syria …

We're in a bombed-out shell of a house in Haswiyeh. I'm trying to upload my report, along with Paul's latest images of the carnage outside. 'I can't get a bloody signal,' I tell him. He squeezes in beside me, sneakily pinching half of my blanket for warmth. 'Let me have—'

The front door slams shut, catapulting me back into the present. 'Hello, it's me. Oh, sorry, Han. I used my key, hope that's OK. I didn't mean to disturb you. I just thought I'd come a bit earlier, to see how you are.'

OK, Jen has let herself in. I kick the blanket away, sit up and turn my head towards where I believe she's standing, rubbing my sleepy eyes. My eyelids open and shut several times. I want to press the 'On' button, but there's only sound and no picture.

'Hi. Come on in. Sit down.' I imagine her scrutinising look, scanning the whole room and taking in the empty bottles on the coffee table.

'That's quite a nightcap for early afternoon! Been shopping on your own?'

'You know, while the cat's away …'

'Honestly, I worry about you, Han. I can't imagine what life must be like for you, but this is *not* the answer. I love you. You're important to me. You've got to stop drinking, love, drowning your sorrows. Make the best of the professional help, and please don't miss any more sessions. We can't help you if you don't help yourself.'

'Professional help! My therapist's idea – making me visualise traumatic events from the past – is useless. It just haunts me even more. I can cope better on my own, rather than having him poking his nose in and wanting to access my diaries and recordings. Don't I have a right to a private life?'

The conversation turns more confrontational and Jen's tone of voice changes.

'Is that why you've cancelled the sessions? Not good enough.'

'And what you are going to do about it? Tell all and sundry? Tell Mummy about your naughty older sister who gets drunk and won't see the quack doctor any more? I don't give a shit. By the way, she'll understand the reference to "quack doctor" – seventeenth century, Gerrit Dou, I believe. Another painting by one of her beloved Dutch artists.'

I leave Jen wherever she's standing in the living room, sniffing around. I need some strong coffee. She follows me into the kitchen, just like a dog.

'Look, I'm sorry. I only want to—'

'Everybody does. I don't need your help, or your pity. I'm OK. I'll manage.'

She watches me making the coffee and doesn't interfere. I sense her invisible tentacles silently wrapping around me. I place the cafetière on the kitchen table.

'You can pour – milk's in the fridge.'

As she leans over, placing the full mug in front of me, I can smell her perfume. Chanel Coco Mademoiselle?

'I tell you what you can do. Help me choose what to wear tonight. What have you got on? Wait, stay where you are. Don't tell me …'

I go and fetch my Colorino Talking Colour Indicator from the bedroom – another gadget present from Rob. Then I feel her velvety dress and scan. It responds: 'Dark blue.' Jen sounds impressed.

'Let's go and scan your wardrobe, then,' she laughs, taking the gadget out of my hand. She complains that there's no light in the hall and bedroom, and that neither of the switches work. 'Can't see a thing in here. Why …?' She's about to ask why I didn't notice it before, then realises, and the question trails away. I tell her where the main fuse box is in the hall.

'Just flick the switch back up again. It's tripped before; must be a faulty circuit.'

We spend ages deciding what to wear – Jen messes around with the colour detector – before we eventually settle on an inconspicuous-looking grey blazer with tailored trousers and matching shoes. Not sure what Jen is doing now, but it sounds like she's rifling through my chest of drawers. I need to stop her.

'Goodness, you've got loads of old diaries and notebooks in here. Can I—?'

'No. Shut the drawer. None of your business.'

'Alright, alright. I won't pry into my sister's secret drawer. Sorry! Let's put some makeup on you, then.'

When we're finally on the tube to the Royal Festival Hall, my mood lifts. I feel a surge of excitement, looking forward to a live performance of Beethoven's Ninth – can't wait! I feel like punching the air to the rhythm of the Northern Line's bumpy rodeo ride, but somehow I don't think Jen would approve.

We arrive at the concert hall in time for a glass of wine at its overcrowded bar. I feel elbows and coats pushing past us amongst a cacophony of voices.

'Do you really need another drink?' Jen asks reproachfully, handing me a large glass of red.

'I haven't been to a decent concert for ages – don't spoil it now.'

We leave it there. Jen picks out bits of background information from the programme. Apparently, the Ninth wasn't exactly a runaway bestseller when it was first performed in 1824, and even throughout the nineteenth century. One of Beethoven's respected contemporary critics called it 'monstrous'. Jen quotes: 'From its first performance up to the present day, the Ninth Symphony has inspired diametrically opposed interpretations.'

Ushers pass through the crowded foyer, urging people to take their seats in the concert hall. I empty my glass, take Jen's arm; we join the slow-moving queue. So nice walking without a cane.

'Does the programme mention that the Ninth was used in political uprisings?' I whisper.

'I don't think so. How do you mean?'

'I was thinking about Tiananmen Square, when the students had it blaring over loudspeakers while blocking the way to the approaching tanks. In the same year, people played it in Berlin to celebrate the fall of the Wall.'

'No, nothing like that, but it does say that Beethoven was completely deaf when he conducted the premiere, and continued to wave his arms when the symphony had finished. Very sad. Why do I bother reading all this stuff to you? I bow to your superior wisdom; you're obviously the expert on old Ludwig.'

As the conductor comes onstage, enthusiastic applause stifles the audience's chatter. The hall falls silent. It takes a few more minutes for the music to start: tuning, listening again, adjusting the strings slightly. Here we go …

I hardly move a muscle for the next seventy minutes. Whatever the critics say, for me the Ninth is emotionally so powerful and structurally perfect, despite its somewhat mysterious opening. I feel as though I'm being dragged on a rollercoaster of emotions throughout the long piece, with that pounding scherzo in the second movement and the magnificent 'Ode to Joy' at the end.

'Thanks, Jen. That was amazing – great choice. You know me so well.'

'Glad you enjoyed it. Let's head back home. I'm happy to stay over at yours, if you want me to. Rob asked me—'

'I know. He's overprotective, but I don't want to be micromanaged by him. I'm OK on my own, really. Just get me back to the flat.'

'There's something else you and old Ludwig have in common,' Jen says, with a false note of controlled serenity in her voice, as we exit the tube station. 'I read it in the programme. He kept loads of notebooks, journals and letters, which revealed a very different side to his life. His quick temper, depression, and struggles with his increasing deafness.'

It was so obvious that she wanted me to talk about the contents of my chest of drawers, find out whether I'd used my diaries and notebooks as a coping mechanism for stress and frustration. Maybe I do, to some extent. But diaries are also a part of social history – the 'bottom-up' kind of history, told by the witnesses on the ground. They tell you about the unimaginable sufferings, about war and destruction that goes on in far-flung parts of the world.

In my case, they are also intimate narratives of ceaseless cravings, of longings and disappointments, of the stubborn ironies in our lives. One thing is clear, though: my diary persona is very different from the one the public sees, the reporter on *Channel 4 News*. When I'm on my own, writing (well, dictating these days), it often strikes me that only a tiny proportion of my public-facing life relates to my inner one. I guess that's why my therapist is so keen to scrutinise my recordings. Well, my diaries and notebooks are private – maybe therapeutic in a way – but they're destined never to be read.

Chapter 7

Hannah

'You sure you don't want me to stay at yours tonight?' Jen asks again as we arrive at the flat.

'I had a lovely time, but I won't be good company. I feel exhausted, and I've got a splitting headache from all that drink. I just want an early night. Is that OK? Perhaps we can have dinner out tomorrow – *my* treat.' I hand her my keys.

'It's the one with the straight edge. I can do the door upstairs, though, thanks.'

She pulls me towards her and gives me a big perfumed hug and a peck on the cheek. 'I'll call you tomorrow. Take care.'

As I slowly climb the stairs to the flat, I sense an unfamiliar musty smell – like unwashed socks or perhaps unaired clothes.

'Anybody there? Hello?' No reply. I stop, listen for a couple of seconds, before I turn the key in the lock, then push the door open.

Everything happens in a split second. A hand on my back shoves me into the flat. I stumble and fall over. My arms shoot out as a reflex to soften the fall, but my head thuds into something hard. The pain explodes in my skull, then my body starts to twitch. I vomit and there's acid and a red-wine taste in my mouth.

The door slams shut and I hear a light switch being flicked on. I curl up into a ball on the floor, protecting my head with both arms. I can feel the blood trickling onto my hands.

'I'm blind,' I plead loudly. 'You've got the wrong place. There's nothing to steal here – no money, no jewellery.'

'Oh, wrong place, have I?'

'Leave me alone! I'm bleeding. I need to get to the bathroom.'

'Shut up! Stay where you are, and don't move. Give me your mobile. Now!' His voice sounds threatening. I can't detect an accent. *What's that click? Is he pointing a gun at me?* I am in no position to negotiate. I feel for my handbag, which is twisted round my neck, and search through it frantically. Then I hold up my phone. He grabs it and walks towards the bedroom, I think.

I dab the blood on my head with my sleeve. *Quick. Think! The old Nokia – must still be in my handbag. Got it.* I scramble to my feet and hit my head on the coat rack. *Ouch.*

'Nice bedroom! Are you ready for me? Famous, but not so powerful now, are we? I'm here, can you see me? Sorry, forgot – course you can't.'

What now? Lights! If I switch … Fumbling, stumbling over the rug, skirting the console table in the hall, I can just about reach up and locate the main fusebox. I press on the cover, making it spring open. Main switch? Don't know. So I flip *all* of them down. When the refrigerator noise cuts out, I know that everything must be off. Now we have a level playing field.

'Fuck. What have you done? Bitch!'

I keep silent, so as not to give away my position.

'Think you're so clever, don't you, switching all the lights off. Wanna play hide and seek, then? Shall I count to ten? And, when I find the famous reporter, I'm gonna have some fun. Exciting!'

My head is throbbing. I wipe the blood from my face. *I'll only have a few seconds until he finds the torch on his mobile and starts his search. Where can I hide?* All of a sudden, my iPhone rings in the bedroom momentarily, and then it's switched off. Footsteps come towards me. I'm in the living room now, but I need to get to the bedroom – the only door with a lock. *Shit. I've just dropped the Nokia – he might have heard.* Now he's threatening me again, his voice sounding eerily calm.

'Listen. I'll find you wherever you're hiding. If I hear you shout for help, I'll set fire to the whole fucking flat. You won't even get to the stairs.'

My iPhone rings again. It sounds closer than before. He must have left the bedroom. Then there's a stamping, crashing sound and the phone stops ringing.

'No more bloody calls now. Such a shame about the mobile. Now, where's that torch button? Ah, here we go. Coming to get you ...!'

Clearly he's found the torch. He kicks something out of his way and starts counting: 'One, two, three ...' *Quick.* I manage to feel my way into the bedroom, close the door quietly, turn the key, then dial 999.

'... eight, nine, ten ... Coming! Where are you? Wow, you've been shopping! Look at all these bottles. You must have known I was coming. Let's have a drink together first? Nice gin you've got there.'

He belches loudly. Now he's stomping around in the living room. Suddenly, a bottle smashes on the wooden floor.

'Hiding behind the sofa? No. I reckon you're in the bathroom, freshening up for me. You see, when a woman like you says no, she really means yes. You're just playing around, playing hard to get, aren't you? I like that.'

He tries all the doors until, eventually, he returns to the bedroom. Locked.

The tone of his voice suddenly changes. 'Open the fucking door, or I'll kick it in.'

I need to play for time until the police arrive. 'Alright, I will. But tell me – do I know you?'

'You'll soon get to know me, alright. Now open the bloody door!'

'You see,' I say calmly, 'I think I recognise your voice.'

He's kicking hard against the door while I try to move the bed to block it. But it's so heavy. I'm really scared now. I'll soon be lying tied up, gagged on the bed, waiting for the worst to happen. *Keep calm, Hannah.* The kicks grow ever more violent. *I need more time!*

'I tell you what, John. Because you're my running mate, I'll open up, but give me a minute and I'll put on some sexy lingerie for you. You'd like that, wouldn't you?'

'No. I'm gonna to rip your fucking clothes off, anyway.'

'Well, can you fetch me a drink, then? It *is* you, isn't it, John?'

No answer. A few more moments gained. The police should arrive soon. *Please!* I grab a pair of scissors from the drawer in my dressing table, just in case. He's finally lost patience and carries on kicking the door.

'Stop! Wait! I can—'

'No more games. I'm coming in.'

Craaaack! The door gives way and bangs against the frame of my bed. I make a desperate attempt to push the bed further towards the door, but it barely moves. There's nowhere to hide. What now? The metal bedframe scrapes on the wooden floor. Is he in the room? I crouch in the corner, one hand behind my back.

He *is* in, pulling me by the hair, dragging me onto the bed. 'Nooo!' I raise my right arm to defend myself, but he's seen the scissors and wrestles them out of my hand. His grip feels strong and rough. As I struggle, scream and scratch at his stubbly face, he grasps and squeezes my throat with one hand while holding me down with the other. I can't breathe. He's on top of me and starts to rip off my blouse. As he tries to tear down my trousers, I kick him in the balls. He squeals.

'Fuck you!' he screams and hits me hard in the face. My head is spinning. I'm ready to give up. Then, at the very last moment, we both hear the sound of a police siren. He freezes for a couple of seconds, then jumps off me. I hear him running towards the door of the flat, shouting, 'Bitch! You think you've won, but I'll be back.'

When the police arrive, I haven't moved. I can hardly breathe. Lying curled up in foetal position, shivering, clutching a pillow with both hands, I'm unable to answer any questions. It's only when one of them calls an ambulance that I begin to unravel.

'I don't want to go to hospital. I'm alright.'

'We'll see. The paramedics will be here soon to assess you. You've got a nasty cut on your head.' A calm male voice standing close by soothes me, covering me with a blanket and helping me to sit up in bed. The paramedics arrive promptly. I have no idea how many people are in the bedroom at any one time.

'Hello, my name is Amy and this is my colleague, Sean. Can you tell us what happened?' she asks, feeling my pulse. Her voice sounds calming. I describe my ordeal in a few detached words, as though it had happened to someone else, adding 'By the way, I'm blind,' in order to explain my scant account.

'I'm going to clean your head wound and put some Steri-Strips on your cuts now. Is that OK?'

She then asks everybody to leave the room, while she helps me to dress. I suddenly burst into tears, giving the lie to any pretence that I was unaffected by my ordeal.

'I only met the jogger twice in the park and he seemed friendly enough at the time. It's all my fault, I know. Why on earth did I tell him where I live?'

'It's definitely not your fault. You mustn't blame yourself, love.'

Amy puts her arm around my shoulder and eventually persuades me to have a CT scan, 'Just to check for any sign of concussion. Are you able to walk to the ambulance?'

The nurses and doctors take over in the hospital's A&E department, asking more detailed questions, reminiscent of the last time I was in hospital when I lost my sight. Later that day, the female police officer continues her line of questioning. Whether I could describe him – size, hair colour, any unusual features … *No, I can't. I'm blind, for fuck's sake.* Maybe I haven't mentioned it to them. The only clue I can give them is that I may have recognised his voice, a guy called John – I don't know his surname – but he told me he lives in the same road as me.

She assures me that they've taken some DNA samples and will immediately start a house-to-house enquiry.

By the time the results of the CT scan come through, Jen is sitting next to me in the waiting room. All clear, thank goodness.

'I should have twigged that something was wrong when Rob rang after the concert to tell me you'd hung up on him twice,' Jen says apologetically. 'And I should have stayed with you after the concert. I'm so sorry. I'll take you home to mine for a bit and you can stay as long as you like.'

I'm staying with Jen until Rob's back from Germany. Curled up on her sofa during the day, I'm in my little black rabbit hole, clenching my fists, wanting to scream out loud. Losing control over my life for a second time feels like hell. Damaged goods, that's what I am. When I get up, I pace through the flat like a wounded animal.

I ask my phone. It's Saturday, 12.20. Rob will be back soon. I can't face him right now, so I ask Jen to talk to him about my ordeal before he takes me back home. He comes in with a bunch of sweet-smelling roses and is not at all judgmental about my news.

'It's not your fault, darling. I'm so sorry I wasn't there to protect you. You OK now?' There's a new energy to the hug I haven't felt before – undemanding, unselfish and sincere. For a brief moment, I think, *We're OK, you and me*, but I would have liked *him* to say it. Instead he says, 'Any time you want to talk about it … let's get home first.' No comment on my head wound from my guardian angel.

'Did the police take any fingerprints?' he asks as soon as we get in. 'And didn't you hear anything before climbing the stairs to the flat?' his line of questioning continues.

'I don't know.' I can't bear to give him a blow-by-blow account, reliving the horrific event.

How did the flat hunting go?' I ask, to distract him.

'Not bad at all. The Consulate already had a shortlist of three for me to choose from, all of which I checked out. I picked a modern one-bed apartment overlooking the Rhine. It's only for a year. I think you'll like it when you come to visit me. You *will* come and see me, won't you? We'll make sure that, in future, when you're here on your own, you'll be safe.'

It takes him less than a day to look into extra security – CCTV, alarm, more gadgets. Why not a stun gun or, even better, a 24/7 bodyguard? Mind you, I don't tell him I suspect I might have recognised the rapist's voice. His reaction would have been quite different, I guess. I don't want to go there. The police assured me they'll be making every effort to find John, if that's his real name? I wonder. Probably not very high on their priority list.

A couple of weeks later, everything, apart from my slow-healing scars, is back to normal, the new normal. I have a brand-new iPhone with a pouch to wear on my arm. *Very considerate, Rob.* He also wants me to wear a panic alarm round my neck from now on. So now I don't even feel safe in my own flat. Whatever next? Electronic ankle tag? *How much more remote control would you like to have, Rob?*

Chapter 8

Jenny

'I can't believe you're going to sign this.' Hamish barks at me, glancing dismissively at the application.

'Why not? Just because *you've* been in the same boring job for the last seven years doesn't mean *I* can't do something more challenging. What's wrong with that?' I grab a pen from my handbag, poised and ready to sign.

'I'll tell you what's wrong with it. You're applying for your sister's job. You're chucking in a secure position at the *Observer* for a one-year contract with Channel 4. And all this just before you jet off to Berlin with Hannah to explore further treatment options for her.'

'Why shouldn't I apply for her job? I do an awful lot for Hannah, but I cannot be her carer. And I have a right to my own career. I'm just as well-qualified as her. My boss at the *Observer* was really sorry to lose me.'

'I don't doubt that. I enjoy reading your articles; they're really good. But—'

'Look, it's been five months since her accident. Nothing's changed – no improvement whatsoever. She's on disability allowance; she can't work as a war correspondent any more. Actually, she may never work again.'

'We don't know that. And how do you think *I* feel, knowing you'll be reporting from a war zone, dodging the snipers? Isn't one crazy sister in the family enough?'

'So this is about you and not Hannah, then? She hasn't even agreed to go to her clinic appointment. The main reason we are going is to see Rob in Düsseldorf. She hasn't seen him since he started his secondment a month ago.'

What follows is a protracted and bitter dispute about our future: plans for starting a family, Hamish's concerns about my security and being away from home for longer stretches of time. When he sees me signing the papers, he gets up and leaves without a word.

I wonder if I've thrown caution to the wind, and failed to realise how much Rob and Han's relationship suffered under the strain of her stressful and dangerous job. But then I'm not like her. I don't take unnecessary risks. I remember, all too well, her daredevil attitude: 'You know, Jen, if your pictures aren't close enough, you're not good enough.'

See what happened to you, Hannah, when you got too close! For you it has always been more bravado than bravery! I'll show you, Hamish and Dad – and everybody else – that this is not the only way to get a great story out. I'm able to have a successful career, too, just like my big sister.

It's early February and we are on our way to visit Rob. He didn't use his free flight back to London last month – apparently he was too busy finding his feet in his new job. But Hannah tells me he does ring her regularly, always at seven in the evening – sometimes they have a virtual dinner together, pretending they're back in Dans le Noir. I bet he cheats, though!

As we step out of the airport terminal, a few uncertain snowflakes are eddying down, but melt as they try to settle on the wet ground. For seconds they sparkle in the neon light of the streetlamps, then die away. With Hannah taking my arm, two small cases in tow, we follow the signs to the S-Bahn. There's always a sense of unease when you first arrive in a new country, with a language you don't speak, and you're trying to get your bearings. Hannah is keen for me to give her a running commentary; she gets impatient when we stop in front of a ticket machine.

'What's happening? Talk to me.'

'I can't work out how to buy a ticket from this bloody machine. It's all in German.'

'*Na und?*' she throws in. No idea what she's saying. Just showing off her scant knowledge of German. The fact that she's been here before doesn't really help now. Great! I'm pressing more buttons. As the queue behind us grows longer, I get stressed and give up. We walk back to the taxi rank outside. At least the taxi driver understands English, although I have to show him the name of Rob's street on my phone. I should have put Hannah to the test and let her pronounce this strange name.

'Come on in, you two. So good to see you.'

Rob hugs me first, then draws Hannah towards him and kisses her. For a few moments, the stiff professional civil servant is gone and instead these are the eyes and mouth of somebody who seems to love deeply. But I'm not sure. Did he ever really love her? With eyes closed, they slip into each other's world, which they no longer share.

'You OK?' he whispers, gently stripping off her coat and taking her hand. 'I'll show you around.'

He's obviously learned how to guide her by now, while describing the studio flat's layout in some detail

94

and letting her feel where things are. It's super-modern – large fortified glass windows, good-sized lounge/diner, plus bedroom with a king-sized bed. Looks like I'll have to spend a couple of nights on the sofa bed. I'm most impressed by the swish marble bathroom with walk-in shower and bidet.

It's already dark, but Rob and I step out onto his covered balcony overlooking the Rhine.

'That's a fantastic view!' I gasp.

'Tell me – what can you see?' Hannah raises her voice behind us.

'The river is huge, Han. Loads of reflecting lights, bobbing up and down in the slow-moving current. How romantic is that! There are some boats anchored on the embankment, too.'

'It can be quite noisy during the day.' Rob dampens my enthusiasm as he ushers us back into the flat, and guides Hannah to the dining-room table.

'I wasn't quite sure when you'd arrive, so I thought we'd have a German *Abendbrot*.' He places the large meat platter with ham and prosciutto closer to Hannah. 'Meats are on your left, darling, and the cheeseboard, gherkins and tomatoes on your right. And a selection of rye and sourdough breads right in front of you. Dig in!'

'You see, Han? He's already gone native.'

'The bread smells delicious, Rob. Thank you.' Turning to me, Hannah adds, 'Don't like dark bread? When in Rome …' I shrug, impale a gherkin on my fork and rest it against the side of my plate.

Having covered all the small talk, the journey and the 'How have you beens?' Rob cautiously steers the conversation towards our trip to Berlin. He's read up about the 'revolutionary' treatment at the clinic. Their researchers are now using stem cell technology to explore possible treatments for sight loss, he explains at length.

'Well,' Hannah takes a perceptible pause for thought before she speaks. 'All I can promise – and I said this to Dad, as well – is that I'll go to the appointment and have a chat. That's all I will do at this stage. OK? Sorry, I'm tired now. Rob, I can't work out all the different settings. Would you mind running me a bath?'

Rob does so, running it to Hannah's preferred temperature and adding some scented pine bubble bath. The underfloor heating clicks on, her towel warms on its rail, the extractor fan whirrs quietly above. Hannah jumps in with a splash. Rob dims the light and brings her a large whisky.

Through the half-open door, I pick up a few snippets of their conversation amidst the gentle ripple of the bathwater.

'When we chat on the phone, I can never tell how you're feeling. Tell me honestly now?'

'You really want to know? I have stopped smiling, Rob. There is no return grin when I smile at people, so I've just stopped. I want to understand blindness, seek its meaning. How else can I hold onto my humanity?'

'But you're coping so well with everyday life. You hardly need any help at all now – unlike most people in your situation. You've even started your creative writing with the help of all your gadgets. Isn't that something you've always wanted to do? From what I've seen so far, you're bloody good at it, too. You should get some of your short stories published.'

'"Coping with everyday life?" Ha. Everyday life in a black hole, you mean. Do you know what a black hole *is*? I asked Siri. A collapsed star crammed into zero space from which not even light can escape, so nobody on the outside knows what life's like inside. *I* do. And do you know what it feels like to be brutally attacked in your own flat? *I* do.'

Rob closes the bathroom door when he hears me getting up.

He finally surfaces, almost an hour later, having put Hannah to bed like she's a child. A very different relationship from the way it used to be. So sad. As soon as she's in a new unknown environment, she's completely out of her comfort zone and has to depend on others, which she utterly hates. Very different from home, where she seems to be OK on her own. I wonder what will happen to their relationship once Rob's secondment comes to an end.

'Sorry, Jen. Hannah's gone to bed. She wasn't feeling very well. Glass of wine?'

He returns with a bottle and two glasses, which he puts on the coffee table next to a vase holding a bunch of wilted yellow roses. He moves them out of the way.

I can't help commenting. 'Thanks, Rob. These look a bit past their prime!'

'Yeah, they didn't last long. I should have thrown them away, I guess.'

'So, how's the new job?'

'Good. Lots to learn, and a nice change from the London treadmill. They are even paying for a language tutor twice a week, so I can brush up on my rusty German. What about you? Any more jobs for Channel 4, filling in for Hannah? Hamish tells me Eric sent you to The Hague – something to do with negotiating the prohibition of chemical weapons in Syria?'

'Yes, that's right. It was a one-off. Eric was pleased with me when I filed my news item on Assad allegedly agreeing to the destruction of his chemical weapons arsenal. All very protracted and difficult to verify, though.'

'The papers say there is compelling evidence that sarin *was* used in Homs last month. The National Security Council will be discussing the incident next week.'

I change the subject. Eric has already told me that a trip to New York is imminent, but hasn't confirmed the date yet. If I told Rob that I am actually *working* for Channel 4 now, would he react in the same way as Hamish?

'So, what have you got planned for us over the next couple of days?'

'Well, I can certainly show you round the *Altstadt*, the old part of the city. There's always live music in some of the pubs, which I know Hannah will enjoy. Oh, and Monday is *Rosenmontag* – it's carnival season here. There'll be Umtata music everywhere, endless parades of people in funny costumes and people on floats, throwing sweets and little bunches of flowers into the crowds. It's quite a spectacle.'

Three days later, and Hannah and I are sitting in a comfortable quiet train to Berlin. Rob has had to go back to work, and I am glad to leave the hustle and bustle of the carnival festivities behind. I hated every minute of it, having to push our way through the throng of drunken spectators, being approached by complete strangers – beer in hand – grabbing your arm and wanting to sway with you in time to the noisy music. Hannah loved the whole spectacle: the concoction of different noises, the smell of alcohol and bratwurst. She didn't mind people brushing past us. She even shared a glass of beer with a complete stranger.

'Did you enjoy the visit?' I ask her, once she's taken her headphones out.

'Where are we now?'

'About halfway, I reckon. Just passed Hanover station. So, I'd say about another two hours to go.'

'Yes, bloody great party, the German carnival. It was fun. And the people were really friendly.' She leans back in her seat. 'What did you think of Rob's flat?'

'Very nice place, all very mod. I loved the bathroom.'

'It all smelled brand new. I mean, the sofa and the carpets. I'm surprised he didn't buy any flowers to welcome us, though. Or did I miss them?'

'No, there weren't any.' I must say, I did have my suspicions, but didn't want to worry Hannah unnecessarily. 'I'm starving. I'll get us some sandwiches from the buffet car.'

'How are you feeling about tomorrow, then?' I ask, as we tuck into our tuna sandwiches.

'Well, I'd rather go shopping on the Ku'Damm with you.'

'The what?'

'You know, the main shopping street in Berlin – Kurfürstendamm, but they call it Ku'Damm.

'But you promised Dad to—' She's suddenly sitting bolt upright, her expression stiff and angry.

'I know. I *will* go to the clinic, but I'm not agreeing to another long hospital stint. I'm not a bloody guinea pig, however "ground-breaking" their treatments may be!'

'OK, OK. You need to decide what's right for you.' The frown on her forehead fades away, eyebrows raised.

'And I do need a pair of new shoes and new trainers. So you can help me choose …'

Eight o'clock the next morning, we arrive at the clinic for our appointment. Why do they start work so early? A young woman sitting close to us in the waiting room is reading to her child. I guess she's about five, and wearing incredibly thick glasses. She points to a page in an illustrated children's book.

'What's this lady doing, Mummy?'

'She's feeding the ducks.' The mother looks up and explains her daughter's eye condition in broken English.

'Look,' the little girl says to Hannah, touching her knee to attract her attention. 'You've got the same boots as the lady feeding the ducks.'

'I'm afraid I can't see – my eyes are very poorly,' Hannah replies, turning her head towards the girl.

'Mine are, too, but the doctor said she'll make them better. She's a nice lady. She gave me a sweet last time, because I was very, very, *very* brave. I think she'll make your eyes better, too.'

'Do you think so?' Hannah's whole face beams with the youthful smile I know so well, but haven't seen for ages.

'Yes,' she replies, with a slight lisp. 'But adults don't get sweets.'

My phone buzzes in my handbag. It's Eric from *Channel 4 News*. I excuse myself and take the call outside. He insists in no uncertain terms that I have to fly to New York tomorrow for an interview with the spokesperson for the National Security Council. It's 'all set up', apparently. From there, straight to Damascus to interview the opposition leader.

My plea for mitigating circumstances falls on deaf ears. 'They do flights from Berlin to New York, you know,' he says with a callous voice. *How on earth am I going to explain that to Hannah?*

When I return to the waiting room, an elderly gentleman is sitting in Hannah's place and the mother and child have gone. *God! Has she done a runner?* The receptionist assures me that Hannah is in the consultation room and that I'm not allowed to interrupt the session. To relieve the tedium, I start booking my flights and let Hamish know by text that I'll be away on business for a few more days.

After an hour's wait, a grey-haired lady with a friendly smile leads Hannah back into the waiting room. By the look on Hannah's face and the faint appearance of a smile, I can tell that the doctor has established a good rapport with her patient. There's a softness in her voice when she takes Hannah's hand, saying, 'We'll do everything we can for you. Ah, that must be your sister. See you again soon.'

We all do everything for you, Han, but get very little recognition for it. We have our lives to live, too, you know. And that includes my career!

On our way back, Hannah wants to stop for coffee in what she calls a *Konditorei* – a posh café where they make their own cakes. However hard I try to elicit some information about the consultation, she keeps her cards very close to her chest. 'They need to run more tests and another CT scan,' is all I manage to get out of her. I'm surprised that she has agreed to undergo more 'non-invasive' tests, though.

To prepare her for my news and put her in a positive mood, I agree to go shopping with Hannah in the afternoon and round off the day with dinner in the Lebanese restaurant close to our hotel. She's always loved Lebanese food and orders lamb kibbeh, which comes in the form of croquettes with a minty yoghurt dip and crudités – all easily eaten as finger food. Pitta breadcrumbs trail down her nice sweater, but that's OK with me. The fine wine and the soft traditional music create an atmosphere that allows me, finally, to find the courage to tell her that I need to fly to New York the next day.

'If your boss sends you there,' she says, shrugging her shoulders, 'you shouldn't really argue with him. Enjoy the trip.' I'm surprised she responds in such a nonchalant tone. 'Can you order me some arak, please?'

'But I can't leave you here on—'

'I can get a train to Düsseldorf, no problem. Don't worry. I'll be fine. And I need to stay here for a few more days, anyway.'

Her drink arrives a few minutes later. The waiter puts it down in front of my nose.

'Bitte schön.' I pick it up and push it into Hannah's outstretched hand.

'God, what an awful aniseed smell. How can you drink that stuff? It's like that French drink. What's it called?'

'No, it's better than Pernod. You ought to try it.'

After too much fine wine and arak, we head back to our hotel, where I let my heavy head sink into the soft pillow on my bed. I want to walk into Hannah's mind, understand her sudden mood swings, discover what makes her tick. I've always found myself comparing my life with hers. Even now, with her predicament, I admire her ability to go through life confident and fearless, coping with everything that life throws at her. Will there be a point in her life where she resigns herself to her fate? Or does she now believe there is a glimmer of hope that she may regain some of her eyesight? She's already made an effort to learn new skills, tackle the iPhone and keep up with all the news reports. Does she have any plans to return to working life? As what? How will she react when she finds out I have taken over her job?

One way or another, I am confident she will take charge of her life, do things herself, on her own, no charity needed. But I don't think she can ever go back to her previous job – not as a war correspondent, at any rate. So I don't feel guilty now, doing her job. My colleagues seem to appreciate the reports from the younger 'Tring sister' as a trademark of serious journalism, even if Eric hardly ever does.

Whenever I compliment Hannah on her achievements, she hardly acknowledges my praise. Strangely enough, the only approval in life she seeks is Dad's, despite their frequent rows. His comment about her most dangerous assignment in Haswiyeh – 'Saw you on telly today, my famous reporter' – filled her with endless pride.

Even her diaries are written in perfect prose. I managed, finally, to read a couple after the intruder emptied out her bedroom drawers. Amazing style! So literary, laced with heavy doses of Henry James and Graham Greene. Too difficult for me, however – I only get about half of all the allusions and references. And starkly different to my style in my first two years as a journalist, when Hannah helped me to clean up my sloppy journalese. Well, that was a long time ago. So why's there still this lingering doubt whether I will ever fully grow into her shoes? Do I even need to? Well, at least my colleagues think I've got all the investigative and communication skills required for the new job.

When I wake up from my snooze, Hannah is already asleep. We part company the next morning with a heavy heart and, for me, with mixed feelings veering between relief and a bad conscience.

Chapter 9

Hannah

'Welche Etage?' A female voice asks as I enter the lift, swinging my cane in narrow arcs ahead of me. I've forgotten whether the breakfast room is on the first or ground floor.

'Zum Frühstück, bitte.'

'First floor.' She's already noticed from my accent that I'm not German.

'Would you like me to show you to the breakfast room?'

'Ja, bitte.' I carry on regardless. Shortly afterwards, another friendly voice, this time male, approaches.

'Darf ich Ihnen helfen? Ich bin der Ober.' Ah, the waiter is taking over from the lady in the lift and is guiding me to my table. There's smooth jazz music playing as we shuffle past the quiet chatter of neighbouring tables.

'Coffee or tea?' He takes my order and offers to bring my breakfast to the table. He even tells me where everything is as he puts each item in front of me and pours the coffee. The croissants are still warm.

'Very kind. Vielen Dank.'

Alone in Berlin. That sounds like a book or film title. It's probably been done before. Or how about 'Alone and Blind in Berlin' for a spiced-up sensational melodrama. Am I excited? Erm, scared and excited at the same time. Does that sound weird? Well, I've been here before, but a long time ago. Must've been – let me think – about five years ago. I reported on the Barack Obama's visit, summer 2008. Berlin was buzzing. It was the kind of hysteria usually reserved for musicians and film stars, with Berliners hanging off lampposts just to catch a glimpse of him – a real festival atmosphere, a summery gathering of love, peace and loathing of George Bush. The young and the pierced, some with guitars slung over their shoulders, others barefoot, jammed up against each other to cheer on a man who seemed to have become the world's most popular politician.

I had travelled to Berlin to report on what Obama called his 'improbable journey' to the heart of Europe, luring the city's young in their tens of thousands to stand in the evening sunshine and hear him spin his dreams of hope. Not for America this time, but for the whole world.

Later that day, I remember meeting this rather handsome Austrian guy who worked for a German TV station. It didn't take me long to realise that he had a crush on me. Or maybe he was just bowled over by the whole love and peace atmosphere. I don't know how to explain this, but he had this rather unorthodox idea of trying to make our parts fit together like a giant jigsaw puzzle, incorporating an insane yoga bridge position. Didn't work for me! Anyway, that's enough nostalgia.

I have another appointment at the clinic today. Although it's on Kollwitzplatz – walkable in about fifteen minutes from my hotel – I order a taxi and wait in the lobby. I'm not familiar enough with the GPS on my phone, and don't want to be late.

'Frau Hannah Tring? Ihr Taxi.'

'Yes, thank you. Ich bin blind.' *Where did that come from?*

'Do you want a hand?' A female voice. Youngish, helpful. Suddenly, I feel her hand around my elbow. It's almost always women who offer; men are afraid to touch, for fear of causing offence. Then there are the men who use it as an excuse to grope, but I don't want to talk about that now.

At Kollwitzplatz, I fish out a 20-euro note – thanks to Jen, I only have twenties in my purse – and hand it to the driver.

'It makes twelve euros, ja?' She counts the change into my open hand. 'Five, six, seven, eight. I bring you to the door, ja?'

'Vielen Dank!'

Professor Gisela Fink, my neurosurgeon, has some good news for me. Her voice sounds calm and confident.

'The CT brain scan shows that the blood clot behind your eyes is now much reduced and hardly visible. And yesterday you said that you're not suffering any serious headaches. Your blood test confirms you have neither diabetes nor high cholesterol, and your blood pressure is normal. So that's all good. However, we did notice a further complication, which is most likely why your eyesight has not been restored.

'Both of your corneas were badly damaged by the trauma, and this has resulted in a bilateral limbal stem cell deficiency. As you know, we're currently pioneering a clinically approved treatment which may help you. It's called Holoclar®, a stem cell treatment for the eye.

The procedure's been successful in a small number of patients, but there's no guarantee it'll work in your case, unfortunately.'

No hard sell there. No case of over-promise – unusual for a private clinic, but rather reassuring.

'So what would *you* do if you were in my position? And what does the treatment involve?'

'It aims to restore the cornea by transplanting lab-grown stem cells into the damaged areas of the eye. The procedure is always done under general anaesthetic. You'd be treated as an outpatient, so there's no need to spend the nights before and after the operation in the clinic. You may want some time to think about it. It's entirely up to you. I can assure you, we'll do everything we can to restore your vision.'

I decide to *walk* back to the hotel, so switch on Google Maps. I need to find my way through the park to Kollwitzstraße and follow the instructions: 'Turn right in two hundred metres.' I can feel everything my cane is telling me: the gentle undulations of the park's path, the border between the path and the lawn, and the varying textures of the pavements, once I've turned into the road. After about a kilometre, it's left into Belforter Straße and then a right turn into Straßburger Straße close to my hotel. 'You have reached your destination.' *How easy was that?*

I slip off my shoes, help myself to a beer from the minibar and sink into one of the old-fashioned wing chairs by the window. I'm undecided. *What if the op doesn't work? I can't take any more disappointments.* The feeling of loss, of being let down, or even of betrayal after weeks of promising hospital treatments in London, has turned me into a grumpy grouch. I don't wish to get my hopes up again only to become entangled in another web of disappointment.

In Jen's absence, who can I ask for a second opinion? Rob? Dad? Both predictably biased and ready to smother me in consolation cream if things don't work out. Someone I can trust to give me a dispassionate opinion. I ask my iPhone to read out all my contacts one by one. I'm shocked at the number of friends and former colleagues I haven't been in touch with since my accident. But ringing long-lost friends would mean explaining what has happened to me, listening to their expressions of empathy and pity and gratefully accepting their well wishes for a successful operation. So I stop halfway through the alphabet.

Instead, I search for contacts in Berlin. Two hits! Rudi, the Austrian contortionist, and Holger, the German reporter I met in Beirut last year, whose parting shot was 'If you're ever in Berlin ...' *Should I ...?* No, I'm not falling for that awful cliché. He was probably too drunk when we met to remember me, anyway. And, when I get back to Rob tomorrow, I don't want there to be any secrets.

Instead, I text Paul. 'I'm in Berlin for a couple of days and would appreciate your advice re my eyes. Wanna give me a call?' I haven't heard from him since Christmas, when he told me that's he's on another assignment in Kabul. He said he was staying on for another month, so he must be back by now, if not already on another mission.

I go for a bite to eat in Dolcini, the Italian restaurant next to my hotel. I'm sitting somewhere near the door, with a double espresso, waiting for my food to arrive, and listening to the audiobook of Julian Barnes' *Sense of an Ending*. There's a passage in it where the protagonist, Tony Webster, talks about fading and unreliable memories.

I stop the recording and muse over his description. I'm sure he's right. When we narrate our own life stories, reconstructed from distant days, we adjust, embellish, make cuts here and there – shaping it into a more or less believable story *about* our life.

But then there are those unalterable stories which never fade away and can never be adorned; stories that will always haunt me. The boy and his mother blown up in front of my eyes, women gunned down by snipers while running to buy bread for their children, and the carnage following a bomb explosion in a crowded marketplace. Those memories will remain with me for the rest of my life, however much I want to eradicate them. It's like trying in vain to scrub away the layers of hard-coated grime from the sides of the bath. How can I forget—?

And how can I forget the trauma of the horrific sexual assault? The rapist's threat, 'I'll be back', haunted me for weeks afterwards. Fortunately, the DNA sample and the fingerprints on one of the bottles helped the police to arrest and charge the suspect with attempted rape and serious bodily harm. It wasn't John, the friendly jogger. In fact, he assisted the police in tracking down his casual running mate, Tom. He must have overheard me, blurting out my address.

I jump when I feel a hand on my shoulder.

'Una pizza calzone, signorina. Buon appetito!' the waiter announces. I take my headphones out and stuff my phone in my pocket. I'm famished. It's one of the few Italian meals I can eat in public without making a mess. I wrap the serviette around the calzone, pick it up with both hands and take a big bite. Then suddenly my phone buzzes in my jeans.

'Hey, it's me, Paul. What are you doing in Berlin?'

'I have some news,' I say, sounding like I'm about to announce I'm pregnant.

'Good? Bad? To do with the food in your mouth?' He laughs. 'Shall I ring you back later?'

'No. Sorry … I'm visiting a clinic about an operation that might give me some of my eyesight back.'

'Chances of success?'

'Chance of seeing everything.'

'That's … a bold claim.' He pauses, trying to judge my reaction.

'Even fifty per cent or less would enable me to work again. Do you think I should—?'

'You want your sight back, don't you?'

'Of course I do. Imagine what it feels like: every time I wake up, I lose my sight again.'

'Look, if you're worried that we won't be able to work together, I'm sure we can find a way, whether you're blind or partially sighted. You may get fed up with me, though, having to explain and show you things all the time.'

'But what if the op doesn't work?'

'Then I'll get a chance to tell *you* what to do, instead of the other way around.' He laughs, I chuckle. 'But we'll still make a good team. The only thing is, I'm not sure whether the snipers will make allowances for a woman with a cane. On second thoughts, they might, if you're convincing enough.' I imagine him putting a virtual arm around my shoulder and me wriggling slowly out of his embrace.

'Or perhaps I could join the bomb disposal team instead. Tap … tap … tap with my cane, with you holding my hand.' His voice suddenly takes on a serious tone.

'You know, Han, I should have held your hand in Haswiyeh and not let go, not let you approach that suicide kid. I'm really sorry. If and when we ever work together again, I will always protect you.'

I gulp and well up. For a brief moment, the force of memory hits me unprepared. The mother's words – 'Don't shoot, we get belt off him' – pierce through my head. Shots ringing out from behind me, then the numbing blast. Those are the last things I can remember …

'Hannah, you still there? Are you OK?' I take a sip from my cold espresso.

'What if the op doesn't work?' I repeat.

'Go with your gut feeling. I'd love to work with you again, whatever the outcome.'

I'm close to tears and clear my throat to get my voice back.

'You're always there for me without telling me what to do. I like that. So good to hear your voice, Paul. I'll be in touch.'

'Wait! I almost forgot. There's the London awards ceremony in two weeks' time. Remember? Journalist of the Year 2012! We're both invited. I'll text you the details.'

I sit still and upright for a few moments, hugging my phone with both hands close to my chest. There's another tap on my shoulder – this time softer and more tentative – and then the waiter's voice. He puts another plate in front of me.

'On the house, signorina.' I don't know what to say. He puts a small spoon into my hand.

'Dessert – pannacotta. You like? My mother lost her sight, so I know about blind people.'

I'm overwhelmed by the kindness of people here: the clinic, the hotel and now the restaurant. Talking to Paul has lifted my spirits, too. I've decided. I make the appointment to go ahead with the op – one week from now.

Berlin's central station greets me with exciting smells of freshly baked bread, but there are also some stronger ones from the many fast-food chains. My taxi driver kindly takes me to the information point, where the lady from the concierge service helps to buy my return ticket to Düsseldorf and leads me to the lower platform for the Intercity Express train. The hotel reception had told me about this free service – very impressive! As I wait for the train, I overhear a brief conversation between an elderly couple standing next to me.

'Hat schon zwei Minuten Verspätung,' the man complains. *If only!* Nobody would complain in the UK about a mere two-minute delay!

The train doors open with a beep-beep-beep. Moving forward cautiously, I feel a hand on my case.

'Let me take this for you. What carriage do you need? This is coach B.' This time it's a young man's voice.

'Ah, lucky me. I have coach B, seat 24A.' He guides me forward to my window seat and hands back my travel case.

I place it between my legs. If I put it in the luggage rack, I might not find it again, and wouldn't know if someone steals it.

Rob's waiting for me at Düsseldorf station. He takes my case and cane, gives me a one-armed hug and a kiss on the cheek. He seems delighted that I have decided to go ahead with the op and will be staying with him for a few days beforehand.

'So, what did they say at the clinic?' he starts on the way home, in buoyant mood as if looking forward to our new life together. He wants to know all the details. 'Will you have to stay in hospital for a few days? And what does the procedure actually involve? Did they sound hopeful? Shall I come with you to the appointment?' He bombards me with further questions, to which I have no answer and don't wish to discuss, either.

'I hope you like parrots,' he says out of the blue as he turns the key in the lock. There's a loud squawk, followed by some chirping noises. A kind of wet-dog smell wafts towards me – a bit like Angus and Roy after a bath.

'What the fuck …? You don't even like animals. Why did you—?'

'Calm down. It's not mine. I'm only looking after it for a few days while my colleague is away.'

'Hello.' The parrot shrieks. 'Hello.'

'That's very noble of you. Who is she?'

'What does it matter? She's just a colleague.' We leave it there.

The parrot interrupts again. This time he's actually speaking German! 'Tür zu, Arschloch!'

'What's he saying?' Rob asks.

'He's being rude to you, and telling you to shut the door.'

'Just ignore him. Can I get you anything?'

'I'd love some coffee.' I bump into him in the small galley kitchen and tell him about the concierge service.

'You've hardly told me anything about the clinic or the treatment. I can take some time off work to come with you.' Here we go again.

'There's no need to accompany me. Travelling on my own is absolutely fine. And remember: it's an experimental treatment, so it might not work at all,' I add, handing him the clinic's explanatory leaflet. 'There have only been a very small number of successful cases out of hundreds of trials,' I exaggerate, in order to deflate any of his optimistic expectations. 'It's an outpatient appointment, so no overnight stay necessary.' He finally stops asking questions. The silence is punctuated by the parrot's one and only phrase: 'Tür zu, Arschloch!' I burst out laughing.

'He's talking to *you*, Rob.'

'This'll shut him up. He'll stop squawking when I throw the blanket over his cage.' It works.

When prompted, Rob tells me about his work: how they keep him busy, lots of business meetings with German companies re inward investment, and how he's going on a business trip to Paris next week. 'The Quai d'Orsay, Ministry of Foreign Affairs,' he adds, almost apologetically. *Why does he think he has to justify a business trip?*

I unpack a few of my things in the bedroom while he nips out to get us a Turkish takeaway. 'I won't be long – the place is just round the corner.'

I feel tired after the long journey. Stretching out on the soft double bed, I notice that the bed has been stripped – no sheets or pillowcases. I search in vain for new ones in his wardrobe.

'I couldn't find any new bedlinen,' I tell him over dinner. 'Where do you keep it?'

'The sheets have just been washed – they should be in the tumble drier. They're the only ones I have. I'll get them for you.'

I help him to make the bed and turn in before him. Apparently, he has an urgent report to finish for tomorrow's deadline. He gives me an obligatory good-night kiss and tucks me in, like I'm his child. My arms are under the sheets, so he cannot see my clenched fists. A strange itchy feeling creeps around my neck and shoulders, like prickly burrs caught on the inside of a jumper.

'I'll get us some fresh rolls from the bakery in the morning,' he whispers, quietly closing the door behind him. My brain wants to lull me into this strange sense of security of being looked after. Yet, at the same time, it feels very different to when I came home from hospital after my accident. Then, he was sitting by my bedside, reading a very poignant poem from the anthology on my bedside table, which ended in the lines:

But one day, my love,
I'll put fresh flowers in your vase
and light a new candle.

Rob didn't light any candles at the dinner table and I'm sure there were no flowers either. What's changed?

The next morning, I wake up in an empty bed. Hearing some rattling noises from the parrot's cage in the living room, I decide to remove the cover. 'Hello,' he greets me. I sense he's quite close, probably hanging down from his beak at the top of the cage or perching somewhere near the door flapping his wings. I'm tempted to set him free, but then I hear my phone buzz. Next thing I realise … It's not mine; the buzzing noise is coming from the kitchen. *Ah, Rob must have left his mobile on the worktop.* And this is where my searching hands eventually find it. The ping sounds like a text. *I shouldn't.* I ask my phone for the time. 'It's seven forty.' *Now* I'm curious. *Who would text him at this time, before work?* I get the phone to read the text back to me: 'Hi. It's me, Friedi. Can't wait to get back to you and feel you inside me again. Paris next week – yeah! xxxx.'

Chapter 10

Hannah

I hear the key turning in the lock. I have just opened the window and been fiddling with the door of the cage, trying to let the bloody parrot escape.

'What the hell are you doing?' Rob shouts. The parrot seems to have missed the half-open window and is scrambling against the glass. Rob bangs the window shut. The bird screeches, flaps its wings and makes a second attempt at escape. This time it sounds like it's hitting the closed window in full flight. It falls to the ground with a thud.

'*Now* look what you've done!'

'He wants his freedom back, Rob. Like me.'

'Meaning?'

'You've got a message from parrot woman. Or is it the German tutor? Or are they one and the same person? She certainly can't wait to get fucked again. Wait – here's your phone. I'll play you the message.'

'Don't! I can—'

'Please don't say you can explain.'

'Well, what can I say? I've been really stupid, thoughtless … I mean … I felt lonely, and she was—'

'Available? Lucky you. I might be blind, Rob, but I'm not stupid. I suspected this was happening all along. I can read the signs: fresh bedlinen, dead roses in the bin, perfume on your shirt collar, and then the feeble lie about the so-called business meeting in Paris – just to add insult to injury. What exactly do you take me for?'

'I'm so sorry. I didn't mean to hurt you,' he whimpers.

'So, how long have you been having "German lessons"? Actually, don't tell me. I don't want to know. It doesn't matter.'

He tries to put his arms around me.

'Don't touch me.' I wriggle out of the attempted embrace and push him away.

'Listen, I still love you, darling. I cared for you after the accident. We can still—'

'Yes, you've been a loving carer, trying to keep me safely locked up in my cage. It didn't work. It will *never* work.'

He follows me into the living room, unleashing a torrent of words, part apology, part self-justification, some of which I've heard before. There are some spiteful comments, which I ignore. All in all, his remorse comes wrapped up in complaints about living with 'the absent war correspondent' who doesn't seem to want a normal family life any more. Whatever that means.

'Living with you hasn't always been easy. Before your accident, you were away an awful lot, with me fretting, not knowing whether you were safe – not even knowing where you were. And, after it happened, you seemed to disappear into a world where I couldn't follow. Everything was just tumbling down.'

'You're right. I am in a different world now, against my will, but things changed way before the accident. I can't remember the exact moment our worlds drifted apart, where I myself felt lost, where we lost each other. All I know now is that we can never go back.'

'So, don't you love me any more?'

'You talk of love, Rob. I'm not sure whether I ever really felt it. My soul has been in a different room and you didn't have the key. You thought you had it, though.'

No reply. I sense he's looking at me uncomprehendingly, probably shaking his head in despair. It was the way he threw the sentence at me, the 'don't *you* love *me* any more', which, for a moment, made me feel trapped again. I no longer wanted to be the caged animal, pacing up and down the same path, testing the strength of the confining bars.

I need some air, so step out onto the balcony. I hear Rob fiddling with the parrot's cage, to make sure it doesn't escape again. I imagine him and his floozy standing arm in arm on the Juliet balcony, gazing lovestruck out onto the illuminated riverbank.

'Do you remember – shortly before my accident – when we went to see *Romeo and Juliet* at the Globe?'

'What are you talking about now?' His voice sounds agitated and nonplussed.

'Well, at the beginning of the play, there's a famous quote about Romeo. I remember it from school. "He that is strucken blind cannot forget the precious treasure of his eyesight lost." Don't you think that applies to both of us, though in rather different ways?'

'I don't get you. You and your bloody literary references! Can't we talk about us? Is there no way we can—?'

'Kiss and make up? You really don't get it, Rob. It's over. Finished. There is, and never has been, a plan B.'

He follows me into the kitchen and switches on the coffee machine. 'I'll make you some breakfast,' he says, carrying on like I've just said something inconsequential, something said in anger, something I don't really mean. His phone pings again and again. *Is she sending him pictures, as well?*

I've had enough. I grab a bottle of water from the fridge, then go and gather my things from the bedroom. The engagement ring slides easily off my finger and onto his pillow. *There's your memento mori, Rob. Maybe it'll sparkle for someone else one day.* I take a few moments to lace up my shoes, put on my coat, then walk, guided by my cane, out into an unknown future.

An hour later, I'm on a fast train back to the Berlin clinic, digesting what has just happened. Wouldn't we all do better *not* trying to understand why relationships go sour, instead accepting that no human being will ever fully understand another – not a wife a husband, a lover a mistress, nor a parent a child? Discretion and deceit are often divided by the finest of lines, where spouses find solace with other partners while still caring responsibly, and seemingly lovingly, for their disabled partners. All I can do now is try to build a new life, find a way out of this darkness and break the future in gently, like a new pair of shoes.

I keep thinking a lot about the 'what-ifs'. What if the op doesn't work and I'm blind for the rest of my life? Everyone says how brilliantly I've adapted to the new situation. But I could scream when I hear this. I haven't, really. In fact, I need a fucking punchbag!

Dr Fink, my neurosurgeon, turns up in the recovery room when I come to after the general anaesthetic and the gauze is peeled off. I've skipped a day in my life; I don't even remember going to sleep. I feel OK, maybe just a bit woozy. My throat is sore, my mouth very dry. She passes me a glass of water and assures me that the operation went well. She also explains that we now have to wait four to six weeks to see whether the implanted stem cells have managed to repair parts of my damaged corneas. We arrange a telephone consultation for a month's time. There's some paperwork to complete before I can be discharged. She seems concerned when I tell her that there's nobody to take me back to the hotel, and kindly orders me hospital transport.

Kicking off my shoes, I drop my bag and cane onto the bed and sink into the wing-back chair by the window. I ring my parents to let them know that I've had the operation and am not optimistic that it'll change anything. I don't tell them that Rob and I have broken off our engagement.

Two days later, at home, going over it all, I understand. Breaking the news to Jenny and hearing her reaction – 'I never quite knew what you saw in him, but then you seemed pretty desperate at the time' – I got it. I had only just come out of a long-term relationship, at 27, and didn't want to be on my own again. Not very emancipated, I know. But that's when I met Rob. I mean, he was very kind, clever, a safe haven, no major hang-ups … Would we still be together if I hadn't had the accident? I'm not sure. People show their true colours in extreme situations. And, to be fair, I probably haven't been the easiest person to live with, even before the accident. Jen agrees.

'Do you think being with the wrong man is worse than being with none at all?' I ask.

'Most definitely. But it does take courage to leave.'

'Not after his affair, it didn't.'

'Anyway, I believe you both want different things. He's got some very traditional ideas of home and family life—'

'It should have been obvious to him that I'm no homemaker and housewife. He needs to grow up! Or maybe he's found a German housewife in the parrot woman.'

'Tell me. You're sure you've broken off for good? And did you go through with the op after all?'

'Yes to both.'

'And?'

'What?'

'What are the chances of you regaining your sight?'

'No idea. They can't tell you. Minimal, I guess. Out of hundreds of trials, only a very small number have been successful.'

'Well, don't lose hope. It's early days yet. Is there anything I can help you with?'

'Are you free next Saturday? I need to go to John Carpenter House. Can you give me a lift?'

'What? *Press Gazette*? What's happening there?'

'They invited me to accept my "Best Journalist" award.'

'God! You're a bit of a dark horse. Congratulations! That's wonderful. Why didn't you tell me?'

'Paul told me only a few days ago. He rang me before the op in Berlin. And I've only just received the invite in the post. You going to come?'

'I'm really sorry, but I've got to go back to Damascus for a few days, to interview some human rights leaders. I would have loved to go to the awards, though.'

Jen sounds more and more like me these days. The apologies, excuses, even down to the 'I would have loved to go' that I used many times to thwart Rob's plans to go out to concerts, parties or visit friends. The job came first – always.

Jen invites me to stay at hers for the next few days, but I decline. When she leaves, I find my special – and, according to my personal shopper, rather pricey – raspberry gin, well camouflaged behind the elderflower cordial, and settle down with a large tumbler and a blanket on the sofa. My phone tells me it's 2.20 a.m. when I suddenly wake up with some weird dream fragments going through my head. I'm in a safe house in Haswiyeh, helping Rob to save the parrot woman, who's been shot in the back by snipers. Paul's there to film it all. That's all I remember.

A week later, a new inner peace seems to be evolving gradually. It enables me to look to my own resources. In spite of everything that has happened during the last few months, I sense the stirrings of an unexpected, almost tangible, strength within me, in contrast to my physical state. Single again. Perhaps it's not so bad, after all.

Rather than wallow in resentment, I sometimes turn to the piano to soothe and calm my battered emotions. However, my finger memory often takes some time to recover the old pieces I used to play, now that I can no longer see the score in front of me. And, at night, I turn to my side of the bed with relief. No longer will a certain someone crank the bedclothes systematically to the left to mummify himself, and I have the duvet all to myself.

Saturday evening, six o'clock. My taxi arrives in an hour. I'm looking forward to meeting up with friends at the awards ceremony, friends who have known me as a compassionate reporter and appreciate the risks I've taken to get the important stories out. And, of course, Paul will be there. He'll be standing on the podium next to me.

What shall I wear? Colorino is doing the talking: 'Bright red, pale blue, grey, black'. I could go for classic, understated elegance and opt for my pale blue velvet dress with smart black boots. I'm sure that would be Jen's choice. I'm having second thoughts, though. What the heck! I opt for the little red number with my black Louboutin heels and grab my small, black clutch bag.

'Wow, you look stunning!' Paul greets me at the entrance. 'Apart from the lipstick on your chin.'

'What?'

'Only joking!'

'What are *you* wearing?' He takes my hand and rests it on his tie.

'It's red. Like your dress. See! Suitably a-tie-red – attired – as you'd expect.'

I call him a cunning linguist. We laugh.

'I don't think I've ever known you to wear a suit and tie.'

'Well, now I am. Feel and see.'

We leave my coat and cane in the cloakroom and walk in, arm in arm. He whispers, 'Heads are turning. I think they're surprised to see me in a suit.' He hasn't lost his sense of humour.

The chair warmly welcomes everybody and then launches straight into his awards speech. He touches on a few facts from my journalistic career, makes a joke about journalism being a second-best career for failed writers, and finishes on an incredibly embarrassing compliment: 'There have been few female journalists of Hannah's calibre: Martha Gellhorn, Kate Adie and Lindsey Hilsum, to name just a few. She finds herself in good company in this lineup. And we should not forget that she has always been accompanied by her brave photographer, Paul Mason, who's brought her stories to life with his exceptional footage and photography. Ladies and gentlemen, bravery has no gender. Hannah writes about the victims of war; the world needs to know who the real victims of war are ...'

The applause is overwhelming. I can no longer hold back my tears. Paul hands me a tissue, whispering, 'You've got a standing ovation, mate. Well done, you.'

Later on, having had to pose for the cameras with the trophy, we're ushered into another room, where we have to face questions from a motley crew of journalists from various newspapers.

'Andrew Klein, *Sunday Times*. You've reported from many different war zones, including Chechnya, Sri Lanka and Libya. You have a reputation for being the last one to leave the most dangerous places at the most dangerous times. Why do you take such risks, Miss Tring?'

'You shouldn't believe what you hear about me, least of all that which I tell you myself. We always have to ask ourselves whether the level of risk is worth the story. We stay when we think it's important for the world to know. Next?'

'The lady in the pink jacket,' Paul interjects.

'Lucy Bromley, from the *Telegraph*. What made you decide to become a journalist?'

'So, as the chair said earlier on, becoming a journalist is often a second choice. I always wanted to be a writer. Here's a little anecdote for you. I remember my mother's comment when I was proudly presented with the college prize for "Best Short Story". She said, "You can't write about *us*. What will people think?" She didn't understand when I tried to argue that it is actual events that give a story life. I suppose that's why, in the end, I became a reporter rather than a writer, and hunted for stories in the real world rather than in the world of fiction. Another question?'

'Megan Jacobs, Institute for Psychology and Neuroscience. Many of our soldiers returning from war zones suffer from prolonged PTSD. How challenging do you find your job, and how do you both cope with post-traumatic stress?'

I turn my head towards Paul, eyebrows raised. Baring your soul in front of an audience of former colleagues and strangers is the last thing you want to do on a Saturday night after a pleasant and moving awards ceremony. Paul nudges me, asking in a quiet, confident voice, 'Shall I take that one?'

'Yes, please. Go ahead.'

'The answer is simple, Ms Jacobs. We find the nearest bar and just drink a lot.'

Deadly silence. Then, a few giggles from the back of the room, followed by slow clapping.

'Well, on that cue, ladies and gentlemen,' the chair intervenes, 'if there aren't any further questions, please come and join us for a drink in the bar with Hannah Tring and Paul Mason.' Enthusiastic applause.

Paul hooks my arm over his and leads me down from the stage. 'I know it's not the nearest, but let's grab a cab to Wax Bar. They've got your favourite cocktails and some amazing rare vinyl.'

We end up drinking till closing time, reminiscing about joint missions, the good and the bad times. In the taxi home, we chat about the time we first met in Kabul's Serena Hotel. I remember it well. February 2008, I was sent to Kabul to report on a terrorist assault on the hotel compound in which seven people died, including a Norwegian journalist I knew well.

'Do you remember? It was the time of growing insurgency against the International Security Forces.'

'Why wouldn't I remember? I was working for the International Security Assistance Force (ISAF) then. You asked me for an interview in the embassy. The best chat-up line, I thought. But are you sure it wasn't 2009?'

'I should have some notes about this ... Are you taking me home? You can stay at mine if you like.'

It's almost midnight by the time we get home. I wouldn't have felt safe returning home late on my own, but I'm not about to tell Paul about the rape attack – not now, anyway.

I don't want to spoil the evening. Nor will I tell him about breaking up with Rob.

'Make yourself comfy. There's beer in the fridge. Help yourself. I'll just have a quick look to see if I can find my notes about our first meet. Definitely no chat-up lines there … I can guarantee.'

Bedroom – bottom drawer. It takes a while until my smart reader locates the 2008 notebook. As I return to the living room, I can hear heavy breathing and a light snoring coming from the sofa. Paul is fast asleep! I turn down the volume on my phone and start reading the diary entry.

3 February 2008 – Serena Hotel
I'm in the Westerners' Kabul, the city within the city, which is unaffordable and simply off limits to ordinary Afghans. There are hundreds and hundreds of Westerners – mostly military personnel and contractors, but also aid workers, diplomats, journalists and fortune seekers – all swarming around like locusts in what they call the Kabubble. Anything seems possible here. You can enjoy a Budweiser with your imported steak at Boccaccio's, or have a boozy rooftop party overlooking the dim lights of the city at night. It's a weird place.

US and Afghan soldiers still have a heavy presence in and around the hotel, so I feel relatively safe. My first port of call is the Australian Embassy, which is based in the hotel.

The man sitting opposite me in the waiting room is wearing an ISAF badge with a UK flag on his left arm. He is tall, and oozes strength around the shoulders and arms. His weathered face, carelessly shaven, looks at me through narrow eyes like sharp little knives. He holds a folder on his lap marked 'Security Council', and bearing the United Nations emblem. My first thought: Nab him for an ISAF interview. *As I slowly raise my eyes to meet his, I notice a scar on his right hand and his mud-splashed boots. He looks at me as if I have disturbed his thoughts, but the frown on his brow dissolves when I smile at him. We both start talking at the same time and laugh. 'You first.' I tell him who I am and why I'm here. He agrees to meet me for an interview after dinner in the hotel, on condition I agree not to reveal my source.*

My notes don't mention whether or not the interview actually took place. Perhaps it didn't. All I remember is that we sat on the roof terrace, drank a lot and talked until the early hours of the morning. No, I mean serious stuff. He had recently returned from Helmand Province, then left the army to become an ISAF spokesperson.

'I am so tired of covering this senseless war,' he told me then. 'Hey, we're bringing peace and democracy to Afghanistan. Just give us another ten years,' he continued with a wry smile. 'There'll just be more deaths on all sides, more suffering for the ordinary people. All we can do is show the world the true picture of what's going on here on the ground: the dead and the maimed after yet another bomb has gone off, and the newly orphaned children wailing in the streets. There will never be any peace until we've all gone.'

I know. First impressions can often be deceptive, and over time we tend to correct them. But I knew straight away that I had found a kindred spirit, someone who is genuine, someone I could trust and rely on. And that has never changed. Little did I know at the time that we would be travelling together for the next four years and that he would become my companion, my best friend, my soulmate. Should I wake him with a kiss?

Chapter 11

Jenny

I'm back after an exciting visit at the UN in New York, followed by a dangerous and difficult mission in Damascus to interview the opposition leader.

What was supposed to last a day or two turned out to be a protracted wild goose chase. Hours before my arrival, a suspected chemical weapons attack had killed hundreds of rebels in the predominantly Sunni suburb of Damascus. The Syrian opposition accused pro-Assad forces of having carried out the attacks. Khalid was in hiding for days. When he finally texted me his new address, I had just ten minutes' warning to stay away. His safe house was then blown up by an explosion, allegedly caused by a gas leak. After that, everything went quiet. I don't even know whether he is still alive.

Coming straight from the airport the next morning, I return empty-handed to my desk at Channel 4. My new boss Eric slams a copy of the *Observer* on my keyboard. Headline: 'Putin's air support for Assad's troops in northern Syria'.

'Your successor has done well,' he comments, sarcastically.

Allegedly, Russian planes were dropping phosphor and cluster bombs on predominantly civilian targets. Supporting pictures show advancing government forces in the Turkmen mountains and the aftermath of death and destruction. There's also footage on the lunchtime news outlining what's happening in Northern Syria. I'm sure that's where Hannah would have gone. Eric's stony face says it all. 'That's where *you* should have gone!'

I get an even frostier reception at home, as soon as I put my case down.

'Back already?' There's more than disapproval in Hamish's raised voice. 'How can you leave Hannah to fend for herself in Berlin; not take her for her operation at the clinic? Yes, and thanks for your curt text, informing me you'd flown to Damascus at short notice. For what? You didn't even ring that evening to tell me you were OK – there was an item on the news about a chemical attack on civilians in Damascus. Nor did you answer your bloody phone. I tried to ring you, over and over!'

Taking a step towards me, he kicks my case out of the way. It careers into the bedroom door with a crash. I can smell alcohol on his breath, so retreat to the living room. I try to keep calm, to explain that I was not able to use my phone in Damascus, for fear of giving away my location and becoming a government target.

'Honestly Hamish, I felt really bad leaving Hannah to her own devices in Berlin, but I had no choice.'

At this point, his inquisitorial tone picks up again. 'What are you trying to prove by stepping into Hannah's shoes? That you can be a hero in a war zone, too? Be shot at, face an explosion and be maimed for life? Is that it? When will you stop this senseless competition, this constant seeking for approval. From whom? You had a good, secure job at the *Observer* and you threw it all away for this?'

'For heaven's sake. I just wanted a change. And this is a more prestigious job, *and* it pays better.'

'So where does it leave *us*? We see each other even less than before. Rob told me on the phone what happened to him and Hannah. He's staying with his new partner in Düsseldorf for another year, apparently. His idea of a long-distance relationship with Hannah didn't exactly work, and it wouldn't for me, either – especially not without proper communication channels.' He walks over to the drinks cabinet and pours himself a single malt.

'Well, they wanted very different things from life.' I try to defend my sister.

'Is that all you have to say about their break-up?'

'How do you mean? You know she never wanted to settle down. She didn't want children, but Rob did. Her job always came first.'

'Family!' He dismisses my comment with a contemptuous toss of the head and walks into the bedroom. I sit back in the armchair, legs and arms crossed. On his return, he chucks a packet of pills on the coffee table.

'And these are *your* idea for having a family? Why the fuck have we been paying out for IVF for the last two months when you're on the pill? How long have you been keeping up this charade?' he bellows.

'I'm so sorry. I'd only just applied for this new job, and didn't want to be preg—'

'Spare me your excuses. I've heard enough.' He stands tall beside my chair, feet well apart, towering over me with his bad-tempered breathing.

'Remind me, Jen. When did we last make love?'

When did we? I try to think, but the crowded recent past is just one big blur. I was trying to get to grips with my new job at Channel 4. Being at Eric's beck and call is no easy feat. Damascus, Beirut, New York. New York! Do I regret my brief adventure with Mark from the UN? *Yes, I know, Han, it's a bit out of character, so let's forget about it.*

Then, with my sister in Berlin. For the last couple of months, I've hardly been at home for more than a few days at a time. Isn't it understandable – and even commendable – that you want to give your career everything you've got? And then there is the constant worry about Hannah. *How is she coping? How much help does she need? Am I neglecting her?* I'm exhausted. Where was the sex? I can't recall.

'I don't keep a tally. Should I?'

Hamish spreads his hands, palms up, resting his case. He picks up his whisky glass and sits down opposite me. His voice is now calm, but rather stand-offishly so.

'I've got some news for you: I've been headhunted by a US counterintelligence firm, and I'm seriously considering moving to Washington in three months. So it's decision time for us.' He stands up bolt upright again, turns around and fetches his leather jacket. 'I'm meeting some friends in the pub tonight. As I say, we have to decide – make or break?' His voice trails after him like the shreds of our relationship.

I'm at my wits' end. *What now? I'm shattered. Everything's just falling apart. I need to talk to Hannah. But why is she not picking up?* I try her old Nokia brick, which she still carries with her. Nothing. OK – parents, then. They might know where she is.

It's Dad who answers the phone. 'Yes, darling. Hannah rang us from Berlin to say she's had the operation, so now we just have to wait and see.'

'I know, Dad. I was with her in Berlin. But that was two weeks ago. Do you know where she is now?'

'Well, then. *You* should know, if you were with her. Did you see the article about her in the *Telegraph*? Hannah won a prize – "Journalist of the Year"! We're all so proud of her. So where is she now?'

Hopeless. We're going around in circles. Next, I try my friends Cathy and Emily. Both lines go straight to answerphone. *Think!* Then I remember. Paul went to the awards ceremony with Hannah. He must have been the last person who saw her, and he's picking up!

'Hi Paul. It's Jen. Sorry to ring you so late. You OK?'

'Hello, I'm good, thanks. How are you doing?'

'Fine, but I'm just wondering whether you know where Han is? Did you go to the awards with her?'

'Yeah, we had a great time. Your sis got a standing ovation! I took her home afterwards and she asked me to stay the night. Now she's off to Turkey for a couple of weeks' holiday.'

'She's what?'

'Holiday. What's wrong with that? She deserves a bloody good rest. She's gone with one of the tour guides from Traveleyes. She'll be absolutely fine.'

'Didn't you want to go with her? Or did she fail to tell you that she's split up with Rob?'

He pauses for a moment, his voice changing from friendly to matter-of-fact. 'No, she didn't, actually. But I'm off on a job to Bogotá next week, anyway, so it wouldn't have worked. She'll be fine. She might even send you a postcard.'

I can't think straight. Why is Paul being off with me? And why didn't Hannah tell him that she and Rob had split? They've always been such close friends. I'm so tired – I hardly had any sleep on the overnight flight, but I just know I won't be able to sleep. Not now. Not with all this shit in my head. I curl up on the sofa with a cup of camomile tea warming my cold hands. *Is Hamish really serious about living in the States? Where on earth does that leave me?*

Two days later, I meet up with Cathy and Emily for a chat in our usual hangout, the Signature wine bar. I'm late arriving. The girls look like they've already had a glass or two, singing along to a retro pop song – 'I Want You to Want Me'. They both get up to give me a hug, while the waiter brings over another bottle of Chardonnay.

'We missed you last Friday. Remember? First Friday of the month – girls' night out! Your sister dropped in for a drink. She wasn't sure whether you'd be back. Is it true? Has she got someone else? She didn't say, but … Do you know why she broke off her engagement?' Emily bombards me with questions before I can even sit down.

'Wow, steady on. Yes, it's true. Living apart for a long period of time isn't easy, especially in her situation.'

'Oh my God! How's she gonna cope on her own?' Cathy chips in.

'She's quite independent, you know, and I'm always there to help, anyway. At least, for a while.'

'How come?' Emily puts her glass down, raises her eyebrows, her whole face turning into a question mark. 'You're not moving away, are you?' Now Cathy looks alarmed, too.

'Well, nothing's been decided yet, but Hamish has a job offer with a company in Washington, so we're thinking—'

'Oh no!' they respond in unison.

'And what about your new job?' Cathy asks. 'It's going so well.'

'Look, we haven't made a decision yet and it may come to nothing, so don't worry about it. Now, tell me, how are you both doing?'

Cathy takes a deep breath and sighs. 'What do you think? Look at me! I am in a dress that's now too small for me, I have gel in my hair and I haven't slept for two nights. We've both been dating a couple of guys. They looked cute, but turned out to be shits, didn't they, Emily?'

'Yeah, Cath and I have decided to give up on dating for a while and just stay with our best friends: Ben and Jerry.'

The dialogue sounds increasingly 'chick flick'. I'm not in the mood for silly jokes. Would Hannah have told them about her impending holiday? I doubt it. If she had, they would have thrown even more 'OMGs' at me.

Eventually, after a tedious chat about their unhappy relationships and their continuing search for Mr Right, the conversation pivots back to me. Questions about my future, my relationship with Hamish, about Hannah's break-up, and me, taking over her job.

As we leave the bar, the mirrors catching Cathy's profile from every pudgy-freckled angle, she concludes: 'Don't ever let anyone tell you that you can't do this job as well as your sister. If you want something, go and get it. That's what I'd do, anyway.'

On my way home, I can't help thinking that Hannah may have turned up to 'girls' night' last Friday to tell me about her holiday plans, or even to let me know if anything happened between her and Paul on awards night. Not in front of the girls, of course. I mean, she and Paul have always been close friends, but she knows he's married with a two-year-old daughter and she would respect that. She might have told him about breaking off her engagement, but clearly didn't. Respect!

I need to talk to you, Han, wherever you are in Turkey. Stay safe. I really need your advice. I'll try you again tomorrow.

Chapter 12

Hannah

I'm glad I didn't tell Paul. He'll find out sooner or later. Anyway, he was fast asleep on my sofa and we both had too much to drink that evening. It did cross my mind to wake him up with a gentle kiss, but I thought better of it. It may have sent the wrong message and I'm not the kind of woman who'd break up a marriage. Full stop. Also, having just ended my engagement with Rob, I'm not ready to jump straight into another relationship. *See, Jen – I've learned from my past mistakes.*

'Eat, pray and get away' – isn't that what people say after a break-up? Forget the praying, but I do want to escape from it all. By quite literally travelling outside my comfort zone, it should be possible to regain my inner peace, a measure of control and make a fresh start. Paul was so encouraging when I mentioned my travel idea, too, but with one proviso: 'Please don't go solo, will you? You'll need a guide. By the way, I'm off to Bogotá in a few days' time. Will keep in touch. Promise you won't go on your own.'

That's how I ended up with Ivory from Traveleyes, a company that provides tour guides for both blind and sighted people. She's a 21-year-old Ophthalmology student who's getting some work experience. Her name conjures up a whole network of associations – mainly the obvious ones, but I don't want to go there. I imagine her to be pale and white (without the tusks), having escaped from her ivory tower for the duration of the Easter holiday.

She proudly announces that she's had a day's induction on common causes of sight problems and has learned how to help people to get around safely. However, it turns out that I need to do a bit of sight and guide training myself with this inexperienced travel companion.

'Sometimes I link arms with you like this. Just relax your arm down. Does that feel comfortable? Occasionally, I will take the back of your arm, or put my right hand on your left shoulder, which means I'll be a few steps behind you.'

When I tell her that I'm looking forward to revisiting Istanbul, she responds with a muffled 'Oh, I've never been to Turkey.' I have, as a student, and I hope that this trip will rekindle my memories of the many wonderful historical sites. I explain to her that I do rely on my guide heavily, to describe what's going on around me so I can totally immerse myself in the whole experience – the sounds, smells, shapes and colours.

'You see, without your descriptions I can't build up the images in my mind. So, the more detail, the better.'

'I'll certainly do my best. But I may need some prompting if I forget,' she responds enthusiastically.

From our sparse conversation on the four-hour flight to Istanbul, I gather that Ivory has led a fairly sheltered life. She's never travelled anywhere on her own, still lives with her parents and has embarrassing gaps in her geography, which becomes apparent when I mention some of the places I used to report from. She doesn't watch the news and has never heard of the Arab Spring. Could she find Libya, Egypt, Yemen or Syria on a globe? I doubt it. It feels more and more like a role reversal: sighted travel guide needs blind person to see the world.

Istanbul. Our first challenge is to find our hotel on the far side of the city's bazaar. Occasionally, I let go of Ivory's arm, so my hands can explore the overhanging branches of trees lining the streets. I can feel some swelling buds that are about to open, releasing their soft shoots within. Rubbing the buds between my fingers, I smell their delicate fragrance in the warm spring breeze.

'On this map, it looks as if we need to go right through this giant market,' Ivory says, pulling me along unceremoniously. We turn around and make our way back up the cobbled street to the entrance of the Grand Bazaar. There's a cacophony of loud voices everywhere. A scooter or moped passes through the crowd, quite close to us. My guide pulls me to one side.

'Shit!' she shouts. 'Careful. He almost drove over your suitcase. Did you not …?'

She doesn't finish her sentence. She sounds agitated and frightened. For me, the bazaar holds no terrors at all. On the contrary – I love the entire ambience. I'm overwhelmed by the sounds of oriental music, the stallholders' voices, enticing you, and the variety of different smells emanating from the stalls we pass. I stop, attracted by a sweet, leathery smell. Instinctively, I reach out to touch the things in front of me.

'Here, there are lots of handbags and scarves on display,' Ivory tells me. 'But I don't think you should touch—'

'Is beautiful scarf for nice lady,' the shopkeeper interrupts, wrapping a silky-smooth veil around my head. 'And this one for other lady,' he adds.

'No, thanks. We're just looking. My friend is not able to see your scarves.'

'But she wants to *look* beautiful. Is silk – feel, with hand-painted spring flowers. For you, only 150 lira.'

'Feels very smooth. I like spring colours. I'll take it.' I hand over my purse for Ivory to pay.

'How much was that in English money?' she asks, as I linger at the next stall, following my nose. I can smell spices, which heightens my senses and my curiosity. Goodness me – it smells like an aromatic wonderland.

'What can you see?'

This time Ivory provides a lot more detail. 'There are six- – hang on – no, seven-by-three-deep large crates, filled with different spices. All amazing colours: red, green, orange, yellow and various sandy colours. They all have price tags with names in Turkish, which I can't read. Then there are things hanging from the ceiling. Looks like dried herbs and sponges and giant mushrooms. I have no idea what they are. Right in front of you there are all sorts of nuts like pistachios and packs of baklava, halva and Turkish delight. I've never seen anything like it.'

A few minutes later, I stop again, tempted by the sound of glasses being stirred in front of me. There's a slightly musty scent.

'Where are we now?'

'Persian rugs, all sizes and colours. Two men in funny white caps are drinking tea – not very interesting.' A slight degree of petulance has crept into her voice. One of the

143

men, who smells of garlic, approaches me, pushing a rug into my outstretched hand. It feels smooth and plush. The other side of the rug seems to match the pattern on the top, and there's no other backing added to the underside. Paul taught me that this is a sign of a genuine handmade rug.

Having linked arms again with impatient Ivory, I resist her slight pull. One of the men offers us a small glass of sweet tea. Has he sensed a business opportunity?

'Look, is very good quality – handmade!' He begins his sales spiel. I want her to feel the texture and describe the colours to me. But she finds the experience of stopping and looking around exhausting.

'We really need to move on and find our hotel. We're not even halfway through the market yet.'

How can I explain to her that, for me, it's all about the journey, while she's obviously just interested in getting to our destination.

'You remind me of our golden retriever at home,' she says, exasperated. 'He's into everything, just like you: nose straight in, paws straight in, sniffing out everything.'

'That's a good picture,' I applaud her. 'I can see myself in that. We have two big dogs on our farm. They're just like that.'

I begin to see the world in new ways, encounter things I haven't experienced before. Admittedly, I still bump into all sort of objects in foreign places, but then there are also new images in my mind. I sense things differently – the smells, the sounds, the textures – all building up to a new construction of reality. I see more with my brain than I used to. Dr Fink said this would happen to me. She calls it neuroplasticity: the brain's ability to reorganise itself by forming new neural connections using the other senses. Maybe I can prove to Ivory that you don't actually need your sight to see the world.

First morning in Istanbul. It's five in the morning. I've just been woken by a loud prayer sounding from one of the nearby minarets, probably coming from the Blue Mosque, which is not far from our hotel. Incredible. Such an amazing sound!

'That noise gets on my nerves,' Ivory complains over breakfast.

'They use different scales to ours, called *maqams* – Arabic for "position".' I try to educate her. 'The reason it sounds strange to our ears is that a *maqam* sometimes uses quarter tones, a pitch between two semitones, such as a tone between F# and G.'

'It's still very annoying, especially when it happens five times a day.' She must have read this in her guidebook. And then she has a confession to make. She didn't actually pack the guide.

'Never mind,' I console her. 'Travel books don't really work for me, anyway, apart from a bit of history. I have to have other sensory experiences if I am to get to know and understand a place. I usually need some help from a local tour guide to find them.'

The city's tourist office emails us three recommendations, all apparently experts on Istanbul's hidden treasures. With a guide for a sensory tour in mind, I pick Gulya, a food expert and perfume lover. She turns out to be an enthusiastic, touchy-feely guide who goes off the beaten track with us, rather than shadowing the tourist trail. First location is a food market in the eastern part of the city. I can smell oranges and mangoes, before we reach a fish stall with an overwhelmingly strong smell.

'Eww, gross! There's a huge slimy octopus with its head still on,' Ivory shouts out, as she rapidly ushers me along. I would like to experience more of the fish counter, but Gulya seems to have gone ahead. I'm not sure whether we're at another fruit stall now, but Gulya drops a soft peach into my hand. 'For you!' She encourages me to feel and smell it.

'If you touch it, you have to buy it,' Ivory chips in from the sideline. Gulya laughs as if a child has said something funny.

'No, no. You can touch and put back. Or eat quickly.'

We turn into a narrow side street and enter a shop that apparently only sells pickled fruits and vegetables. Gulya exchanges a few greetings with the shopkeeper, then guides my hand along a row of what feel like giant glass storage jars. She describes each of their colours and contents to me.

When I turn around, there's a very powerful smell. 'What's this in front of me?'

'These are jugs with pickled juices,' Gulya explains. 'A delicacy in Turkey that's thought to have healing properties.'

We all give it a try – some of us reluctantly. The juices are made from salt, lemon and mysterious spices, a sensory experience we could have done without, I have to admit.

But I would like to have seen Ivory's disgusted facial expression when she took a cautious sip.

By the end of the tour – we've also taken in a bakery and a fantastic perfume shop – Gulya has completely taken over from Ivory as my sensory guide. When she sees me and Gulya with her arm round my waist, posing for a selfie, Ivory asks in a little girl's voice whether I mind if she does a bit of shopping on her own. We don't see her for the rest of the day. She's obviously fed up with playing a poor second fiddle. Gulya and I spend the rest of the afternoon in a café chatting away.

I have thoroughly enjoyed this off-the-beaten-track tour, avoiding the tourist traps and people snapping away at the sights. It's been a very different experience from my visit as an 18-year-old. Of course, photos no longer work for me as souvenirs. My memories are now made by meeting people, experiencing new smells, and sounds and textures.

After three days in Istanbul, our tour bus heads east into the mountains. We are staying for a few days at a farm high up in the Honaz National Park. Emre, our host, is a beekeeper. He also keeps chickens and goats. He's built himself a high platform, which he calls his beehouse, where he can get close to the hives and harvest the honey. Ivory and I have to wear the full protective gear: a bee suit, hat and veil, and gloves. Emre is apparently immune to bee stings; he doesn't even wear gloves. As we approach the platform, I can hear the buzzing of hundreds of bees. An incredible sound! It resonates with me, reminding me of

Rimsky-Korsakov's 'Flight of the Bumblebee', a really fast 'buzzing' piece which I used to play on my parents' piano.

'I'm not getting up there – no way! It's a death trap!' Ivory describes the platform's rickety structure. Emre lets me feel the supporting beams, then guides me up the ladder. We've reached the top. The humming of the bees grows even louder up high. I find I love the smell of warm beeswax and honey. There's also a pleasant hint of pine and cedar in the air. Emre guides my hand over the honeycomb, with its perfect structure and tiny openings.

'You must come up here. It's amazing!'

Ivory eventually overcomes her fear of heights. She's pleased that Emre lets her harvest some of the honey to take home.

In the afternoon, after lunch, Ivory and I sit out on the alpine meadows, listening in awe to the stillness all around us. It is a unique feeling of calm and tranquillity. I have no sense of passing time. Everything just stands still up here. In the distance, somewhere far away, the muted sound of a cowbell and a bleating goat encroach on the peaceful silence.

'This is the most beautiful place I've ever been in my life.' Ivory speaks in a brittle voice as if she's about to cry. 'I find it difficult to describe.'

'Go on. You can.'

'From where we're sitting, we have an amazing three-sixty view. Snow-capped mountaintops all around, with rugged, steep sloping sides; floating below are carpets of white clouds, looking like huge clumps of cotton wool. And, further down below, as you look into the valleys, there are the green alpine pastures with the odd mountain pine growing in between.'

'Very good. I can see that. You're definitely getting better at describing the world around me. That's great.' She seems to lap up my compliment.

'It's because *you* make me see things in so much more detail. It feels a bit like I'm painting a picture for you.' She rests her hand on my shoulder. 'I would like to have had an older sister like you – adventurous and daring. I feel I haven't seen much of the world at all.'

'Imagine the world as a huge book with thousands of pages. Those who do not dare to travel only ever see one single page.'

'Yes, but don't you think that travelling can also be quite dangerous? My parents always—'

'You know, I'd rather experience the world around me, possibly get hurt on the odd occasion, than not venture out at all.' She removes her hand from my shoulder and takes a deep breath as if to psych herself up for her next question.

'How did you hurt your eyes?' she asks, out of the blue.

'Let's go inside and have a drink. It's a long story.'

Ivory opts for Turkish tea – she loves the small, tulip-shaped glasses it's served in. When Emre offers me some 'lion's milk' – the local term for raki – I can't resist, but I do add some ice cubes to water it down.

'Look, it's turned your drink into a milky white colour. Is that why it's called "lion's milk"?' she wonders.

After a few sips, I relax and give her a journalistic account of my accident. She wants to dig deeper; probes me about how I felt after the accident and how the people around me reacted.

'I was so scared, Ivory. I didn't want to be that blind person. It felt like part of my brain had died. I had this desperate feeling of being shut in, wanting to get out and break through that dark curtain into the light out there.'

She clears her throat to regain her brittle voice.

'I think I would have felt so vulnerable and kept myself to myself. Did you not feel lonely? I would have just stayed at home and listened to audiobooks.'

'I needed to keep positive because, if I didn't, I would've gone down into that dark place and stayed there. When your independence is taken away from you, it affects all the people around you.' I take another swig of my raki. Memories and feelings come flooding back. 'I sometimes dream I can see, and then I wake up and lose my sight again and again. The more the frustration builds, the more it affects your partner and the people around you. It's a long grieving process. You realise your life is never going to be the same again.'

The picture coming into my mind is that of a capsized ship. I pause to regain my equilibrium.

'So, in a way, I've accepted my fate. I refuse to live in nostalgia; I would rather live in reality. That's why I've come here, to see the world again … in a different way. And you're helping me to do that.'

Her chair screeches on the stone floor. Ivory walks over to me, elbows my raki glass out of the way and flings her arms round my neck. Her cheeks are wet with tears. 'I'm sorry.'

'Never mind.' I dab her tears with my sleeve. 'I'm drunk enough as it is. You know, it's our last day tomorrow. Let's make the most of it.' We agree to get up at the crack of dawn and watch the sun rise over the mountains.

Six a.m. 'It's still dawn,' Ivory yawns as we return arm in arm to our spot on the dewy alpine meadows, both wearing woolly jumpers to shield us from the fresh breeze. We settle down on a piece of canvas, borrowed from Emre.

'Let's listen to some music while we're waiting,' I suggest, without expecting an answer. I played the piece late last night, so can quickly retrieve it on my phone. It's a short intermezzo by Massenet called 'Méditation'. It seems to have its desired effect. Not a word.

Then, the early morning sunrise comes like a kept promise.

'Wow! It's magical, Hannah,' Ivory exclaims. 'All the mountains are taking on a rosy tint, and the valleys and trees are covered in mist. It looks brilliant – like a glossy postcard photographed with a soft lens. And look here! Even the dewdrops on the meadows have a silky colour. I can't describe—'

'You don't have to.'

Golden rays of sunlight are dazzling me, overpowering me with too much light. I feel stunned, as if staring into a car's full beam by night. I have to shield my eyes for a while until – that's unbelievable! – until I can eventually recognise a silhouette of mountains around me and a carpet of white clouds hanging over the valleys. It's a very blurred vision, but it's a vision of something! *Is my sight coming back? Five weeks after the stem cell op? Can this really be true?* My gaze remains upwards, away from Ivory, head turning in both directions to take in the stunning panoramic view. I need to hold onto something.

'Ouch! You're hurting me! Let go of my wrist,' she shouts.

'I'm so sorry. I didn't realise what I was doing. I'm so excited!'

I look into her (maybe) brown eyes for the first time. Although my sight is still hazy – I'm gazing through this milky veil – she appears very different from the image I had formed in my mind. Not pale and white, but a face of rosy complexion, freckly and fresh. She stares at me uncomprehendingly when I tell her about the operation that seems to have brought at least some of my sight back. She returns my smile and flings her arms round my neck for a second time.

'That's so amazing! I'm so happy for you.'

'It feels like a magical awakening. All of this is so breathtaking. It's unreal … Now *I* can't find the words to—'

'You don't have to.'

Just as she described the panorama a few moments ago, the rising sun has cast a rosy tint across the morning sky and bathed the mountains all around us in its beautiful hues. But my brain cannot make sense of all the information it is receiving. Oh, my goodness … it's so overwhelming. However, Ivory's face, her body, trees, seem to have no depth. They look like flat paper cuttings. It's only when I touch things that they slowly take shape, regain their depth and jump into focus. I'm sure Dr Fink will be able to explain this when I next get to speak to her.

The tour bus picks us up after breakfast and we say goodbye to the lovely Emre. Instinctively, I grab and sweep my cane from side to side before climbing inside. That's when this weird idea jumps into my head. *What if...? What if I carry on as before? Tell nobody that I can see what they're doing, how they're treating me. How they regard me with all their pity or disdain.*

A worthwhile experiment? I don't know.

Chapter 13

Jenny

'I'm back.'

'Han? You OK? I was worried about you. I kept trying to call, but you didn't pick up.'

'Well, here I am.'

'I'm still at work, so can't talk for long. Paul told me you went on holiday to Turkey. Really? Why didn't you say anything?'

'Yeah, I had a great time. I was going to tell you at your girls' night out, but you didn't show up. I'm calling from the Prêt, near your office. Shall I drop by at lunchtime?'

'Uh, no … I'm not at my desk at the moment, but I can come to yours after work, if that's OK. Really got to dash. Sorry!'

Phew, that was close! If she'd come over to my old workplace at the *Observer*, they'd have told her I don't work there any more. Eric almost gave me away when he rushed past my desk shouting, 'Need your report for the seven o'clock news.'

Tanned, with elaborately coiffed hair and dressed presentably, Hannah opens the door when I ring the bell. With a welcoming smile on her face, she tells me to make myself comfy in the living room while she makes us some tea. It's cold for late April, so there's an electric fire switched on in the corner of the unusually tidy room.

A few bulbs are lit in the standard lamp of Scandinavian design. They reveal a neat pile of books and newspapers on the nest of tables below. Ornaments brought back from far-flung places vie for attention on the mantelpiece – a blue and white ceramic jar sits next to a small bronze Buddha figure framed on either side by Oriental terraria. *Not my taste at all.*

Hannah puts a tray of delicate, tulip-shaped tea glasses on the coffee table.

'These are pretty,' I say, putting one of them into her outstretched hand.

'My travel companion, Ivory, bought them for me in Istanbul.' She puts the glass down and starts fiddling with her phone.

'Here, take a look. She offered to take these holiday snaps for me.' I swipe through the photos: pictures of markets in vibrant colours, Hannah trying on scarves, stalls full of Oriental spices … then a few selfies.

'Who's the woman with the black hair, with her arm round you.'

'Oh, that must be Gulya, the touchy-feely sensory guide who showed me round Istanbul. She was so much fun to be with, letting me experience the markets and taking me to places off the beaten track.'

Then, a few shots of snow-capped mountains, Hannah wrapped in beekeeper clothes with an array of honeycombs and masses of crawling bees.

'Looks like you had some fun,' I say nonchalantly. *Not exactly my idea of a holiday, though.*

'I needed to get away from it all. Rob's affair affected me more than I'd thought. There was no way we could … I just don't trust him any more.'

'No regrets?'

'None.'

'So, what's happening with the flat?'

She just shrugs her shoulders and sips her tea.

There is a brief pause in the conversation. I get up and walk to the window. Traffic is sparse. No audible birdsong. Two fighter jets scar the clear sky, etching visible traces into the blue canvas – two long white lines running in parallel, not crossing over. If they did, they might crash. Sisters!

Do I dare to tell Hannah about me taking over her job at Channel 4? About Hamish's ultimatum to give it all up and move to Washington with him? About my affair with Mark in New York? There are now some extra folds in the fabric of deception. I just can't bring myself to—

'How's Hamish these days?' She interrupts my thoughts. It's like she's read my mind.

'He's doing well. He'll be travelling to Washington on business soon. He said they might offer him a job over there. There's a chance we may be moving to the States.'

'Do you want to?'

I quickly change the subject and ask about Hannah's future plans – work, summer holidays, seeing Mum and Dad. She says she urgently needs to find a job; she's skint, as always. She wants to do more travelling, and maybe sign up for a part-time Creative Writing MA in in the autumn. I reassure her that people with sight loss can find work in every major category of employment these days.

It's probably not easy at all. Especially not for someone who's as demanding as she is.

The fact she's able to carry on without Rob is admirable, but it's also sad in a way, because it confirms that his role in the relationship was always ancillary and expendable. *Am I expendable for Hamish?* Still, it's worth remembering that Rob has been an arse and she certainly can't be held responsible for the break-up.

My mobile rings. 'Caller ID withheld. That must be Hamish.' I excuse myself. 'He always does that – hacker habit. Want to say hello, Han?'

'Yeah, sure.' I put my phone on speaker.

'Hi, darling. You OK?'

'Hi, sweetie, it's John. Can you talk?'

Shite. I quickly turn off the speaker. 'I can't talk now. Sorry. Call you back later.'

'Whoa! Something you want to tell me? That sounded like an American accent. Is little sis having an affair? "Sweetie"! Don't worry – my lips are sealed. You can trust me.'

How embarrassing. But there's something in her tone that's tempting me to tell all – every little salacious detail, every hidden intimacy.

However, my brief account sounds more like the first few lines of an unexciting CV. Forty-one years old, Operations Manager in the UN, previously worked in Washington for the National Security Council, lives in Brooklyn, and … married with two kids.

'We only met a couple of times, in Damascus and New York. He's ever so charming, good-looking and keeps saying that he's fallen in love with me.'

Hannah listens patiently to me pouring my heart out, hands folded peacefully in her lap. Her body language changes as soon as I tell her about my awful row with Hamish – arguing about my long business trips, being away from home, not spending enough time together and, you know, *that*, as well. In the end, I succumb, and tell her that I carried on taking the pill even when we'd started the IVF.

She frowns and shakes her head. *Would she have known? How?* She leaves her unfinished tea on the tray, and goes to pour herself a drink from the decanter on the sideboard. Then she turns around, changes her seat, and is now facing me. In the long-drawn-out discussion that ensues, she's kind and non-judgmental at first, striving to show compassion for the circumstances that led to the affair. However, she's concerned it'll harm my relationship with Hamish further, and the others involved.

'Look, long work stints away from home can take their toll on a relationship,' she says calmly, like an agony aunt. 'I know all about that, believe me. Like Hamish, Rob was always complaining that we had precious little time for each other. But that's no excuse for an affair. I also know how tempting it can be to seek affection elsewhere when you're travelling to far-flung places. But, when *I'm* at work, I don't play around. Never have done.'

'What? Not even with Paul?'

'Certainly not. He's married with a two-year old daughter, you know. I admit, I was tempted a couple of times. We're very close friends and we've travelled together for four years.'

Big sister talk. I carry on regardless, talking about Mark and probably giving far too much away. She looks straight into my eyes, as if she can see me, weighing and measuring my every word, every sentence, against her own moral standards. *You didn't always have high morals ... Remember—?*

'From what you're telling me about John, he may well have a crush on you, but it strikes me he just wants to fit you into his own busy schedule. And, more to the point, he's married with kids. So, I definitely wouldn't go there, especially if you think moving to Washington with Hamish will give you a better chance of keeping the relationship with Mark going. Why don't you talk to Hamish, make a clean breast of it? If he really loves you, he may forgive you.'

'I can't. Not now. He's already furious with me. He's only just found out that when we started IVF I was on the pill.'

'Why on earth ...?' Her voice takes on an exasperated edge. 'He wanted to have a child with you, Jen! And you—'

'I know. It was so stupid. But I've been really busy at work, travelling a lot more than usual and I wanted to wait a bit longer. Anyway, I stopped taking the pill after our row.'

'And you couldn't just *tell* him that? Or did your affair with Mark play a part?'

'I don't know. Maybe. I don't think so. I'm so confused.'

'Just tell him the truth – before he finds out.'

'Listen, I need to get back. I promised to be home by half seven. Thanks for listening. I really appreciate it. I'll sort it out … somehow. I like what you've done with your hair, by the way.'

As I walk back home from the tube, the light drizzle soon turns into a heavy April shower. No umbrella, as usual. For a few moments I shelter under a shop window, hoping the deluge will stop. In the reflection of the glass, I can see my hair dripping with water, smudged mascara running down my cheeks. The rain keeps bucketing down relentlessly. I no longer care, so walk on, stepping right through the puddles. Soon, I'm drenched from top to toe, and with every step my heels squelch a melancholic sigh. My eyes follow the torrents of water heading for the drains. *Just like my relationship with Hamish*, I fear, *if I tell him. It's all going down the fucking drain.*

I turn into our street, enter the building and note that the time switch for the light in the stairwell is still on. I walk up to the second floor, imagining that Hamish must have returned a few minutes before me. Shaking my head like a bedraggled dog, I drop my drenched raincoat, kick off my heels and ring the bell. No answer. I ring again and knock our Morse code distress signal. Nothing. I fumble frantically for the keys in my handbag. The key only goes in halfway. I try again, more forcefully this time. I check I've got the right key. *Has he left his key in the lock?* More knocking, heavier this time. More insistent bell ringing. I pause and listen. Still nothing. I sink down on the doormat, exhausted, nonplussed and extremely wet. The light in the stairwell has run its ten minutes and goes off automatically. I switch it back on and look at my phone. Ten past eight.

What now? Hamish's number is engaged. I slide down, my back against the door.

Half an hour later, Hamish stumbles through the front door downstairs, singing an old Scottish love song:

I once loved my bonnie lassie
She was pretty and classy
Thinking she was pure
as a lily in the dell …

He crawls up the stairs on all fours, half drunk, then stops dead at the top and turns to face me, cowering on the doormat.

'Hello, Jennifer. Help me out here. What rhymes with "dell"?'

'Not funny. I came back at half past seven as agreed. And now I can't get in. What have you done to the lock?'

'So sorry, dear. Apologies.' He laughs. 'It's certainly *past* half past and I'm half pissed. Oh, by the way, I've changed the lock. I presumed you'd made your decision to go to New York rather than come to Washington with me.'

'What are you talking about?'

He unlocks the door, steps over my coat and stumbles straight to the drinks cabinet in the living room. I follow him in, strip off my wet clothes in the hall. I'm baffled to know what he may have found out, and from whom. So I tread carefully.

'I was going to tell you—'

'You don't have to.' He pops his head round the corner like a clown, grimacing. 'You see, there has been this little worm of suspicion, which recently infested our relationship. It's a bit like a nasty computer worm, the kind of malware that always causes major harm to the network. I wanted to make sure my fiancée wasn't sleeping around while she was away "on business". So I hacked your phone. I've read all your sordid little messages.' His voice suddenly turns deadly serious. 'The game's up, Jen. You can stay the night, but you're in the guest room now.'

I dry myself in the bathroom. A few moments later, I'm sitting opposite him, shivering in my dressing gown, arms and legs crossed. His tone is no longer waspish, more matter-of-fact, as he pours himself another single malt.

'You of all people should know that most of my work revolves around penetration testing – finding a way into IT systems to expose their vulnerabilities. So, by comparison, hacking your phone wasn't exactly a challenge.'

My immediate reaction is to sharply protest, but I think better of it.

'I am so sorry, Hamish. I didn't mean to hurt you. It just happened. It's not serious – we only met a few times.'

'Not serious, eh? "I'm thinking about you all the time … I can't wait to see you again … I've fallen in love with you." There's worse, too. Shall I read out some more?'

'Stop … I'll finish it with him. New leaf. I promise you. It was just—'

'Where did it happen? Here? In my flat? In our bed?' He hisses the questions between closed teeth.

'It doesn't matter, Hamish. It doesn't *matter* where.'

'It does to me. In his flat? In New York? Or did you always go to a hotel? Is that why you didn't pick up your phone? How long has it been going on? I've only been checking your texts for the last two months.'

'For God's sake, Hamish. That's enough. What else can I say? It was thoughtless of me. I'm really very sorry.'

He looks wounded when our eyes meet for a few seconds. He's obviously fighting with himself to regain control, before resuming his judgment.

'I find it very hard to believe you could betray me in this way. Would you have carried on if I hadn't found you out? Don't answer that.'

Then he repeats his earlier verdict: 'You can stay the night, but you're in the guest room now.'

I'm not staying. He's chucking me out of his flat. Have I lost him for good? Will he come round if I give up my job and agree to go to Washington with him? Promise to make a new start? Maybe. I'm not sure.

I throw a few clothes and overnight things in my travel case and pick up my car keys. Hamish is slumped on the sofa, watching football. He seems surprised to see me ready to leave, but doesn't get up.

'I'll come round at the weekend. Can we talk then? I still love you.'

No response. I shut the door and leave.

My immediate thought is to go back to Hannah – a daunting but not altogether selfish one. Sharing a flat with her would come with certain duties and moral obligations: caring for my blind sister, helping her cope with PTSD, putting up with her frequent mood swings, being lectured by her about my infidelity. All this, of course, presents me with something of a conundrum.

As I reach for my keys to her flat, it strikes me that I'd have to pretend to still be working for the *Observer*, rather than the *Channel 4 News*. Contemplating the mighty effort involved in this charade, and the likelihood of being found out, I turn on my heels and check into the nearest hotel.

I kick off my heels, drop my travel case and throw myself onto the bed. It's almost midnight. My phone's almost dead. So I text him.

> *Honey. Sorry to cut you off earlier. I was at my sister's and she was listening in. I've got some bad news. Hamish has hacked my phone. He's found out about us. He's read all our messages. I don't know what to do. Call me. Early morning, before work if you can. I'll be on my own.*
> *Love you*
> *xxxxxx*

I'm so confused. I won't be able to sleep now. What else did I expect from Hamish other than bitter resentment? There was a certain finality in his decision not to let me stay more than one night. My apologies, my plaintive words, just washed over him. Could I persuade him at the weekend with a large dose of feminine charm?

The gloomy hotel bar is almost empty as I gulp down my double G&T and swiftly order another. Out of the corner of my eye, I'm aware that a man is looking at me. He's in his forties, with chiselled features and is dressed in smart evening wear. He keeps glancing over, so I flick back my hair and return his smile. He finishes his drink and walks towards me.

'I left the party – got bored,' he says, as our eyes meet. 'Can I buy you a drink?' He undresses me with his eyes.

'No drink, but …' The message is clear. He follows me to my room.

'Turn the light down.' That's all I said.

Chapter 14

Hannah

Jen has just left. I wonder if she noticed any changes, picked up on any clues that I've regained some of my sight. For a start, I left the lights on – she may have thought that a bit peculiar. And, for once, everything in the flat was spotlessly clean. No comment. She did, however, notice I'd had my hair done.

I was still in two minds whether to tell her my good news. But I hesitated, since she was so preoccupied with her own problems. She's in such a mess. What is she going to do? She's such a dark horse – I had no idea she was having an affair. And taking the pill while paying for IVF? Honestly! What *else* haven't I been told?

The moment I saw her flicking quickly through my holiday snaps, bored and disinterested, I made up my mind *not* to tell her. The last photo of me, getting into the minibus still holding onto my cane, reminded me of my maybe-not-so-absurd idea: what if I were to carry on as before? A plan is beginning to form in my head. I'm thinking that I don't have to lie about my regained sight, but by the same token I don't have to tell any unnecessary truths. I just won't disclose what I can see. Pretend and, for once, cheat at blind man's buff – or, in my case, blind *woman's* buff. I'm pretty good with my cane now, I like wearing dark sunglasses, plus I still have the armband.

I walk over to the bookshelf and pull out the first volume of *The Shorter Oxford English Dictionary*: 'Blind-man's-buff. 1590. A game in which one player is blindfolded, and tries to catch and identify any one of the others, who, on their part, push him about.'

There are quite a few people who have pushed me about. *I'll bear that thought in mind …*

As I slot the dictionary back in its place, I notice the small lithograph of *The Two Sisters* by Georges Lemmen, which I had relegated to the back of the shelf. I haven't looked at it for ages. Mum brought it back from Bruges as a souvenir. She gave us both a copy when we were in our teens. I never liked it, but kept it just in case Mother visited. It's an austere portrait of two girls, Jenny and Berthe, similar age difference to ours. Although they are wearing identical dresses, it appears they have little else in common and seem preoccupied by their own thoughts. On the table in the background is a bronze vase with a bunch of dried honesty, which Berthe seems to look at with disdain. Maybe I hated it so much because Jen used to tease me by saying I was Berthe, the plainer sister.

Bin? Maybe later. Large glass of red first. I park the painting on the coffee table, then feel drawn to pick it up again. Holding the wooden frame with both hands, I stare at Berthe. Is she returning my gaze? I freeze for a moment. Then I start addressing her: *What do you think of our sister Jenny? The goody-goody girl, the one with a blonde ponytail and the impeccable moral values? Not so respectable now, eh?* After all that she's been telling me, she's become deceitful and unfaithful. What's been happening to her? I take a big swig from my glass and continue the 'conversation'.

And, Berthe – do you remember the 'Jenny thing', as Dad called it. 'Never ever tell Mummy,' he warned me. 'We will never talk about it. Do you understand? Not a word to anyone.' I swore I wouldn't, Perhaps I'll confront her one day.

I imagine: Berthe with hoodie, trainers, dark sunglasses and cane, wearing a high-vis 'Partially Sighted' armband. The traffic lights show red when she crosses the road, sweeping her cane from side to side. All of a sudden, tyres screech, stopping just in front of her. She screams and drops her cane. 'Ever so sorry,' the elderly gentleman apologises through the open window of his vehicle. 'I didn't see your cane. Are you alright?' Berthe nods, walks a few steps towards the pavement, bends down and picks the cane up from the gutter. First blunder. *You can't see where it is, Berthe! You need to ask for help.*

I'm trying on new stories like new clothes. We're walking along a busy pedestrian lane. A young boy hurriedly approaches Berthe on his scooter. What does she do? She jumps out of the way for fear he might crash into her, shouting, *Oi, watch where you're going.* Second mistake. *You're blind, Berthe. You can't jump out of the way if someone is coming towards you. All you can do is stop and wait for people to avoid you.* She's got a lot to learn.

Enough of this fantasy game. I want to relax and switch off. Now, what shall I read tonight? I pull out a couple of novels and read the blurb on the sleeves. In the end, I settle on *Perfume*, a book by Patrick Süskind I haven't yet read, but it sounds intriguing from the description on the cover. The story follows a boy with an exceptional sense of smell, capable of distinguishing, and later reproducing, a vast range of scents. Yet there is one scent he cannot capture …

As the days fly by, I grow ever more dissociated. *Am I turning into a split personality? It's just a gam*e, I keep telling myself. Occasionally, I catch myself having a whole conversation with myself. I'm alarmed when I Google 'split personality'. Apparently, it's a dissociative identity disorder, often caused by PTSD or childhood trauma. Perhaps I shouldn't have broken off my treatment.

I haven't heard from Jen for nearly a week now. I worry about her. I decide to drop in on her that evening.

It's Hamish who opens the door.

'Oh. Hannah. I wasn't expecting you. Come on in,' he says with a false smile, taking my arm to lead me into the living room. 'I'll take your cane.' There's a stiffness in his posture as he leans in to give me a peck on the cheek.

God, what a mess! Clothes strewn all over the floor, two empty wineglasses and crumpled crisp wrappers left on the coffee table. The small onyx ashtray reeks. It's so packed with cigarette butts, they stand vertically, like a hedgehog's quills.

'Can I get you a drink?' Hamish asks, quietly collecting the glasses while kicking a piece of black lingerie under the sofa. He casts a surreptitious glance at me.

Did you see that? I'm confused. Have they made up? Did Jen tell him?

'Sorry. I'm all over the place these days. Coffee would be lovely. Is Jen still at work?' I follow him into the kitchen. Berthe is commenting on the dirty dishes in the sink.

'No idea, Han. I thought she'd have told you – we split up last week. She's got someone else and in a month I'm moving on to a new job in Washington. There's probably a lot she hasn't told you. That doesn't surprise me.'

'I'm so sorry. I didn't know. She did mention she'd met someone, but said it wasn't anything serious. Did you not talk—?'

'Serious enough, believe me. I checked her phone messages – not proud of that – but I'm glad I found out. It's been going on for months.'

'Would it help if the three of us had a chat together? When's she back?'

'She's not coming back.'

'Well, where *is* she, then? She didn't ask to stay at mine.'

He just shrugs his shoulders and dials her number, more out of curiosity than remorse, I gather. No answer.

'We were going to get married this year, Jen. Were even planning a family.' His eyes are welling up. The ghoulishly pale face says it all: eyebrows lowered and pulled closer together, the corners of his mouth drawn downwards, lips tightly pressed together. Moments later, he straightens up and clears his throat.

'Right now I just want to leave everything behind, and make sure I keep that last bit of self-respect intact.'

He's made up his mind. There is no way I can persuade him to resume talks with Jen, with or without me. I don't blame him. End of an era for the four of us. We hug each other tightly as we say our goodbyes, my head resting on his shoulder. He strokes my hair and says in a soft voice: 'I'm sorry it didn't work out for you and Rob, either. We two must keep in touch, though.' Before he pushes the door to behind me, he adds, 'Leaving party in two weeks at a friend's house – I'll text you.'

Jen's phone switches to answer mode each time I try. It's the weekend, so I can't reach her on her business number, but will try her friends later. She's not returning any calls.

Monday morning. Jen's friend Cathy tells me that she's living in a hotel close to my flat. I wonder why she didn't come back to *me* when they broke up. Very strange. I feel compelled to go and see her at her workplace. But, first of all, I need to see Eric, find out whether I can get my old job back. I can't live on Disability Living Allowance and I shouldn't any longer, anyway.

It feels like a culture shock going back to the Channel 4 office. They've refurbished the whole place – well, at least where *I* used to sit. No more open plan, just lots of small soundproof cubicles, and no names anywhere. I hated hot-desking in my previous job. There's no privacy. You leave your mug, biscuits, lipstick or anything else on your desk and they all go walking the next day, never to be seen again.

Glancing into the gaps between the cubicles, I see quite a few new faces, all busily typing away on their keyboards or talking on their phones. Even former colleagues hardly notice me. Maybe it's the dark glasses.

However, Eric has spotted me. He's as beigely dressed and pale-faced as the last time I saw him. He steps out of his glass cage, shouting in his typical exuberant voice. 'Hello, Hannah! How are you? Good of you to come and see us. We've all missed you.'

'Hi. It's good to be back. I've come to have a chat with you about—'

'Yes, of course. Come back to my new "crystal palace" after you've seen her. She's over there, second workstation on the right. See you in a bit.'

I see a young woman's back sitting at her desk. She has short auburn hair, pressed down with heavy headphones, and is watching a news item. I can smell her fragrant perfume. Chanel Coco Mademoiselle. *Who the hell am I looking for?* I walk past the next few workstations. Eric seemed certain I was meeting someone here. *I'll have to ask him what he meant.* So I turn round and walk back along the other side of the row. Then, suddenly, I do a double-take as I pass the penultimate cubicle and stop dead. *Fuck! It's Jen – she looks like a different person.* She glances up from her screen, drops her headphones and rushes over to me.

'What are *you* doing here?' Her mouth is wide open.

'I could ask you the same question.'

'I … I work here now. I can explain.'

I can't believe what I'm seeing, and raise my voice.

'A minute ago, I thought I could smell your perfume. Now, I smell a rat. My God! You've stolen my job, haven't you? Last week you came to me pouring your heart out, telling all, and you didn't have the guts to tell me that you'd taken my job? Not only did you cheat on your fiancé, but you also betrayed your own sister. What sort of person—?'

'Not here, please,' she says forcefully, like an angry schoolteacher. 'The conference room is right next door. Come with me!'

She grabs my wrist like I'm a naughty child and pulls me away from the turning heads staring at us in disbelief. I wriggle out of her clutches, reluctantly following her into the quiet room. We sit at opposite ends of a wide glass-topped table. I'm still wearing my dark shades, so I can see her eyes. But she can't see mine.

'Eric called me a number of times after your accident to fill in on a couple of assignments that were earmarked for you. When it became evident that you would not be able to return to your job, he asked me to apply for it.'

'And you couldn't tell me that?'

'It was never the right time. You were recovering for weeks in hospital. You were depressed. I went with you to the Berlin clinic for further treatment—'

'Where you left me to fly off to New York to screw your lover.'

She leans forward in her chair, pointing her index finger at me. 'How could I tell you? You were suffering from PTSD, but wouldn't accept any help, and you broke off your treatment. You had – and probably still have – a serious alcohol problem.'

'That's none of your business.'

'Tell me, then. When should I have told you?'

'You had a perfectly good job, but no, you wanted mine. Always have done.'

She stands up and walks the length of the table, backwards and forwards, delivering her defence.

'Perhaps I was sick of playing second fiddle to you. You, the famous war reporter, on telly all the time, lapping up Dad's praise, as well as the media acclaim. "Journalist of the Year"! I'm sick of watching you bask in the admiration of our friends and fellow journalists. You, taking pity on me, helping little sis to become a better journalist by

173

sprucing up my prose, making me sound like you. Now *I* am carrying on the Tring torch. I'm doing your job – differently, but just as well. They soon won't know which of the Tring sisters is or was the famous one. I've become you, with all that material greed and hunger for status. And I hate myself for liking it.'

She spreads her hands, palms up, resting her case, then returns to her seat. Now it's my turn to get up.

'Whoa! Wait a minute. Material greed? Me? I couldn't care less about money. Status? Depends what you mean by that. Sure, I like being in the limelight. But responsibility comes with that, too. Responsibility to discover the truth about what's really happening in the world. More to the point, it gives me a chance to shape public opinion, to influence political decisions, and – if you're lucky, like me – to save lives.'

'You never knew the difference between bravery and bravado. When you said to Paul after your accident, "Looking back on it, I'd say it was worth it," I couldn't believe it. That was reckless.'

'You don't know what you're talking about. You haven't seen what I have seen. You've never looked into the haunted eyes of a starving child, never seen the frightened faces of women and their kids, huddled together, sheltering underground from bombs and artillery fire. Never witnessed traumatised mothers, hurrying their bandaged and blood-soaked children onto a makeshift hospital ward, dodging snipers and artillery shells. If you had, you'd understand.' I take a deep breath, then continue.

'And do you want to know how I cope? I run. I run until there are no memories in my head at all – not of Beirut, of

Kabul or Haswiyeh, or anything beyond the sensation of gasping for air and pain in my cramping legs.'

There is a gaping silence, during which she fiddles with the drinks machine until it spits out one of those underwhelming powdered coffees. I realise that she's watching me with one of her little frowns.

'And you've come here just to embarrass me in front of the staff?'

'No, I didn't know you'd stolen my job. I came here to ask Eric whether I could have it back.'

'How *can* you?'

Her face turns into a big question mark, eyebrows raised. Demonstratively, I take off my sunglasses, fold them up slowly and put them on the table in front of me. My eyes latch onto hers.

'You see, I *am* honest with *you*, and always have been. So, I'll tell you my news. The stem cell operation worked, after all. At the end of my holiday, most of my sight came back. It feels like a new lease of life. So, I *can* start working again now.'

Jen lets out a happy scream and rushes over to me, her impulsive hug almost pushing my chair over. Her tears wet my cheeks, and with every sob her chest heaves.

'Oh, my God! I don't know what to say. I'm so happy for you.'

To my surprise, this is the moment, as she pulls her chair up towards mine, that she decides to *really* tell all. No more secrets. She recounts how Hamish had hacked her phone, read all her private messages, changed the locks and threw her out of his flat. She didn't want to come back to mine, fearing I'd soon discover she no longer works for the *Observer*. She even tells me about her one-night stand in the hotel.

'Look, you must stay at mine. I won't take no for an answer. We're not selling the flat for another six months or so. Rob is probably staying in Germany, anyway, with his new woman.'

'I'm not sure how long I'll be staying in the UK, either. You see, Mark said he'd find a job for me in New York, possibly at the UN.'

'Let's talk about that tonight. Don't make any hasty decisions right now.'

There's a knock on the door.

'Excuse me, are you going to be much longer? We've booked the room from eleven.'

'We've almost finished,' Jen apologises, then closes the door again.

'There's something else you should know: Eric has been in touch with Paul. He's in Bogotá, shooting a film for Channel 4's *Unreported World* about the Revolutionary Armed Forces of Colombia (RAFC). I'm supposed to fly out there and manage the project. I don't think I can. After the split, I feel so exhausted – mentally and physically. Do you think you could go instead? You'd be working with Paul again. Extra bonus!'

Eric is very pleased when I tell him my good news. He agrees to me flying out to Bogotá in Jen's place. I'll be working for him as a freelancer, at least for a while.

Jen is more than happy to move in with me. We are going to pick up her stuff from Hamish's flat.

She laughs at my parting shot. 'By the way, I'm not so sure I like what you've done with *your* hair.'

I'm excited to see Paul again, to travel and get back to work. He assured me a while ago that he'd be happy to work with me, blind or not. So maybe I won't tell him quite yet. And he'll be expecting Jen, anyway. I hope he likes surprises.

I'm going to do some research on RAFC. All I know about Paul's mission is that this powerful terrorist group is currently negotiating a peace deal with the Colombian government. Eric suspects that RAFC is using this rare access to Western media coverage as a marketing ploy – suggesting an image of a peace-loving organisation, fit to be recognised as a political party, one that can ultimately join the government. Not an easy task for an organisation that is funded mainly through kidnapping, ransom and the production and distribution of illegal drugs …

'They'll only let you film what they want you to see,' Eric warns me. 'So you'll need to tread very, very carefully.'

I only have a few days to get up to speed on the subject *and* settle Jen into the flat.

Chapter 15

Hannah

In theory, home is the place where you grew up, the place where you lied to your parents when you returned late at night, not telling them that you'd been skinny-dipping in the neighbour's pool and had sex. Home is where you grew up with your sibling, comparing and competing, striving and struggling for your parents' love, wanting to be different, shaping your own identity. It's a place which triggers happy memories, but also some pretty unpleasant ones.

Going back to Chalfont St Giles means admitting that this neglected Georgian house and its surrounding countryside still has a hold on me. It's as if I need to check that my roots haven't withered away, that the apple trees are still in the same place, thriving, and that Mum and Dad are OK. Maybe I go back from time to time just to understand how I became the person I am today, to dissect the soil I grew from. Of all my family members, it's probably only Dad who has this sense of belonging, this closeness to the countryside, such an attachment to the soil. There's a bit of me that feels the same, although I don't indulge in nostalgia.

I've only been back once since my operation. I didn't want to relive the feeling of being completely useless at home, of discovering how much my mental pictures of Mum and Dad and home had faded. How I hated not being able to see their faces and needing to be guided through my own home like a dog on a lead!

I sensed that they were both shocked at my blindness, that I was no longer the daughter they knew. But how well did they really know me? I always used to avoid answering questions about my job. And it was only when Dad told Mum to watch my reports on the *Channel 4 News* that she began to worry about me and actually ask questions. She wanted to know if I was safe in these 'terrible places'. 'Are reporters affected by PTSD like soldiers?' she'd enquire. I always reassured her that I was fine, that I never took unnecessary risks.

The moment Mum opens the front door, Angus and Roy shoot straight past her, jumping up at me with welcome barks, paws up on my chest, thrusting their cold snouts into my face. Mum notices immediately that I'm not wearing dark glasses and walking without a cane. Before I can open my mouth, she looks straight into my eyes.

'Is it really true? Can you ...? Jen told me that—'

'Yes, Mum. Almost. Still a little hazy at times, but my sight has mostly come back.'

She wraps her arms around me and showers me with kisses and tears. The dogs bark even louder and perform a jealous dance around us.

'Come on in,' she says, picking up my bag. She insists on carrying it up to my old bedroom. Halfway up the stairs, she turns round and whispers. 'Dad's in his snug. He's not very well. Jen will have told you ... but he'll be delighted to hear your news.'

I'm not sure what to make of her comment. Jen didn't tell me anything about Dad. I go and peer through the door, which is slightly ajar. He's fast asleep and looks quite normal. Possibly he's lost a bit of weight. I lean over him and kiss him gently on the cheek. The first thing he says when he opens his eyes is, 'Hannah! Is what Jen told us true?'

'Yes, Dad. It's good news.' He pushes himself out of his chair awkwardly, and struggles to stand up, then clumsily wraps me in a bear hug. I'm shocked at how fragile he is.

'I knew it! I told you! That's fantastic, my love.' He falls back into his chair and coughs. 'How did they manage to do it? I assume it was done at that Berlin clinic I found for you. Sit down. I want to hear all about it.'

At the end of a long chat – Mum brings in cups of tea and biscuits – I pick up a book that's lying face down on the side-table by his armchair, though it's half-hidden by a *Hunting Time* magazine with its headline, 'Shooting Time'. Dad takes one look at the book and waves his hand dismissively.

'Your mother bought me this book. Not very interesting.' I turn it round so I can read its title: *Cancer – A Signpost to the Future*. I'm devastated. Our eyes lock.

'Since when …? How long have you …? Nobody *told* me. Am I the last to know? Why, Dad?'

I fling my arms round his neck and well up, leaving a wet imprint on his checked shirt. When I sit up again, he dabs my eyes with his cotton handkerchief. He screws up his eyes and looks at me as if to check whether I can really see again. Then, after a pause, straightening up, he gives me a look that silences me. His eyes say, 'Let's not talk about it any more – it's not going to change anything.' And, with a brief inclination of his head, his gaze turns into a gentle smile. I close my eyes and nod in agreement.

I learn later from Mum that his lung cancer has invaded the surrounding tissue and metastasised to other parts of his body. He won't even consider chemo.

The conversation over dinner soon turns into story time, Dad trying very hard to steer away from the 'C' topic. However, Mother navigates bluntly back to the subject, hoping I will assist her in talking him round to accepting some kind of treatment.

'You know what you've got, right? Can you not even say the word?'

I frown and look at her reproachfully.

'What I've got?' he echoes. 'Life. I've got life, Mary. It's a terrible affliction with a hundred per cent death rate,' he says, grinning all over his face at his joke. Mum rolls her eyes and shakes her head. I struggle to keep a straight face.

Undeterred, he makes another attempt at storytelling. He has this knack of opening an anecdote with an attention-grabbing statement. He then makes sure the poignant ending is something that resonates with you long after the story is over. Horror stories and tales that involve shooting are his favourites.

'Hannah, did you know that, in the war, your grandad was shot by a sniper before he killed him?'

'Yes, we've heard that one before,' Mum interrupts. 'It's horrible. Not at the dinner table, please.'

'*I* haven't,' I pipe up. Dad ignores Mum's plea.

'Well, this man shot Grandad straight in the face with a low-calibre rifle. The bullet cut through his upper lip and ricocheted off his false teeth. The impact of the bullet made him fall to the ground, but otherwise left him unhurt. So he rolled onto his side, picked up his machine gun and killed the sniper.'

He carries on with another anecdote, less cruel, less depressing, but the damage is done. My head is spinning. The same images return, rerun for the umpteenth time. I'm back in the Syrian ghost town of Haswiyeh. From a safe distance, Paul and I are watching the snipers aiming and shooting at anything that moves. Dead bodies are left lying in the street.

As I leave the table, I hear Mum's faint voice: 'Hannah, your dessert …'

I check my phone. It's just gone seven, still light enough for a run. I quickly change into my sports gear and leave. I run down the unmarked lane and, for half a mile I skirt round the squish of mud and horse shit, before turning left over the turnstile into the unfolding Chiltern Hills. The cool spring breeze fills my lungs and calms me down. Another mile or so, and I reach the abandoned ramshackle barn where Jen and I used to hide and look for bats. The corrugated-iron roof – rusty and loose – flaps noisily against its rotten skeletal structure. A little further on, I reach our neighbour's lichen-covered gate, hanging off its hinges, secured only by a piece of barbed wire. Close by, in the middle of nowhere, is a remnant of a dry-stone wall. That's the place where Dad taught me to shoot. Some months afterwards, Jen and I 'borrowed' a shotgun from

Dad's collection while he was away on business. We never told our parents about that nearly fatal accident.

I'm on familiar territory here – like old times, coming home. But it's not like that any more. One minute it feels like I'm seeing my old world restored again, then the next it is only smashed to pieces by Dad's news. The human body is so fragile and unpredictable. I just want to keep on running.

On my return, Mum looks up from her Renaissance art book and says patiently, 'We need to talk, Hannah, when you've had a shower. Dad's gone to bed.' She's desperate for an ally, to persuade him to start chemotherapy as soon as possible.

'He never listens much to me ...' I know what's coming next is, '... but he might take your advice.' This is only partially true, however. I remind her that there'd been a bargain. He recently agreed to halt his madcap idea to build a scramble track and, in turn, I had to promise to consult the clinic in Berlin. I don't really want to be drawn into this. Not because I don't want to help him, but I feel I don't have the right to tell him how to live his life, or what's left of it. Long hospital stints, chemo with all its side effects. I might not even choose that life for myself.

Over the next few days, I make an effort to distract Mother from the 'hopeless situation'. We drive out to Coombe Hill – a National Trust place in the Chilterns – and visit a couple of old churches, having lunch in Merlin's Cave. I still have my head in the menu when she cheerfully catches my attention.

'Hannah, darling ...'

I'm not fooled by her smile and I know that sweet tone of voice.

'Do you seriously think that Dad shouldn't ...?' she says carefully.

'No. I don't think I have the right to tell him how he should live out his life.'

The waiter arrives and takes our order. Mum doesn't want to eat anything, so I'm lunching on my own under her watchful gaze.

'But couldn't you just have a word ...?' she begs again.

'I will talk to him before I leave, but I can't promise anything.'

There's something irritating about her efforts to make me feel guilty for not intervening, for not 'helping'. Helping *him* or *her?* I wonder.

On the way back, I try to divert the conversation by explaining to her why I've chosen the life I have and that I'm going back to it, freelance in the first instance. I don't tell her, for obvious reasons, that I'm off to Bogotá in a few days' time. When we step out of the car, she reminds me once again to 'have a word'.

Later, we sit down with Dad for afternoon tea and home-made scones. Mum makes her excuses after a few minutes. Dad already smells a rat and comes straight to the point.

'You understand, don't you, sweetheart?'

'Understand what?' I say, playing the innocent. He looks at me with his honest, pale face. There's something vulnerable in his gaze and, though I do understand, I'm uncertain whether I should say so. We're quiet for a while, but he keeps his eyes focused on me, like a child asking for permission to get down from the table. I can't take the staring game any longer and look away.

'I guess I do. And you don't have to spell it out,' I say quietly.

He takes a deep breath, leans back in his chair and smiles. As he moves, a flash of pain shoots across his face for an instant before he's comfortable again. Seeing his happy smile is what matters to me, more than anything else. Just when I think our quiet understanding has reached its conclusion, he leans forward again and that vulnerable, childlike look returns.

'What do you think?' he whispers. 'Chemo, or just have some fun on the way out?'

How can I answer that? He *knows* Mum has asked me to talk to him about it. He *knows* it's not something I can answer either way – choosing between two ways of dying. I sit there, frozen, unable to put into words what's going through my mind. He places his big, heavy hand over mine and says, 'You don't have to answer, love.'

'I think,' I say, knowing that Mother probably won't forgive me, 'I think there's some hunting spirit in the old man still.'

His big smile needs no interpretation, but he carries on reaffirming our bond anyway by saying, 'You and I have always understood one another, haven't we?' He resumes his comfortable pose. 'So, where are you off to next?'

I give him an honest answer, which doesn't seem to faze him. He seems pleased that I can carry on with my journalistic career.

'Always someplace new, always on the go. I can't imagine what it's like, being permanently on the move. That's one thing you don't get from me,' he laughs, and coughs. Almost as an afterthought, he throws in: 'Be somewhere else, when the time comes.'

The next morning, it's time to leave. I load up my rental car and say my goodbyes. Mum sheds a few tears and slips a plastic box with some left-over scones into my shoulder bag. Hugs and kisses all round. I look at Dad as I turn on the doorstep. I want to cry. There's a note of defeat in his voice. At the back of my mind: *Is this the last goodbye?* Drips of rainwater trickle down on me from the leaking gutter overhead. It's beginning to rain.

There are a few messages and emails on my phone when I return home. Jen tells me that she's taken a few days off work – now that I'm going to Bogotá in her place – and she's off to New York. Perhaps, after all, the affair with Mark *is* quite serious.

Eric has sent me a brief file containing information about the task in hand and the arrangements Paul has already made with various RAFC contacts. The whole project shouldn't take more than a week. The last message is from Hamish, giving me details of his leaving party before he leaves for Washington. His wealthy friend Julian is hosting.

Saturday night, nine thirty. As the taxi approaches Totteridge, the houses become progressively grander, the streets leafier. I'm late, as usual, a habit I must have picked up from my South American friends. It may be considered a little rude here, but rocking up late has its advantages. This way, you can skip the instantly forgotten introductions, skirt around the edges of the party, listen in and decide who you might actually want to talk to.

Julian's place is one of those ultra-modern designer houses, built in the Bauhaus style, a kind of symbiosis of wood and glass. Multiple sliding glass doors, Bauhaus dining chairs and a single vase of white lilies on the oblong table.

The party is in full swing, buzzing with a cacophony of voices. The sight of bare skin and hips gyrating to the rhythm of loud salsa music is a welcome distraction from the worries of my recent visit home.

Since the house layout is mostly open plan, I quickly find my way to the marble-floored kitchen. This is where small groups hover around the island, having staked out their pitch by the food and drink. I grab a drink and stop for a moment, not sure which group of people I should join. Hamish spots me and links arms.

'Hannah – so glad you could come. I'll show you round … and I must introduce you to Julian. It can't be easy moving around in a strange place without your cane. You look stunning, by the way.'

'Thanks. Well, I've got some good news.' The music drowns out the rest of my sentence.

Don't tell him just yet. Let's play.

Hamish leads me through a studio, densely plastered with modern, mostly abstract paintings.

'So, what's your news? By the way, Julian is a bit of a mad art collector.'

'Hmm … I'm working again, part-time. Paul and I are going to do a documentary on RAFC and report on their ongoing peace negotiations with the government.'

'On what? And where?'

'RAFC are the Revolutionary Armed Forces of Colombia. Paul's already in Bogotá.'

'You're amazing, always on the go, despite your … I hope Paul will look after you. It's a dangerous place.'

We walk a few more steps into a large, minimalist living room. Three white sofas sit at right angles on a tiled black floor, facing a glass coffee table. Opposite the seating area hangs a supersized TV on a whitewashed wall. All surfaces are clear of ornaments and knick-knacks. Several Miró-style paintings decorate the otherwise empty room. First impression: clean, sleek, distant and cold.

'Ah, Julian. Meet my almost sister-in-law.' Apart from his mouse-coloured curly hair, he looks like a middle-aged car salesman – slick blue suit, matching waistcoat and brown pointy shoes.

'Oh, hello. How very nice to meet you. Hamish has told me about your terrible, terrible accident. I can't imagine what it must be like for you. You see, we recently ate out in Dans le Noir. I know it sounds a bit decadent for us to go there, but it was a real eye-opener, if you'll excuse the pun.'

Hamish breaks the embarrassing silence.

'Hannah was on TV quite a lot before her accident. She's a well-known war correspondent.'

'I'm afraid I don't watch the news these days. All these ghastly things happening in the world that one really doesn't want to know about.'

'Is that so? What does one do, then, with one's time?' I mirror his upper-class-twit accent.

'I buy art. I recognise the value that our vibrant young artists bring to the community. My investment helps them to develop their work, build their reputation. It allows them to evolve and create more value.'

'A real patron of the arts, then,' I say in a sarcastic tone. He doesn't get it.

'Yes, but I support contemporary artists only, although I do have an early Picasso over there by the window, see?'

It's definitely not a Picasso. His pointing gesture turns into an 'Oh, hello!' to someone admiring the painting. He turns halfway round and says with a false smile, 'Very nice to meet you, Jenny.'

'Hannah,' I correct him, but he's already gone.

'Sorry, Han. He's a bit of an absent-minded eccentric. Not a real friend,' Hamish apologises.

'Just someone with a big house, and full of hot air,' I add.

'I tell you what. Since you're going to Bogotá, you may want to chat to a couple of my friends from South America, especially to Lucía, who I believe is actually from Colombia.'

Lucía is a petite young woman. She is wearing an off-the-shoulder ruffled dress, and its ivory colour contrasts beautifully with her brown skin. After a brief introduction about my travel plans, she jumps straight in with an overwhelming degree of enthusiasm.

'If you want a lovely beach holiday, you must go to Cartagena – my favourite. It's on the northern coast.

We call it the "queen of the Caribbean coast". It's also a UNESCO World Heritage Site. And there's lots to see—'

'Sounds great.' I interrupt her flow. 'But I'm going to Bogotá for work. I'm a journalist. We're doing a documentary on RAFC.'

'Oh no! The so-called People's Army,' she says with a contemptuous toss of the head. 'They're a bunch of criminals – drug lords and brutal killers. Steer clear of them. And I'd be very surprised if they let you do any filming or interviews.'

She takes her mobile out of her handbag and gives me the name of a friend in Bogotá, should I get into trouble.

Shouting and laughter come from the billiards room next door, so we move to see what the hilarity is all about. They're playing beer pong. On opposite sides of the covered table are a number of plastic cups, arranged in a triangular shape. Each of the cups is filled with what looks and smells like vodka, not beer.

Lucía asks me to explain how to play the game.

'Each team takes turns to throw a table tennis ball into the other team's cups. Once one lands in a cup, the opponent has to drink its contents and the cup is taken away. OK?' We both join in. There are just two cups left. The last game is between me and a young woman called Joy. She's wearing a tight red miniskirt and a baggy silk blouse – very low cut – which doesn't leave much to the imagination as she leans over the table to throw her ping-pong ball. I manage to win in the end, but I encourage her to have an extra 'solidarity' shot with me, just to show the boys that we can hold our drink, too.

Joy is teetering on her heels towards Hamish, who's just entered the room, and stumbles into his arms. There's just enough time to catch her. She's pretty drunk and her plea for another drink turns into one big slur.

'Could I have another little brandy, darling? This vodka stuff is disgusting.' Hamish looks at me, trying to hide his embarrassment. He helps her to a chair.

'Ah, I see you've already met Joy. She's a colleague from work. So what can I get you, Hannah?'

'A glass of red for me. Thanks, Hamish.'

There's loud music emanating from upstairs. They're playing old AC/DC songs, fast-paced with a heavy beat reverberating through the floorboards. Joy grabs my arm and pulls me towards a spiral staircase. She's not waiting for Hamish to come back with our drinks.

'Wanna dance? Come along – we'll show the boys we can dance, as *well* as drink.' She holds on to me with one hand, kicks off her heels, then pulls herself up the banister with the other hand. As soon as we start moving on the dance floor, a group of men form a circle around us, googly-eyed, watching our every move. Joy is getting into a sexy mood, and starts playing with her long black hair, doing a hip roll and booty dip. Her movements are shouting, *Look at me!* I leave the circle when she starts unbuttoning her blouse, revealing a black lacy bra, not unlike the one Hamish kicked under the sofa when I last visited him at his flat.

The circle of men surrounding her draws closer. They begin clapping to the sound of the bass beat, shouting, 'Off, off, off.' She has their full attention and carries on playing a seductive game for a while. I'm not sure whether to interfere, to pull her out of the predators' circle. All I can hear from where I stand is their 'Off' shouts, shortly followed by a chorus of 'Yeah' and loud applause, just as Hamish returns with our drinks. He realises immediately what's going on, turns the music *off* and the light full *on*. The crowd disperses, leaving Joy in the spotlight, covering her boobs with both hands. She seems to sober up in seconds, then she runs out.

'Sorry, Hamish. That was partly my fault. I shouldn't have encouraged her to drink even more after the game was over. Perhaps go and check she's OK? I'll be off soon.'

On my way out, I say my goodbyes to Lucía and a few others, then Hamish, who is holding Joy upright with his arms around her while chatting to Julian. In the background, his South American friends are dancing to salsa music again.

'Thanks for the invite, Hamish. I see she's in good hands. In future, tell her not to leave her underwear on the floor in your flat,' I say, lowering my dark glasses onto my nose. He looks perplexed.

I give him a peck on the cheek and turn to Julian. 'I think you'll find that your so-called early Picasso is actually a copy of a collage by Matisse. I saw the original in the Pompidou Centre in Paris a year ago.'

'I thought your sister-in-law was blind?' he says to Hamish.

Chapter 16

Hannah

I think back to Hamish and Julian's shocked faces at my parting shot, and it brings a smile to my face. I wonder what they will have made of it. I feel vindicated in suspecting that people are more likely to cheat when they think you can't see them. I'm considering whether I should play blind woman's buff for a bit longer and put Paul to the test, too. *Rubbish, I trust him completely.* But it may be a useful resource in our arsenal when dealing with RAFC. They may feel safe with a blind woman and let me 'watch' what I'm not supposed to be seeing.

I'm really looking forward to working again, particularly as Paul has assured me we'll still make a good team – successful operation or not. I know it doesn't feel right that I haven't told him my good news yet, but I wanted to tell him face-to-face, look into his eyes again.

Bogotá. El Dorado International Airport. Arrivals. Suitcase clutched in one hand, I hold up an A4 sheet reading 'PAUL MASON' with the other, my cane tucked under my arm. I haven't seen him since the awards ceremony and I can't wait. A basket of conflicting emotions hits me all at once: the joy of being able to work with him again, but I also feel unsure whether I'm still up to the job. And then there's the fear of the unknown, dealing with RAFC. The whole scene fills me with a sense of foreboding.

I want to shout out loud and wave as soon as I spot him among the crowd. *Shush. Stay put. Don't move. You can't see him, remember!*

'And who's this lady masquerading as her sister? Hannah! What a lovely surprise.'

Paul greets me with a beaming smile. I let go of my case, my cane drops and I fling my arms around him.

'How come you—?'

'Long story. I'll explain later. Jen's flown to New York instead.'

'OK. Let me take your case. You hold onto my arm.'

I pick up my cane and link arms as instructed. On the way to our car, I lower my dark glasses a fraction so I can take a proper glimpse at him. I'm comforted to see he's in good shape, still a charismatic figure with tall, dark good looks. And, aside from a nicely trimmed beard, his appearance hasn't changed at all. It's been seven months since our near-fatal accident.

'How are you? And what about your eyes – any improvement? How's everyone at home?' he asks as he guides me into the car.

'It's too early to tell.' I skate evasively over his pertinent question. 'But there's loads of news at home – mainly depressing stuff, though.'

I tell him about Dad's cancer, and reveal that both Jen and I have broken up with our partners. He listens quietly as he navigates us through the heavily congested traffic.

'I'm so sorry to hear that,' he says. 'We can talk about it properly over dinner if you want. You'll have my full, undivided attention then, if that's OK. Traffic is absolutely mad here. Crazy drivers.'

As we approach our hotel in the city centre, surrounded by densely packed high-rise buildings, Paul gives me a brief low-down on the place. I look out of the open window and let my eyes roam about the busy streets.

'Imagine a mini New York against a backcloth of alpine mountain reliefs. That's what this place looks like – too many cars, too many people. It's not far now. And do let me know when you get fed up of me describing things to you all the time.'

We have a lot of catching up to do, so we meet in the lobby for a drink before dinner. We skirt around the difficult topics for a while, though. I show him my holiday snaps from Turkey. Unlike Jen, he pauses to take a good look at each photo, smiles at the ones taken in the bazaar and comments on the selfies.

'Looks like you had fun. And made some friends, as well. Did you have two different guides?'

'No, the one with her arm round me is Gulya, my sensory tour guide in Istanbul. She went off the beaten track with us. Great fun – always up to some mischief or other. You'd have liked her.'

Out of the corner of my eye I see the name 'Sylvie' light up on his buzzing phone.

'I'm sorry. I need to take this.' He excuses himself and steps outside. Through the window by the hotel's revolving door, I see him shaking his head and gesticulating angrily. His face looks glum as he comes back into the lobby.

'Everything OK?'

'Yes, fine. Sorry we were interrupted. Do you want to tell me about Rob and Jen, then?'

'There's not a lot to report, really. They both had an affair – apparently, for quite a while – and Hamish and I gave them their marching orders. No regrets. For *me*, it's been difficult for some time. First, being away from home for long stints, and then my accident made things worse. I lost my independence. All Rob wanted to do was keep me safely locked up in a cage, clipping my wings. Clearly, it didn't work. Anyway, he seems happy now he's got his parrot woman in Düsseldorf.'

Paul bursts out laughing the minute I tell him the parrot's catchphrase – 'Tür zu, Arschloch!' – and when I describe its repeated attempts to escape as I tried to set it free. He's still chuckling when the waiter comes with more drinks.

'And what about Jen? Her new relationship. Is it anything serious?'

'I don't know. The guy's married with two young kids. I've told her I don't approve. Does that make me seem old-fashioned ... narrow-minded?'

'Not at all. I agree that being away from home for long stretches puts some strain on a relationship. Not many couples seem to survive that.'

He empties half his glass in one slug, then folds his arms across his chest, takes a deep breath and sighs.

'I don't know how much I've told you about Sylvie. Talking about this part of my life is like I'm discussing another person entirely, a young man in a story who wakes up one day to find himself with a child and a woman he hardly knows. Although, like you, I've never been home for extended lengths of time, I still miss my little Freya very much. But, as Sylvie and I never married, I've got

little chance of getting custody of her. How can I, anyway?'
He pauses for a short while. 'That's what the phone call
was all about. She's moving out.'

'Did you never want …?' My sentence trails away. We're
both distracted by people milling around in the lobby. And
there's a lot of new information for me to digest.

He leans forward, resting his chin on his hands. His
speech is slowing down, with long silences, as he struggles
to shape his thoughts.

'… Kids? Yes, but not at that time. You know, with one
sprawling limb I try to hold down the past, smoothing the
present with the other, yet at times like this I also want to
dig the earth to find out what is buried for the future.'

'Well, for the immediate future you'll have to put
up with me. I hope you won't have to dig *me* out of any
trouble.'

I'm not sure if my flippant reply will help him bounce
out of his sombre mood. So I move my chair close to his,
our foreheads almost touching. Then I put my hand on his
head, tousling his hair until it stands up on end.

'There. Now, *that's* a great look!' I say with an impish
smile.

He grabs my hand and returns it to my lap. 'You've
always been trouble, but I don't mind,' he says easily. His
face is brightening up. Then, out of the blue: 'Are you
hungry yet? When shall we have dinner?'

'I'm fine with a liquid dinner for the moment,' I reply,
checking my watch.

He glances at me suspiciously. 'You've changed, haven't
you? What is it you're not you telling me? Let's see …'
He stands up, smooths his hair down again and grabs an

orange from the fruit bowl on the table, then throws it at me. 'Catch!'

My reflexes kick in, and I do exactly that.

'I knew it! You're such a lousy actress.' He heaves me out of my chair and wraps me in a hug. 'Since when do blind people check their watch for dinner time? And you were very quick picking up your cane from the airport floor, I noticed.'

We unfold from our embrace and look into each other's eyes. A warm and tingly sensation travels right through me.

'How much can you actually see? And since when?'

'My sight came back – well, most of it – at the end of the holiday. I couldn't believe it.'

'That's fabulous. Amazing!' Another squeeze. 'We'll have to celebrate. I'll take you to the best restaurant in town.'

'OK. I'm game. How very perceptive of you, Mr Holmes.'

There's a hint of smugness on his face as he takes my hand to lead me out of the lobby.

After dinner, he briefs me on his action plan and all the meetings he's set up for interviewing and filming RAFC representatives. He agrees that playing the blind woman might give us some unexpected insights – we may be able to assess better whether they're seriously committed to a peace deal with the government or just putting on a show for the media.

Having discovered a green space with benches near the restaurant, we start chatting about old times. First Kabul, where we met for the first time. We also talk about other assignments. Not so distant, but equally dangerous ones: Libya, Nigeria (the Boko Haram insurgency) and the most recent one in Syria. Slowly, almost subconsciously, we slip into the past, reliving some of the horrific conflicts we witnessed together.

'I've had enough of Afghanistan, Han. I stayed there too long. Sometimes the ISAF soundtrack still haunts me at night. The dull "kot-kot-kot" of the M2 machine guns, the crunching of frozen puddles underneath the heavy armoured vehicles, the deafening noise of the Chinooks passing above us.' I put a soothing hand over his.

'What keeps *me* awake at night is our last stint in Syria. Us crawling through that scorching tunnel, filled with diesel fumes, in order to get to the abandoned people in Haswiyeh ... I can still see the women and children trapped in bombed-out houses, begging for food.' I pause to wipe a tear from my cheek. In the spaces between my words I hear the screaming of shells. 'Snipers and shells everywhere, Paul.'

'Sshhhh ... Don't, Han.'

He puts his arm around me and draws me closer. I bury my head in his open jacket. We stay in this safe bubble for a long time.

'You know what?' he restarts cautiously. 'Our first meeting with RAFC isn't until tomorrow afternoon. So, if you're up for it, in the morning we're good for a short hike in the mountains.'

'I'd like that.' I straighten up. 'Let's walk.'

We stroll slowly down the street, past busy bars and restaurants. The air is teeming with conversation. Paul's arm sits around my waist, my hand nestles in his back trouser pocket, and then his phone buzzes.

It's Eric. He wants to know if we've joined up and are ready to go. Out of curiosity, I ask Paul why Eric sent him and Jen to Colombia, of all places. It's not exactly a war zone.

'Do you know what Eric said when I told him I'm tired of covering failing wars? "Well, find us one where there's a remote chance we might actually be winning." That's how I came up with Colombia's RAFC. I've been here a couple of times before, and have some contacts. So I told him it would make an original contribution for *Unreported World*. And he agreed entirely.'

'To me, it sounds like the pressure to be original has taken over from the need to be first with the news. I get that.'

We stop in front of a cosy-looking bar. I'm expecting an invitation to have another drink. Instead, sporting a self-assured grin, he announces, 'I was also hoping to get to know your sister a bit better.'

'Hey!' He gets a gentle elbow in his ribs and we both laugh.

The next morning, we set off for an easy hike to Mirador Aguadora. Although the sky looks menacing – we're in the middle of the rainy season – a few rays of sunshine nudge their way through the clouds. After a two-hour walk, as we climb higher, the vegetation is becoming more sparse. For a few moments we're shrouded in clouds and mist, but we soon reach the top and are rewarded by a spectacular panoramic view over the sprawling city of Bogotá.

Paul takes his Rolleiflex and a film out of his rucksack. Loading this old-fashioned camera takes ages.

'My grandad had one of those ancient cameras, similar to yours. I remember – I must have been about ten – when he showed me how to load a film. What a kerfuffle. And all before you could even take your first picture.'

I'm getting a bit bored, so start snapping away on my iPhone.

'You've made your point, thank you. I need to be careful not to rip the perforated edge,' he mumbles, unperturbed, closing the lid and winding the film on until a '1' appears in the minute window. He finally sets the shutter speed and the distance.

'So, what's so special about this camera?' I ask.

'Well, for a start, it has two reflecting lenses, so I can look down on this beautiful, sexy woman.'

'Oh, shut up!'

'And, more technically, it's a six-by-six-centimetre square-format camera, so if I want a horizontal or vertical photo I can shoot square and edit later, without losing too much detail from cropping.'

The Rollei's shutter clicks several times in my direction, so I fool around, acting out a couple of suggestive poses. Paul follows me round, taking a few close-ups from different angles, until I hold my hand in front of the lens. Finally, he puts the camera back in his rucksack, grasps my arms and places them round his neck. Our eyes lock.

'May I kiss you? I've always wanted to.' The juvenile sentence comes out of nowhere. We hold each other's gaze until my eyes answer his question. We kiss briefly. Then again – this time, long and passionately.

'I have no idea where this is going,' I say, leaning my head against his shoulder. My heart is pounding. His hands slip down onto my buttocks, caressing me gently. I reach down to feel him, arousing him.

'Does it have to go anywhere?' he whispers.

'Perhaps. It might.' I'm a little disconcerted by his question. I slowly ease out of his embrace. But, for a moment, I look at him as the person I may want to spend the rest of my life with, the person I may want to have children with. *Too early? Is either of us ready yet? Will we ever be?*

'I think we'd better make a move.'

We're approaching the city from the south, past the slums of Medellín. Simple, brightly coloured houses with misshapen bricks and corrugated metal roofs are jammed against the hillside, stretching for miles. Crowds of children play in the dappled sunlight on a potholed and waterlogged street. We watch from afar.

'Look, they're playing Cinco Huecos. Five Holes!' Paul says. 'I've seen this before. You try to throw coins into the holes, and the person who scores the most hits wins the game and keeps the money.'

The game suddenly takes a sinister turn when it is interrupted by two other bystanders, older boys with rifles slung across their shoulders, who fire a warning shot in the air and seem to be ordering the kids to stash their winnings into a linen bag. The taller of the boys picks up the bag and gestures to them to disperse. He fires more shots into the empty potholes, which cause the water to splash up like little fountains, spilling over the younger boys' bare feet. They all run off in a panic, while the two boy soldiers laugh, raising their rifles above their heads in triumph.

'Don't!' As I'm about to approach them, Paul takes my arm. 'See the insignia on their arms? They're junior gang members of RAFC. Quick – let's walk away before they spot us.'

Back at the hotel, Paul explains. RAFC used to 'clear' their territory of opposition by using boy soldiers to distribute flyers, ordering people to leave their homes. Then, a few days later, they would deliver funeral invitations bearing the names of residents who refused to move out.

Our first meeting takes place in the hotel's conference room. While Paul is welcoming the two RAFC reps, Pablo Sánchez and Raúl Gómez, I make a slightly later entry with my cane and dark glasses. Pablo is short, bald, thick-necked, and has a constant smile etched on his face. His sidekick is a tall, serious-looking bearded guy with narrow eyes. They both wear combat uniforms with RAFC insignia – in yellow, blue and red – on their left arm.

Paul outlines the details of our planned report. He tells them we would like to include questions on who they are, their aims, the reasons for their struggle and how they're financed. I sit next to Paul with my laptop, taking notes and pretending to be his secretary. For most of the talk, they seem quite candid. However, they don't want to be referred to as 'rebels'.

'We're freedom fighters, the people's army.' Pablo interrupts Paul and insists that the blind *señora* records this correctly. Another correction follows from Raúl when we talk about the strength of the people's army.

'No. Eighteen thousand, not fifteen thousand, freedom fighters throughout Colombia,' he insists. He then adds, 'We have advantage over State: they have bureaucracy and less resources. We not bother with bureaucracy; we just solve problems.'

They're not so forthcoming with details about their 'resources'. We know that they're funded by kidnap and ransom, extortion and taxation of various forms of 'economic activity' – and, of course, the production and distribution of illegal drugs.

Pablo is giving us a 'history lesson'. It's a narrative that reflects their own role as saviours from the chaos of many different factions, who have been fighting each other for decades.

'You see, for many years we had, and still have, the guerrillas and the narcos and the right-wing paramilitaries, all at each other's throats, fighting and killing. Over the years, we have carved out order in the turmoil, like a man with machete hacking a path through the jungle. And people pay us to keep them safe, to protect them. It's just like raising taxes. We like to call it vaccine.'

The chilling image of the hacking machete is instantly eroded by a loud blast coming from somewhere close by. It triggers the hotel's alarm system. Everyone rushes out into the open. Paul immediately hails a taxi to take us to the bomb site.

I scan the streets nervously, fearing a second blast or an attack on first responders, and also worried about putting ourselves at risk. *This is not the time for rational thoughts. Fuck it – let's go.*

A few minutes later, we arrive at a scene of destruction and mayhem. Where there used to be a lively market, now there are dead bodies. Some lie under the skeleton structure of the market stalls, absurdly garnished with the pulp of fruit and vegetables, like a scene from a Dalí painting. Police and first-aiders are tending the wounded and carrying them into ambulances. Paul takes a couple of shots of the devastation, then helps me look after injured mothers and wailing children.

'Animales!' yells the woman next to me. She's holding her crying baby, swaddled in makeshift bandages. I sit with her until one of the medics arrives and takes over. Paul makes sure all of the children are either reunited with their parents or, at least, have found someone they know.

The scene is too horrific to describe in detail. Although we have both been in situations like this before, the shock remains just the same. Nothing prepares you for this carnage. And it doesn't make it any easier to cope with. It's the stuff of nightmares. Violence and destruction seem to be stitched into the fabric of daily life here.

As expected, the government calls off all negotiations with RAFC until they can establish who the culprits are. The attack bears all the hallmarks of RAFC. Will they claim, or deny responsibility for, this attack? Apparently, the assault killed ten civilians and fourteen government soldiers.

Early evening, and the El Irish pub is already teeming with people. We find a space outside, where we have a few drinks to help us digest what has just happened on the ground. I want to stay focused, and begin to type up our report.

Paul scans through his photos and asks from time to time, 'This one?' I nod, thinking, *Will this make people stop and care? Or will they just mumble 'How awful' across their breakfast table? And then just carry on as usual over their coffee and toast and boiled eggs?*

For a while we remain silent, writing, cropping photos and ordering new beers as soon as our previous ones are finished. Paul interrupts me just as I'm thinking about a hard-hitting headline.

'I think this one should go on the front page. It'll stop people in their tracks, make them read on past the strapline.'

It's a close-up of the yelling woman with her baby, with me kneeling beside her trying to calm her down. And, in the background, the devastated marketplace.

'Agreed. You always find a detail that makes people stop and look. It also makes me realise how much war photography needs the written context, you know. Without it, scenes of life's extremes can easily become propaganda or be dismissed as fake news.'

'Indeed. So good to work with you again, Han,' he says in a soft voice, leaning over to give me a kiss. 'Tomorrow morning, before we fly back home, I need to do some filming for the RAFC documentary – a few shots in the mountains.'

It's almost midnight. I'm struggling to get to sleep, mulling over the day's events. My mind walks me through the aftermath of the attack, and similar disasters. Images of the dead and the wounded are scattered in front of me. Little toddlers, orphaned … their desperate, innocent faces. They keep haunting me, merging into each other, assimilating into a Bosch-like hell. I look at my phone. It's now half past one. I send Paul a text.

'Are you still awake?'

Chapter 17

Hannah

Paul calls me once he's seen my text.

'Yep. Still awake.' Soft guitar music is playing in the background – and the sound of maracas. Clearly, he's not in his room.

'Where are you?'

'In the bar downstairs. Pedro's giving me his life story while pouring free drinks. Would you like to join us, or shall I come up to you?'

Paul is a little unsteady on his feet as he stumbles into my room. He slumps down on the edge of my bed. I reach towards the minibar to get myself a drink.

'Thanks, Han, but I think I've had enough already this evening.' His speech is slightly slurred.

'I did notice. Couldn't *you* sleep either?'

He pads down the duvet with his left hand, gesturing to me to sit down next to him. Despite his drunken state, his touch is gentle as he strokes my hair and caresses my face. Soon, his hand glides up my thigh. I stand up, then slip under the duvet, still in my pyjamas. He peels off a few layers and follows suit. As though we have a silent agreement, we just kiss and cuddle, gradually falling asleep in each other's arms.

The next morning, a ping from my phone wakes me up. I turn myself round. Paul's gone. He's sent me a text.

Sorry, love. I couldn't bring myself to wake you. You looked so peaceful and snug. I don't remember much about last night, I'm afraid. Did we … ?
Filming should finish early afternoon.
See you soon. Stay safe – and stay in 'blind' mode, just in case we're being shadowed. We'll get a flight back to London tomorrow.
Can't wait! Xxxxx

Exhilarated by the prospect of going back home with Paul, I step out of the lift and walk towards the breakfast room, inwardly smiling as I sweep my cane from side to side.

Suddenly, I hear something like 'Es ella. Es ella, la mujer ciega,' before some men grab me from behind, press duct tape over my mouth and flex-cuff me. Having dragged me out of the back door of the hotel, they bundle me into a van. The rickety vehicle has no windows, so I have no idea where they're taking me. And why. Ransom? To extort money – but from whom? Or to prevent us reporting on the atrocities in the marketplace? Will they do the same to Paul?

Fortunately, they don't deem it necessary to put a paper bag over my head, so when we stop I can see where we are. Calle de San Miguel. And there's a church at the end of the road. They drag me into an old, dilapidated building. The faint sign over the door reads 'Asilo de Manicomio'. Is this some kind of asylum? Ominous … What's this all about? My head's spinning and I'm desperate to escape –

by whatever means. At the end of a dark corridor, we enter a small, windowless room. The metal door slams behind us with a thud. Then the men release their grip.

'Well now. Who do we have here? Another pretty one,' says the plump 50-something woman behind the desk, bearing a frozen smile. She looks like a stereotypical 'madam' – heavy eye makeup, bright red lipstick, false lashes. The bags under her eyes resemble tiny purses, stuffed with the memories of a disappointing life. She puts her cigarette down for a second, then types 'New entry' into her computer. Seemingly, it's the cue for the men to rip the tape off my mouth.

'Ouch! You've got the wrong person,' I protest. 'I'm a British journalist.'

'Haha. Of course you are, treasure. We have all kinds of important people here. There's a Mona Lisa, a Marilyn Monroe, as well as a feisty Joan of Arc, to name just a few. But a blind journalist? No, not so good. But we have good job for you here.'

'Please let me go. I've got a plane to catch tomorrow.'

'Name?'

I feel that if I resist I'll be met with crushing retribution from the two rebels still standing guard next to me.

'Hannah Tring.'

'We have good job for you here, Anna,' she repeats firmly. 'You start tomorrow. We take photo later.'

'It's Hannah! I don't want your bloody job, whatever it is. I need to leave … *now*.'

The madam makes eye contact with the men and, like a dragon, blows angry smoke through her nostrils.

'Check the *señora*'s bag,' she says, sour-faced. 'Then take her to her room.'

They empty my rucksack onto the nearby table, and confiscate my phone, cigarettes, a nail file and a tiny bottle of gin. The madam shakes her head and tuts, taking great pleasure when she quotes the 'house rules' to me: 'No smoking, no sharps, no alcohol, and definitely no phones.'

The two rebels – I now see the RAFC insignia on their arms – escort me to my room, which is more like a prison cell, with its window bars. One sharp cut with a bush knife and the flex on my wrists pings off.

'Lunch at twelve in the restaurant,' one of them mumbles. The next minute, they're gone, leaving the door unlocked. Bewildered and utterly puzzled, I stand in the middle of the sparsely furnished room, wondering what to make of this Kafkaesque situation. *Will there be guards outside the door 24/7?* Before I have time to check, a female rebel – like her comrades, also armed and in uniform – strides into the room without knocking. A rotund middle-aged woman with spiky black hair, over her arm she carries a green bath towel that matches the colour of her uniform.

'Come and take shower,' she announces in a commanding voice that leaves me in no doubt that this invitation, my second shower of the morning, is not optional. For me, being led naked into a big cement room and hosed down with disinfectant has stark associations with the Second World War. I fear the worst.

Luckily, after a thorough inspection, she hands back my clothes and escorts me through the dismal neon-lit corridor back to my room. I lie on the bed for some time, recovering from this humiliating ordeal. My skin itches and reeks of bleach. I fish out a small tube of hand cream from my rucksack, squeeze it and rub its contents all over my body, in an attempt to obliterate the strong chemical smell.

So, what are my options? I have no mobile, no way of contacting the outside world. Will any of the other inmates have managed to smuggle in a phone? I still have my spiral notebook and pen – I could write a message pleading for help and shove it through the window's metal bars. But, finding it outside a mental asylum, would anyone take it seriously? Doubtful. The only chance of escape will be from the workplace, wherever that may be. And what kind of work are they going to make us do?

Looking forward to lunch and an opportunity to contact other inmates proved a mistake on several fronts. First, all seating in the 'restaurant' – a primitive canteen-type hall with wooden benches – has been assigned. One of the minders directs me to a solitary seat away from the others. Second, the 'paella' is just a pulp of mushy, sticky rice mixed with overcooked vegetables. If I turned the bowl on its head, the meal would definitely stick to the bottom, like a reluctant blancmange.

Watching the women in the canteen, lunching in small groups at various tables, something strikes me as rather peculiar. They're all immaculately manicured and coiffed, and quite a bit younger than me – between 18 and 25, I'd say. I continue to observe them covertly. Then I notice something else. They move in a strange, yet familiar fashion, hands stretching out like feelers, obviously searching for the position of the cutlery, their bowls and drinks. It suddenly dawns on me. Of course: they're blind! But why are they incarcerated in a psychiatric hospital? Have they all been abducted? Where are their relatives? And what kind of work have these lovely girls been assigned to carry out?

Oh my God ... No! I truly hope I'm wrong ... I certainly need to stay in character. I'm one of them now. However, I have an invaluable trump card.

After lunch, my minder takes me back to my room. Two till four is siesta time. We're not allowed to leave our rooms, except to use the only toilet at the end of the corridor. There are twelve rooms on this corridor; mine's at the far end. The fat guard sits right in the middle. She's supposed to enforce the no-contact rule during quiet time.

I use the excuse of a toilet break. When the guard sees that I'm used to walking and feeling my way along the wall, she just shouts, 'Hurry up!' and stays put in her chair, carries on reading her paper. On the way back, I slip quietly into the room next door to mine 'by mistake'.

'Who's there?'

'Shush! Don't be frightened. I'm in the room next door to you. My name is Hannah. I just want to talk to you.'

'We're not allowed during siesta,' my neighbour replies timidly. 'We get severely punished if they find out ...'

Juana is a petite 20-year-old with a wasp-like waist and a beautiful brown complexion. When she eventually calms down, she tells me how she ended up in what she thought was a care home for the blind.

'I lost my parents in the civil war. I thought I'd be safe when they brought me here …' She pauses and begins to sob.

'May I hold your hand?' I walk towards her bed, to sit next to her. 'What is it that they make you do here?' I ask.

'I feel so ashamed, but if you don't do what they want, they beat you brutally. What can I do? Every night, they pick three or four women to go to the house with the loud music. They give us drugs, so we don't remember a lot of what they do to us. But I remember enough, and I cry every night. If I could see, I'd kill them – even if I died for it.'

'Will they come again for you tonight?'

'Yes, I'm sure. It's my turn tonight. They will come soon. We get food in the club tonight.'

'Is it always the same people who take you to the house? Do they recognise you?'

'No, the *señora* gives the taxi drivers the room numbers of the women to take.'

'Listen – and tell no one. I was blinded in an accident, but most of my sight has come back. If you let me go in your place tonight, I might be able to escape and summon help to get you all out.'

'But that's so dangerous. They will kill you. They have knives and guns.'

'Don't worry. I'll be careful.'

I explain to her that my room is next to hers on the right. I stay where I am. So now it's her turn for a toilet break, and time to swap rooms. I just hope it all goes to plan.

Four blind women, including me, holding onto a rope, are led out of the psychiatric hospital by a taxi driver. I make sure that I sit in the front passenger seat, so I can see where we're going. Rather than moving further out of town towards the slums of Medellín, we seem to be driving into the city centre. We arrive at Club Exotica, in the middle of a mini Soho. All around us are bright, flashing neon lights and shopfront displays advertising strip and peep shows, massage parlours and pornographic films. Unlike in Amsterdam, where I've seen sex workers posing behind glass windows, here half-naked women walk openly in the streets wearing thongs, fishnet stockings and skimpy dresses, watching as potential clients scout out who it is they find most appealing. It feels surreal.

All eyes are on us. A throng of males, prowling the pavement like sex-hungry wolves, observe us walking through the doors of the club. A man standing beside the doorman is obviously expecting the influx of 'fresh meat'. He leads us down to the basement. Its walls display nudity in various, incongruous contexts: the seating area of a plane, on the front of a fire engine, pushing a supermarket trolley. Another 'madam' awaits us in a small dressing room. She orders us to strip off and put on a see-through negligée, before we go on stage in front of 'the people's army' – around ten men, mainly in uniform, some still carrying weapons. The older ones have first choice. A bald, bespectacled man in his sixties with a friendly smile comes up onto the stage, takes my hand, then leads me back up the stairs to a room on the first floor. He carries a gun, stuck in the side of his belt. My adrenaline kicks in, ramping up my fight-or-flight response. I mustn't let on that I can see where he is.

'Where are you?' I ask, hands outstretched.

'I'm putting some music on for us,' he explains, with a kind smile. 'My wife and I always dance together ... She die last year. I miss her very much. Not worry – we just dance.'

He doesn't speak much after that. All he wants to do is hold me in his arms and sway gently to the music. Nothing else. A lonely man who just wants human companionship. Lucky for me, but not so fortunate for him. He's picked the wrong woman tonight. His hands are on my hips when I remove his gun slowly from the holster, swiftly freeing myself from his embrace. Holding the cocked gun to his temple, I force him down on his knees.

'What are you doing? Please. Don't shoot. I thought you were blind?'

I'm now standing over him. 'Shut up. Take off your jacket ... and belt.' I check him for other weapons. He doesn't seem to be carrying a phone. 'On your front, arms on your back.'

He squeals as I dig my heel into his back. I tie both hands with his belt, and pull his trousers down to the ankles. I cover him – head and body – with a sheet from the bed. My heart is still racing.

'If you shout or make a move, I *will* shoot you.'

Having turned up the music, I slip quietly out of the room dressed in his combat jacket, which is just long enough to cover my bottom. I rush downstairs, waving and smiling to the men walking towards me, girls in tow. They seem amused by the 'joke': me, wearing a uniform jacket, with little underneath and showing my legs off. Wolf whistles and cheers, audible in spite of the thumping music echoing throughout the place, follow me as I hasten towards the exit. Even the doorman buys the prank and lets me dive into the crowd. There's plenty of cash in the guy's wallet for a taxi back to our hotel.

The moment Paul sees me entering the hotel bar – it's way beyond midnight – he freezes, mouth wide open. It takes a couple of seconds for it all to sink in, and for him to make sense of my desperate state and my ridiculous appearance.

'My God, what happened? I was so worried. I've been looking everywhere for you, and your phone was switched off.'

'Yes, I'm just feeling a bit weak. I need to …' My voice breaks into unintelligible croaks, then my legs give way beneath me, as the adrenaline drains out of my body. I'm about to faint. He catches me just in time; carries me to my room. Replacing the combat jacket with a bathrobe, he props me up on my bed against the pillow, then fetches a glass of water. I'm still shaking as I tell him about my ordeal. My voice trails off slowly, as though the words are stuck in my throat, unwilling to roll off the tongue.

'I was so afraid, Paul. It was so degrading. I've never felt so humiliated.'

'You're here now, though. You're safe. You've made it.'

And, in the silence that follows, I feel him squeezing his arms around me. My arms reciprocate.

'You were so brave and clever to fool them.'

'I'm not so sure about being brave. I was forced to fight, in order to survive.'

'Bravery is not being afraid to *be* afraid. You're a true survivor. But now we have to leave before they find us and take revenge. I have somewhere we can stay tonight.'

'But we can't abandon those girls.'

'There's nothing we can do right now. Let's talk to the British Embassy and the police tomorrow.'

Next day, we're at the police station, trying to persuade them to immediately liberate the women from their captors. They seem strangely relaxed, and reluctant to take any action. Instead, they patronise us and belittle our demands.

'Prostitution in Zona de Alto is legal,' they argue. 'In this part of the city only,' he adds, almost by way of an excuse.

'These are not your normal sex workers. They're blind women – imprisoned in an old psychiatric hospital in Calle de San Miguel and then transported against their will as sex slaves to Club Exotica. The people we're talking about are pathetic criminals. Using blind women, so *their* faces will never be recognised.'

'And how do you know that, lady?'

'Listen—' Paul is struggling to retain his poise.

I don't want him to interfere, so I continue to talk over him. 'Because I was there. I was kidnapped from my hotel, because they thought I was blind.'

To prove my point, I put on my dark sunglasses and wave my cane in front of their faces. They eventually get it.

Finally, in the early afternoon, the police raid the psychiatric hospital. I advised them beforehand that the women would be safe in their rooms during siesta. Paul and I watch from a safe distance, filming as – one by one – the women are led to safety and the culprits are arrested. Two of the male guards resist, and are shot point-blank in front of us.

I grab Paul's arm.

'Look, that's Juana. The one I swapped rooms with. Juana – you're safe and free,' I shout at the top of my voice.

She turns her head towards us.

'Muchas gracias. You are hero!' she responds.

We return to London the next day, physically unscathed, from yet another place of conflict and brutality. An assignment that seemed like an expedition into the cultural heart of darkness. At least we return with a credible achievement, though. We can report a minor victory over cruelty and suffering.

For the first time, Paul and I hold hands on the plane. I have butterflies in my stomach like a bloody teenager. We start talking at exactly the same time.

'Do you think—?'

'Should we make—?'

'Make what?' he asks. 'You go first.'

'Plans?'

'You mean, when to finalise and file our reports?'

'That, too.'

'Oh, and us working together again?'

'Yep, that as well.' How many nudges does he need? Or is he just playing silly buggers?

'Oh … us? Well, I could move in for a few days and see how it goes, I guess.' He gives me one of his mischievous smiles, then turns his face to receive a kiss.

'What was *your* question, then?' I ask.

'I was going to ask if you might consider carrying on as a freelancer and try your hand at writing a bigger story. I always felt your articles, your prose, are just like a rehearsal, an hors d'oeuvre for a much meatier project.'

'Well, I do have plenty of material, heaps of diaries and notebooks. But I'm not sure if I'm really good enough.'

'*I'm* sure you are. Let others be the judge of that. I can visualise your book in print: "On the Front Line: The Collected Journalism of Hannah Tring". But, to make a real impact, you may need to include some excellent photographs. I may be able to help you out there. What do you reckon?'

Chapter 18

Jenny

Mark and I are lunching in a cosy Mexican restaurant. We're sitting on a secluded patio framed by stunning magnolia trees in full bloom. Mark is wearing jeans and a white short-sleeved shirt, and sporting a chunky Omega watch. He's got the kind of face and physique to stop you in your tracks – very much the tall, dark and handsome cliché – plus a perfectly trimmed black beard. He tells me that May is the prime time to visit New York City. It's the month when the locals drop the cold-weather caveats and get back to eating and drinking with their friends and loved ones on pavements and patios and in backyards … without having to consult their weather apps.

We skip the pleasantries about flight and hotel. It was all pretty eventless, apart from the fact that I was sick on the plane – a first for me. And highly embarrassing.

As we raise our champagne glasses to toast my arrival, Mark announces that he has booked a private helicopter ride to Niagara Falls. Wow! He's also organised a personal assistant to take me shopping on Fifth Avenue, followed by a special spa treatment. He's planned an exciting agenda for my trip.

'The only downside to arriving on 8 May,' he apologises profusely, taking my hand, 'is that I won't be free tonight, sweetie. It's Mother's Day, and I have to show my face at home later on. I'll make it up to you, I promise. And, while you're here, I'll make as much time for you as I possibly can.'

Really?! Not exactly what I had in mind on my first day in New York: sitting alone in a hotel room, watching American soaps, while he's having a celebratory meal with his wife and kids. And how much time will he *really* have for us? Or will he merely fit me around his busy work schedule? I'm sounding a bit like sceptical Hannah.

Sex in the afternoon is equally disappointing. A rushed affair in an air-conditioned hotel bedroom, and not remotely as I remember our previous encounters. He directs me as though we are making a porn movie: 'Do this,' 'Do that,' 'A bit faster …'

I phone Hannah in the evening, but her mobile seems to be switched off. *She must surely be back from Bogotá by now.* I wonder how her trip went. Will she and Paul stay as just close working colleagues? Now that she can see again, she may want to go back full-time to her old job.

The next few days fly by, each one filled with John's meticulously organised agenda. Great fun, though, especially exploring the shopping paradise on Fifth Avenue with the five hundred dollars' worth of gift vouchers from John. He's so generous. He excuses himself for a few hours here and there, when he needs to attend UN meetings. Fortunately, he can work from home most of the time.

On our penultimate night, after he's been talking at some length about his domestic situation and all the reasons why he can't leave his family just yet, he comes out with an extraordinary proposal, which is prefaced by a long-winded and rather convoluted backstory.

'Barbara's sitting her entrance exam for the Graduate School of Journalism in ten days. She'd be delighted to have someone like you help her run through some sample papers. Her main concern is the news writing part, which includes notetaking during an interview. I've already told her that someone from Britain's Channel 4 is coming to interview me, and that she can sit in on that as a practice run. I thought we could invite you to stay for lunch afterwards. Then it's your turn to offer her some help preparing for the exam. And I'll suggest that you could stay with us for a couple of days. That way, you and I will be together a bit longer and it'll give me more time to hunt around for a job for you. The house is big enough to afford us some privacy. You can stay in the self-contained annexe, which has a separate entrance. Barbara's out a lot during the day – tennis, yoga, shopping – and the kids are with their grandparents next week ...'

I'm gobsmacked by this proposal. Moving in with his family? *Absolutely no way!* I really don't know what to say.

'I can't. I've got my return flight booked for Sunday, and have to be back at the office on Monday.'

'Surely you can stay another week, while I try to find you a good job at the UN.'

I check out of my hotel a day early. Intrigued? Well, I'm curious to know what the competition looks like; how I measure up. We're almost exactly the same, heightwise – both five foot six, if I'm lying and adding an inch. But that's where the similarity ends. She's somewhere in her early forties, I suppose, with dark, shoulder-length hair pulled back by a pink hairband to reveal a pair of sparkly earrings. She's wearing a matching pink tennis top with a white trim, and black leggings. Her eyes, grey-blue; her forehead and smile, frozen. I hold out my hand to greet her.

'Hello, Mrs Marin.'

'Barbara. Do you play tennis? Any good?'

'I used to play a lot in my teens, but—'

'Mark used to play, didn't you, darling? But he's got a chronic knee injury now. Haven't you? Poor man. Golf's his game now. Has to wear a knee brace. He plays with the old guys at the local club. Do *you* think it's a sport?' She laughs, searching my face for a sign of agreement. 'I mean, hitting a stationary ball, then chasing it from hole to hole. What kind of sport is that? They even have someone to carry their goddamn golf clubs.' She turns to face John, who is standing next to me, tight-lipped, embarrassed.

'When's the interview, darling?'

'Miss Tring is ready to do the interview now. I told you she'd be here later this morning.'

'It'll have to be after my match, I'm afraid. Nice to meet you, Miss Tring. We must play. Tomorrow?'

'Jenny – please.'

She's off. Mark slams his phone down on the table and loosens his tie.

'That woman! Never listens. And, as for appointments, she's either late or misses them altogether. She's a bloody law unto herself.'

It's the first time I've seen him really angry. He goes and brings up the luggage from the car, handing me a key for the annexe. We spend the next two hours online there, searching for jobs over a sandwich lunch. There are a couple that sound interesting: assistant editor at the *Boston Post* and reporter at the *New York Times*.

'I can also pull a few strings at the *Times* office for you,' he says, edging closer. I decline his flirtatious invitation for a quickie. It makes me wonder whether for him the essence of sex lies in the anticipation, the wooing, the plotting and the secrecy.

Her ladyship finally surfaces late afternoon, freshly showered, pen and notepad in her hand. The agreed interview is about cybersecurity at the UN. I quiz Mark about his role as operations manager on the different types of current cyberattacks, his risk mitigation strategy and the organisation-wide approach to cybersecurity, as well as on their professional development programme.

Mark seems impressed. 'That wasn't exactly a walk in the park! How do you know about these things?'

'My ex-boyfriend is a hacker – a "white hat" one. Those are the good guys, who try to find a way into an organisation's IT system or network in order to expose its vulnerabilities. They can also hack into people's smartphones if they suspect anything untoward.'

Mark and I exchange a faint smile of complicity. Then, Barbara and I compare interview notes. Oh dear! For a start, she obviously didn't understand the questions. Her sparse notes are a mess of half-finished quotes from John's elaborate, and occasionally evasive, answers. I'm going to have my work cut out with her.

'That's a good start, but you need to summarise the answers in your own words. I'd be happy to spend a bit of time with you on that, if you like.'

'Splendid idea,' Mark butts in. 'Jenny is staying in New York for a few days. She could help you prepare for your exam. What do you reckon?'

'That would be very kind. We would, of course, pay you. Where are you staying at the moment?'

Mark picks up the line and throws in the bait. 'Right at the other end of town – not wildly convenient, alas.'

'Well, couldn't she stay with us for a couple of days? We were going to play tennis tomorrow anyway.'

She's swallowed it. I order a fake taxi, say my goodbyes and sneak out to let myself into the annexe. Late-night visits (and more declarations of love) now assured.

Afterwards, when he's crept back into his single bed, doubt creeps into my mind. *Will this surreal scenario actually work? There are now three in this relationship.* Even if Mark and Barbara did divorce, would he want to remarry? I'm not convinced. I think that secretly – or unconsciously – he may still yearn to be reconciled with Barbara and scurry back to her and the children with his tail wagging.

But I'm not ready to give up just yet, however uncomfortable this game of complicity makes me feel.

The next day – I've now *officially* moved in – I suffer a humiliating defeat against the much older, but more agile and aggressive player. Barbara hits fully through her ground strokes, comes to the net at the earliest opportunity, and slices the ball so that it curls backwards, wrong-footing me every time. Her serves are accompanied by a loud grunt, which I find really off-putting. Most of her double-handed backstrokes are outright winners, and yet she still swears loudly if one goes into the net. My game's pretty pathetic.

I'm on the defensive all the time. I fall into a lethargic sulk as she closes all of our matches 6–1.

Afterwards, Mark joins us for a drink. Barbara checks her phone to see what she's doing next.

'Haven't you got any work to do, John? We're off to hot yoga now.'

'I'm sure Jenny has things to do – workwise, I mean.' He gives me a stern look.

What can I do? I raise my eyebrows, shrug my shoulders.

'Shouldn't you be revising for your exam, anyway?'

The metal legs of the chair screech on the patio as Barbara stands up in defiance. With a brief inclination of her head, she says to me, 'Coming? We're off.'

'I'm sorry I played so badly,' I say, on the way to our next adventure.

'No worries. At least you don't suffer from dodgy knees like John.'

I've never been to a hot yoga class and, looking back now, I certainly wouldn't recommend it. It's very humid: about thirty-five to forty degrees in an undersized gym bubble. There's soft music playing in the background.

We start with some basic poses, which the instructor calls out by their Indian name, all ending in '-asana' – healthy in name only. I haven't a clue what they all mean, so I just try to ape Barbara's movements as best as I can, sweating profusely in the process. We move dynamically between the different postures. Barbara whispers their English names, too, for my benefit: Cat, Cow, Downward Dog, Plank and so on. Some seem a tad suggestive, and

I wonder whether my hosts used them as foreplay in the early stages of their marriage. Then, the chanting and humming begins.

Around thirty minutes in, we crouch on the floor, sitting back on our heels, heads on the mat. Barbara sighs and shakes her head. 'Stay down – it's a relaxing child's pose.' Unfortunately, my feet go into a spasmed cramp and I have to give up. I'm knackered. Finally, a lukewarm shower restores my normal body temperature.

I apologise over lunch, pretending to suffer from asthma, and finding it difficult to breathe in such high temperatures. She laughs. 'It'll be cooler in the mall.' She talks incessantly, never taking a breath, it seems. Mostly it's free-flowing stream-of-consciousness stuff. I'm tempted to drop a subtle hint, the one Han used to tease me with – *heard of Mrs Dalloway?* – but I hold back in the end. Anyway, I'd only draw a blank.

In the well-earned coffee break with my new shopaholic friend, she talks candidly about her psychotherapy sessions.

'The good thing about my therapist is, she helps me to take a realistic view of my life, makes me see what's achievable and what's not. New York is a brilliant place to be when you're feeling good, any way you slice it, but not so great when you're feeling down. Over the years, she's helped me to solve our monogamy problem, or "the marriage monotony problem". Mark and I are children of the sexual revolution. We thought things would change once we were married, but we've stayed in the omni-fucking mode – instant gratification, without feeling guilty about infidelity – which suits us both. He's a good person at heart, a loving father and a caring husband, believe it or not. But with women he's like a boy with a new toy. He likes the adventure, the first kiss, the first fuck. It's like an adrenaline rush for him: over all too quickly. Then, the whole damn thing starts again from new. But I'm always there for him. I'm his place of safety, playing happy family.'

I listen in awe, feeling a mixture of emotions: confusion, fear, outrage … and even admiration at the way she dissects their life in such a detached way.

'I don't understand how you can still—'

'Live together? You see, everyone has their love story. Most of them fizzle out after a while. And then, for some, the journey begins again, until you give up or settle into a different routine. However, therapy also has a nasty habit of unravelling you. The longer you pull on the thread, the more flaws you find. That's the point when you want to run away from your life or, in my case, dabble in a bit of nose candy, and some other stuff.'

Over dinner for three in a posh restaurant, I feel that I've become an accessory in their loose, guilt-free liaison.

Mark enquires about our exam preparation progress.

'All going swimmingly well,' she lies. 'Have you found Jenny a job yet?'

Damn! I shouldn't have mentioned that when she asked me about my future plans. John's perplexed look says it all. He struggles to regain his composure.

'Sure, we've scanned a couple of promising ads out there. We can have another look later.'

'See, Jenny? The journey begins again.'

His face transforms into an enormous question mark: eyes screwed up, as though he is looking straight into the sunlight. 'What have you two been plotting?'

That evening, I keep the door to the annexe firmly locked. An unpleasant feeling continues to gnaw away at me, but I can't quite pin it down. Something's wrong, and I don't know what it is. Did she tell me all this shit to warn me off? Does she even *have* a therapist? Probably.

I'm sick in the morning, then Mum calls. She's hysterical, and in floods of tears.

'They found Dad in the woods,' she cries.

I'm speechless for a moment. I dread to think what she means. My heart begins to race.

'Are you still there, Jenny? I can't believe he's dead. Where are you now? You have to come home immediately. I need you both here. Where's Hannah?'

She struggles to answer my 'when', 'where' and 'how' questions. I explain that I'm in New York, but will get the next plane home. I have no idea of Hannah's whereabouts; only that she's on holiday in some distant place in South America, where she can't even be reached by phone. She's never there when you need her.

I throw everything into my suitcase without folding any of my clothes. Then I catch a cab to the airport without informing my hosts. The shock of Dad's death lingers throughout the whole flight, swelling into a deep sadness that follows me all the way home. I don't answer John's numerous calls when I'm at my parents' house.

A week later – still no sign of Hannah or Paul – we are celebrating Dad's life, with the help of a few neighbours and Mum and Dad's friends. It's a very different affair to anything I've attended before. I'm glad we're not crowded into some old cemetery chapel, having to endure endless readings. There is no minister of religion running the show, and we don't have to stand and sing and pray, then sit and stand and sing again. It's exactly how Dad wanted it to be. We are all sitting comfortably in a semicircle in my parents' large lounge, listening to a few short speeches given by family and friends, recounting anecdotes, recalling happy memories.

We watch the slideshow I put together: a collection of Dad's photos at different stages of his life. Some of them – the ones of him shooting and carrying a gun in the woods – are met with deathly silence. Others, pictures of both Hannah and I sitting on his lap as girls, evoke an upbeat 'Awww …' reaction.

On a table in front of us, surrounded by a sea of flowers, sits the urn, alongside an oversized black-and-white photograph of Dad. It's Mum's choice – a little too grainy for my liking. He looks benign, yet somewhat pensive.

Later on, we congregate around his grave in the local cemetery, dig the urn into the ground and perform the 'Earth to earth, ashes to ashes …' gestures, while friends keep a tactful distance as they wait their turn. We decided not to scatter the ashes (this *is* against Dad's wishes), but to bury the urn instead. I think I hear Mum whisper a faint, almost imperceptible 'I love you' as she pays her last respects, but I can't be sure.

That evening, when everybody has left, Mum and I both slump into comfortable armchairs, limp with fatigue and weary with the burden of excess emotion. The stillness is oppressive. It's the awkward silence of an incomplete family, full of unacknowledged thoughts and worries about our futures. Even the dogs lie motionless on the rug in front of an empty fireplace, seemingly mourning their beloved master.

'Cup of tea, before I go up to bed?' she asks, as if normal life has already resumed. Next to a number of sympathy cards, I notice last week's paper, bearing the headline 'Blind journalist Hannah Tring and cameraman free hostages from sex slavery'. What on earth is *that* all about? When he sent me a brief text saying Hannah had returned safe and sound, Paul was obviously keeping me in the dark. What sort of adventures has she got herself embroiled in? They sound horrific!

The next morning, I'm sick again, so I go to Mum's local chemist. I recognise the young woman behind the counter with her auburn hair and bright red lipstick – she used to work in the pub. Her white uniform sits oddly on her. I detect a trace of schadenfreude behind the friendly façade as she hands me the pregnancy test.

I read the instructions carefully. The ten-minute waiting time feels like an eternity. Nine and a half minutes ... I look at the windows of the rectangular piece of plastic. The blue line across each is firm and assertive – positive. *No-o-o-o! It can't be. We always used a condom – or did we? Read the instructions again!* 'Hormone pregnancy tests have been shown to be over ninety-nine per cent accurate in lab tests … It is more likely you will get a false negative than a false positive, if there is an error with the test.'

Shit. I'm ninety-nine per cent pregnant! My heart's racing. *What now? Who can I talk to? Who can I trust?*

Chapter 19

Hannah

As I close my laptop to receive my lunch tray from the flight attendant, I notice Paul swiping through pictures of glaciers and people hiking in mountainous terrain.

'Ooh, beautiful! Where's that? May I see?' Paul pulls the table down to receive his meal, then reluctantly passes his phone into my outstretched hand.

'Stunning landscapes! And look at this emerald-coloured lake ... Where *is* this?'

'It's in Chile's National Park, Tierra Patagonia, at the edge of Lake Sarmiento. It's also a UNESCO biosphere reserve.'

'I'd love to go there sometime,' I say enthusiastically, handing his phone back.

'We *are* going there – if you want to, that is.'

'What do you mean?'

'It's all booked. It was meant to be a surprise. All I have to do is press "Pay now". I was hesitant about finalising the booking, because there's one thing you need to agree to first: it's a digital detox resort. There's no TV, phone reception or Wi-Fi in the hotel. All digital devices have to be handed into Reception on arrival. But in their stead, you have emerald lakes, soaring mountains and amazing wildlife. Seems like a pretty decent swap to me.'

I pull him over for a lavish kiss, almost knocking over our lunch trays. I hesitate for a moment, imagining what it would be like having no phone on holiday. News, friends, Twitter, everything's usually just a swipe away. I find it almost impossible not to constantly check my emails or social media. I'm so used to having a smartphone now, but, then again, I'll be with Paul on our first – romantic? – holiday … so I agree.

'Maybe it won't be too bad, unless one of us falls into a crevice, or is kidnapped! What dates have you got in mind? We could …' I leave the sentence hanging in the air in anticipation.

'Well, there's another snag. They only have one slot available. So we'll have to fly tomorrow.'

'What? No, I can't. I need time to get things ready, and we have to file our reports.'

'The flights aren't till late afternoon. We've got all morning to repack our cases, and the reports are almost ready to go, so where's the problem?'

'I have a whole list to check before I go on holiday.'

'OK. So that's it, then,' he says, disheartened, as if the whole thing is now off.

'We agree.' He opens up the booking website on his phone, and is just about to press the 'Cancel' button …

'No, wait,' I panic. 'It's such a lovely idea.'

His finger hovers over the button – then, click.

'Too late.' He switches off his phone. 'All booked now. I'll help you pack,' he says with a wicked smile. His cheese roll drops onto the floor as he gets an elbow in his rib.

'Oh my God, Paul! Have you really? Do you always act on impulse like that?'

The booking confirmation flashes up on his phone. Although I'm used to being sent on assignments at short notice, this one feels very different. I shake my head in stunned disbelief at this daring move. It seems more than an invitation to go on holiday. A declaration of love, perhaps?

'Sometimes spontaneous decisions work out better than well-planned ones,' he says. 'Look, we both deserve time out from war zones; otherwise, we'll crack under the strain. I've always wanted to go to Patagonia, a place at the end of the world, unspoiled by civilisation. My grandfather went there once, as a young man. He walked for days across the Andes from Argentina to Chile's Tierra Patagonia. Setting off into the unknown, he hardly knew what he would find there. This place was like a rumour, he told me. He wasn't even sure whether or not it existed.'

I take another look at Paul's photos – the place looks so idyllic. *I can't believe we'll be there in a couple of days.* Then reality kicks in. I need to finish writing our report before we get back. I push my tray over to Paul's side, retrieve my laptop and start editing.

We arrive back at my flat late in the evening, fully expecting to see Jen. She's been living with me since Hamish threw her out of his flat. I can't wait to hear her news from New York. I hope she's found real love there, but I'm not holding my breath, to be honest.

There's a half-emptied suitcase in the bedroom. *Where's she off to this time? Always in a hurry. Hey, some of the clothes in that case are actually mine!* She always used to steal my clothes when we were teenagers. Old habits seem to die hard.

While Paul goes to collect our takeaway, I unpack and repack my case for our holiday. I'm not even halfway down my checklist. I make him a bed on the sofa, assuming that Jen will be back at some stage and will want to creep into the double bed next to me. Also, I don't want her to assume that Paul and I are an item. Well, we're not ... or are we?

The next day, we make it to the airport just in time. Jen didn't turn up after all. *Never mind, I'll ring her when we get to our resort.* The whole journey takes a lot longer than expected. There are no direct flights, so we change planes in Madrid and Santiago. From there to Balmaceda, which is only halfway to Patagonia, then onwards by hire car.

It's almost midnight when we finally arrive at our destination. Exhausted from the long journey, we sink into a super-sized double bed.

We're in a small, family-run hotel, a retreat set on steep green hills with awe-inspiring views over Lake Sarmiento. Unlike most hotels we stay in on work assignments, there's no self-service breakfast. We have no idea what we're ordering from the breakfast menu, thinking that three out of the five main items will do for both of us: *pastel de choclo*, *espanadas* and *porotos granados*. The large hot meals arrive, more resembling lunch or dinner. With a bit of tasting guesswork, we establish that dish number one consists of minced beef and onions; the second is a kind of *calzone*, filled with cheese and various vegetables; and the last is a bean stew. All very delicious, but a tad unusual for breakfast.

'There is, of course, *desayuno continental* at the bottom of the menu in very small print,' Paul points out during our meal. It's only then that I notice other guests are having a normal breakfast. And, surprisingly enough, a normal and animated conversation. Of course! There are no phones to check, swipe or stare at. I almost forget we had to hand ours in at Reception.

'Shit, I forgot to ring Jen. Do you think they'll let me borrow my phone back just this once?'

'I doubt it. We've all agreed to abide by the rules. We'll contact her when we get back. She'll be OK,' Paul reassures me.

Back in our room, I lie on the bed reading a brochure about the different outdoor activities on offer – horseback riding (where else would you sit to ride a horse!), glacier hiking, mountain biking and catch-and-cook fishing. Paul is next to me on the bed, at full stretch, his hands cupping his head, eyes closed. I'm trying to read his face, his inner thoughts. I want to know if he's serious about our budding relationship. I should know him by now. I do know that beneath his upbeat veneer lies a deep empathy with others and a natural confidence that makes him such a pleasure to spend time with. No matter what environment he finds himself in, he always seems to adapt quickly and smoothly, and that's what makes him such a superb team player and colleague. But, emotionally, he's still a massive unknown to me. True, we've kissed, touched – we've even slept in the same bed – but no more.

I stroke his forehead and press a gentle kiss on his lips. His mouth opens a fraction. I pull back, letting my fingers trace the outline of his lips. He takes my hand and drops little kisses into my palm. I pick up the brochure I've been reading.

'Fancy any of these outdoor activities?' I ask.

'More than any indoor ones? Let's see.' He scans the open page and points. 'That one, catch-and-cook fishing.' He jumps out of bed, grabs a pen from the bedside table and, pretending it's a fishing rod, throws his imaginary line in my direction.

'Look, I think I've caught a big one! Move your head towards me … slowly … a bit more … more. With his right hand, he turns the pretend crank clockwise, reeling in his catch. 'See? There! Just need to descale it and make a real meal of it.'

More kisses follow, but more passionate this time.

'OK. Stop. That's enough,' I laugh, throwing my pillow at him. (I dread to think about his imaginary play had he chosen the horse riding.) Pillows fly to and fro across the room. Laughter and screaming. I hide under the bedclothes to shield myself from further missiles, then he pulls back the duvet, pressing his pillow gently onto my face – no longer than a second or two.

'Got you! Hooked.'

'No,' I scream at the top of my voice, panicking. 'Don't *ever* do that again!'

'What's the matter? It's just a pillow fight. I didn't mean to hurt you. I'm sorry.'

My heart is racing and I gasp for air. I push him away. He waits, then passes me a glass of water from beside the bed.

'What's the matter, Han? I've never seen you like this before.'

'You didn't hurt me, but for a few moments I felt I was reliving an incident from my childhood.'

I then tell him about my childhood trauma, which Dad used to call the 'Jenny thing'.

'It was a few days before Jen's sixteenth birthday. I was ill in bed with pneumonia, coughing and wheezing a lot. I felt breathless even when resting. Jen was furious that she couldn't have her birthday party at home, nor was she allowed to go out to celebrate with her friends in case she spread the contagious illness. On the night of her birthday, she came into my bedroom, disturbed (and annoyed) by my constant cough. Holding a pillow in her hand, she shouted, 'Shut the fuck up.' She then squeezed the pillow over my face, which made me choke. I couldn't breathe and struggled, shouting for help. Dad came in just in time.

'The next day, he sat us down for a serious chat. Jen cried a lot. "Never, ever, tell Mummy," he told us. "We will never talk about it again. Do you understand?" We both swore we wouldn't. The incident was never referred to again. I'm sorry, Paul. I'm still chasing the dragons of my childhood.'

He puts his arms around me and holds me until I stop shaking. The playful humour, the banter, goes in a flash. Instead, sadness lingers for a while. His soft kisses feel soothing, turning the morning's prelude into a different kind of intimacy. But one that could develop ... Should I make the first move? *What's holding you back, Han? That's not like you!* I hear Jen at the back of my mind. My hand moves onto his thigh. Our eyes lock.

'Do you fancy an easy walk in the mountains?' Paul asks innocently. 'It's not on the outdoor activity list, but it's good for the soul.'

I touch up my makeup while Paul gathers a few things into his rucksack, including his Rolleiflex camera. We're off. The early-morning fog has evaporated, but the sky is still coated with a fine white veil that softens the gleam of the sunlight. We walk in silence for an hour, sometimes hand in hand, and on steeper slopes in single file. The magnificent landscape lies all around us. Snow-capped mountaintops with rugged, steep sloping sides, while floating below are little white clouds, looking like puffs of cotton wool. Further down, in the valley, there's Lake Sarmiento, reflecting the mountain panorama in all its emerald glory. We stop to take in the amazing view, breathing in the total silence.

'This is such a special place. Thank you for bringing me here.'

I give Paul a huge hug. Having taken his Rollei out of his rucksack and balanced it on an elevated rock, he rushes back to me, arm round my waist.

'Time for an old-fashioned selfie. Smile!' The self-timer clicks; the shutter opens and closes in quick succession. 'First photo of "us",' he smiles.

As soon as my lips touch his, he puts both arms around me, pulling me closer, deepening the kiss a little. Then, holding my face in the palm of his hands, he looks into my eyes. He takes a deep breath and says simply, but seriously, 'I love you.' His words drop like soft feathers into the warm spring air. I'm lost for words and kiss him passionately –

all tingling and fireworks. I can't hold back my tears any longer. My heart, the most guarded part of me, is opening up, slowly, very slowly – like a spring flower.

'I love you so much. I'm so happy. And I do want to meet your little Freya when we get back.'

'You'll love her,' he says, clearing his throat to get his voice back. We remain in our embrace for a long time, until the silence is broken by a strange humming sound. In the distance, below the snowline of the mountains, we spot a herd of red-furred guanacos – a kind of small llama – grazing in the dense scrubland.

'Aren't they beautiful?' I marvel. 'A whole family. Look at the two little ones! Strange sound they're making, though.' Paul imitates their humming, but one octave lower.

'I think that sound means they've given their consent to our relationship.' He grins.

As we climb higher into the mountains, the weather changes noticeably within minutes. The sky turns into one dark grey flannel, the temperature plummets. Having donned our rain jackets, we decide to go back; too late, however, to escape the lashing shower. We're completely drenched.

Back at the hotel there's clear sky – not a spot of rain. The girl at Reception asks brightly, 'What happened to you two?' Between sneezes, and pauses to wipe the water from our faces and clothes, Paul says, keeping a straight face, 'Well, you see, our ship sank and we had to swim the last five miles.' She hands us the keys without a word.

'I think she's still thinking about that,' Paul chuckles all the way up. 'Do you want to jump into the shower?'

'You go first. I don't mind. I need to wipe off my makeup first.'

I peel off my wet clothes, one by one. Trousers, T-shirt and knickers; then I pile my bra on top and, leaving the wet bundle on the floor, tiptoe starkers into the bathroom.

'Any room for me?' I ask, pressing my nose against the steamed-up shower door.

'For you, always. You must've been reading my mind. Come on in. Sorry, it's a bit of a squeeze.'

I nervously expect him to scan my body 'for approval' as I get in, but his eyes are fixed on mine, full of unspoken love. I step towards him to let the warm water cascade over my hair and back, our bodies now touching. He pulls me closer for a long kiss. I can feel his hands caressing me all over. Mine respond by exploring unknown territory.

'Do you … in the shower?' he asks with a tremor in his voice.

'Bit narrow … I can think of other places I'd rather …'

A little later on, we are lying on the bed on our bath towels, bodies still wet, two lovers with their arms and legs entwined. There's a question in his eyes, and a smile hovers over his lips. He waits. He doesn't ask, but I simply say, 'Yes.' Easing slowly out of the embrace, he begins to kiss my face and body. He travels like a light butterfly, brushing me here and there with a hot, dry, almost burning, kiss. Then, his body becomes weightier, challenging me, pressing me for an answer. I cannot resist the strong current that pulls me in. Bodies arching, floating together on gentle waves. When the moment comes, I let go of my self-control and let him in. Everything's focused on that moment of gratification. Time stands still. Bliss. Heaven. Release.

The room has a great stillness and softness about it. As we lie in each other's arms, it feels as though we are at the centre of a large, slowly turning wheel where there is complete silence, utter radiance and pure sensuality. I arch my neck slightly backwards so that my lips can meet with his. Then the sweet-tasting kisses gently fade. Gradually, we drift away from the centre of the wheel towards its periphery, feeling a touch of friction as we become aware of the birdsong outside.

'I'm famished.' I hear my own feeble voice coming from far away. Neither of us stir. We remain in the same position, spooned together, peaceful and complete.

'Me too,' he croaks.

My throat is dry and feels a little sore. 'I think I'm falling in love,' I whisper into the pillow, as though the words are too fragile to be uttered aloud, 'but I'm still dying of hunger!'

'And me,' he repeats, having regained his voice.

'Which – in love or hungry?'

'Both, I think. We should get up and go downstairs to eat,' he says, not moving.

'You first,' I breathe. 'I can't move just yet.'

We almost miss dinner. There's an odd mixture of guests from all walks of life in our retreat – a teacher, a health club manager, a firefighter, an event coordinator, a pilot, a physio and a surgeon – all of us working in high-stress jobs. As we enter the restaurant, Sophie the physio and schoolteacher Bernie invite us latecomers to join them. As new arrivals, we're interested to find out how they're coping with digital detox, having been here for almost a week. They're both candid about their experience and their reasons for being here.

'I hated the first couple of days,' Sophie admits. 'I felt completely out of my comfort zone, cut off from my friends, colleagues and all social media. Every morning, for the first three days, my hand automatically went to the bedside table to check my nonexistent phone.'

'And *I* thought there'd be at least a telly here for me to watch some of the important football fixtures. I had the whole schedule for this week's Championships on my phone. So it was a definite thumbs-down from me, as well,' Bernie adds.

'And now?' Paul asks.

'Well, the outdoor life is amazing here. We've been on several boat trips, had a few riding lessons and done some mountain biking. Really great fun. So you forget about the phone after a while. Cheers – at least the alcohol is flowing!' We all clink glasses.

'We've met some fascinating people here, haven't we, Bernie? And had the most amazing, really deep conversations. I think it's all about balance, because there's lots of positives about the technology we have today … I just think it's healthy to find the right balance in life. Being on social media … it's often a kind of echo chamber. You connect with people who are more or less like you, have the same interests, follow the same people online. But it closes your mind. Being here, in the real world, opens it up again.'

Sophie pauses and takes another sip of orange juice. 'You know what I found most shocking? I hadn't read a single book in three years. And I was like, "Wow, how did that happen?" Then I realised it was all about my attention span. My focus had gone,' she says.

'I think there's a lesson in this. I realised that neither of us can even watch a movie without checking social media ... and yet I confiscate my students' mobile phones if they bring them into the classroom. Fuck multitasking! Then, when they use their mobiles outside the classroom, there's all this bullying and sexting. It's so stressful to deal with it on a daily basis. I don't have an answer—'

'I'm so sorry,' Sophie interrupts. 'We've been hogging the conversation long enough. What about you two, then? What made you choose this place?'

'Paul persuaded me to take some time out. We both need the opportunity to completely switch off, having worked together for four years in war zones. And I'm glad he did. You begin to see different sides of the person you think you know.'

'That's right. We've only just discovered each other. Literally,' Paul adds, squeezing my hand under the table. Sophie smiles. Bernie looks nonplussed.

'Working in a war zone. Wow – how do you cope with that level of stress?' Sophie wants to know.

'Don't!' I glance at Paul, shaking my head. 'He gave a rude answer to that same question at a recent press conference.'

'But an honest one,' he pings back. 'A little drink, now and then, does indeed help. But we also talk a lot ... Good old-fashioned conversation, face-to-face.'

'And I write a detailed diary after the official reports, which helps me to digest things. But this here is a piece of undiscovered world for me. I love this kind of escape, and being together for the first time without a work assignment feels extra-special.'

'It's difficult to describe being in this peaceful place with Hannah, without fearing for our lives. We feel relaxed and connected to the world like never before.' He pauses, looking around at the other guests, who seem to be listening in to our conversation. 'Isn't it bizarre, folks, that this super-connected digital world we live in can lead to us all feeling more disconnected than ever?' There's respectful applause all around.

Over the next few days, we try out all the outdoor activities, sometimes in the company of other guests, sometimes on our own. Occasionally, however, the mornings just slip through the sheets and we miss breakfast.

'Life's too precious to fritter it away on social media,' Akilah, the surgeon, tells us on our glacier hiking trip. 'People page me all the time in the hospital, when I'm on call, and sometimes even after work, so I don't want to hear any more bleeping when I finally get some rest at home. I hope my children will come here one day. I find it quite sad that I can't have a proper conversation without them constantly reacting to pings on their phone like Pavlov's conditioned dogs.'

At times, the conversation takes on a rather personal and philosophical angle. We agree with Akilah that, in jobs like his and ours, it's difficult to maintain a steady and close relationship.

'This place makes you rethink your priorities in life,' Paul says. 'There'll be some hard decisions to make when we get back home.'

'Yes, for years I've always wanted to be that superhero female journalist, show the men we can be just as good, if not better. But, at the same time, I wanted to have a home with flowers and the smell of a Sunday roast – lamb, rosemary and fresh thyme. But it hasn't happened ...'

'I'll cook for you, Han. And, regarding your reputation as an outstanding war correspondent, you don't need to prove that any more.'

'You two seem to have found love out here,' Akilah says empathetically, as we stop for a snack at the bottom of a slippery, icy slope. 'I envy you. Hold on to your relationship, nourish it, and don't let it slip away.'

Chapter 20

Hannah

I'm struggling. My world has irreversibly changed again. I've hardly slept or eaten for the last two days. I'm on my own during the day, back in my little black hole, despite the fact that I can see again. There's so much I still wanted to show Dad, talk to him about, make him feel proud of me for. And now he's gone forever. Now I fall back on my oldest coping strategy – my diary.

22 May 2013
11 a.m.
Dad told me on my last visit home, 'Be somewhere else when the time comes.' I can't help thinking that I should have been there for him, to help him die a better death. If there is such a thing. When I saw that headline in his hunting magazine, 'Shooting Time', it didn't cross my mind that's what he had planned. I saw him go from a robust, happy family man to a frail old boy, resigned to his fate, making a dismissive gesture at my worried face. It was like he'd merely been dealt a bad hand at cards. Did I say the wrong thing when he'd asked me, 'Chemo, or just have some fun on the way out?' I now realise the tragic irony in my answer: 'I think there's some hunting spirit in the old man still.'

I wanted you to be proud of me, Dad. Your opinion was always the thing that mattered to me. The standards I set myself were yours. And now? I love you, Dad. I wish you could have met Paul. You would have really liked him. We may have a family together one day. You know what a friendly surgeon said to us on holiday? 'Hold on to your relationship, nourish it, and don't let it slip away.'

I told Paul that I wouldn't be good company for a while, so he's half-heartedly gone back to his house to sort out things with Sylvie. Also, with Jen still living with me, it would be a bit crowded in my small flat. She's been very supportive, and seems to have dealt with Dad's passing much better than I have. It's almost like she's relieved not to have to compete with me for his love any more.

But she has other things on her mind now, of course. Her morning sickness has been going on for weeks, and she's no idea whether to go ahead with the pregnancy, desperately wondering when it could have happened, hoping it's Hamish's. Even if it is, I fear the relationship is beyond reconciliation.

Early evening. Jen's back from work. She glances at the half-empty wine bottle on the coffee table, eyebrows raised. Maybe it's just my imagination, but I think I can already detect a small bump. I can't stop staring at it. She straightens out her jumper as though she's noticed my gaze.

'Oh, why not! It's still early days.' She sighs, grabs the bottle and returns with a half-glass of red.

'It's all about choices now. Important ones.' I open the conversation.

'Bad ones, in my case. Past *and* future.' She empties her glass in one slug.

'Are you going to keep it? And whose is it, do you think?'

'I don't know, Han. Mark and I have always been careful, I swear. But I came off the pill immediately after that awful row with Hamish, so there's a slight chance—'

'He always wanted a child with you, Jen. And you went along with all that IVF stuff, knowing full well it couldn't happen while you were on the pill. And now it has. How ironic is that? Things could have been so different for you two.'

'Strange, isn't it? Mum and Dad always thought that I'd be their best bet for a grandchild. Now look at *you!*' She bends forward to touch my ring. 'Engaged – you and Paul. Maybe more of a chance now?'

'By the way, I went to Hamish's leaving do a few months back. We've kept in touch since he went to Washington. As far as I can tell from the odd email, there's no new love on the horizon yet. So, you never know …'

As my sentence trails off, her face softens into a brief smile. Running a nervous hand through her hair, she tells me she couldn't, nor does she intend to, manage the rest of her life alone, especially not as a single mum. She shifts uneasily in her chair for a moment, then changes the subject.

'Now, tell me what happened to you in Bogotá.' All of a sudden, she seems calm and curious.

'Dinner first – it's in the oven.'

The account of my ordeal is rather matter-of-fact, more like a police report, skimming over the harrowing details, a much-sanitised version of my emotions at the time.

This time, there is no sisterly accusation of 'more bravado than bravery'. And for me there's no appetite to relive the emotional upheaval. I've had my fair share these past months. Maybe I should resume my PTSD therapy ...

Our chat makes me think about starting a family. Raising a child is such a huge responsibility. I'd be making a 24/7, long-term commitment to provide physical and emotional support to the life we'd be bringing into the world, a world of constant conflicts. As would Jen, if she goes ahead. Then there's a vital question: do we both have the necessary support network to help us juggle job and baby? Would I be ready for it, with all my emotional baggage and addictions?

I steer the conversation back to her pregnancy.

'If you knew for certain it was Hamish's, would you want to go ahead?' I begin cautiously. She puts her knife and fork down to consider the answer.

'It depends on his reaction to the news. And, of course, whether there's any chance of getting back together. I really don't know. But, then again, it should be my decision, regardless of what he does or doesn't want. What do *you* think? And how about you and Paul? Does he want a family with you?'

'I think there's a slim chance Hamish might come round eventually, if he knew for certain the baby is his. I know Paul definitely wants kids, and a sibling for little Freya. It's me who's undecided. I carry a lot of baggage, Jen.' I pour myself another glass of red. 'You know I've struggled for years. I battle with drink, and with food. It's difficult to escape the culture we're immersed in, a culture that's obsessed with youth and bodily perfection. Just look around you – TV, magazines, social media. At 30, I find myself engaged in a hopeless quest to make my stomach appear like it was when I was 18. It's a losing battle, I tell you, and I'm so tired of fighting this war against myself.'

'Wow, that's quite a confession! I get the alcohol and the food, but not the hankering after bodily perfection. You're tall and slim, so definitely no complaints in that department.'

'There's one more "confession", if you want to call it that. Your famous war reporter – the one who's on telly all the time – used to think she wanted to be in the limelight, have noise and people around her. What she really needed was the opposite: moments of peaceful, relaxing silence; silence you can breathe in, silence that makes you feel whole again. I experienced that for the first time on our Patagonian holiday.'

'You mean that detox escape thing?'

'Yes. No need to be so scathing. You should try it one day. It makes you reassess what's important in life.'

Her phone buzzes on the table. She leans forward to answer it. But, when she sees the caller's name, she switches it off.

'That's exactly what I mean. You can't resist for a minute, even while we're talking about stuff that matters. Is Mark still stalking you?'

She nods sheepishly.

'Do you think I should try to go back to the *Observer*? I could work from home a lot more, should I have a child. I'm tired of jetting off to different conflict zones all the time, Han. Now Eric wants me to fly out to Damascus again next week, to interview a former government scientist who claims the Syrian government is employing chemical weapons. I think he'd be pleased to have you back full-time.'

'Paul and I have decided to stay freelance, make time for each other and also do some writing – or, in his case, start up a photography studio. You have to decide for yourself which job makes you feel most comfortable.'

We leave it at that. There will be other tough decisions for her, and more misery to come, when I tell her that Paul and I are looking for a house and I'll soon be selling the flat.

A week later, I have my first appointment with the therapist, the one who treated me when I lost my sight. All I remember is his quiet, gentle voice and an unsuccessful attempt at eye movement desensitisation, which I hated. Dr Roberts is a tall, bespectacled slim man, wearing a blue cardigan over his white shirt and tie. He's interested to hear about the stem cell treatment in Berlin and, after a preliminary discussion, suggests taking me back to the trauma incident that initially caused my sight loss. We spend the next two sessions retracing my steps: from the explosion in Haswiyeh to the devastating experience of waking up blind in hospital, followed by the protracted struggle to adapt to a life in a world without light. When we explore how my blindness has affected my relationships, he asks me about Rob, and then Paul.

'You said Paul always travelled with you and was there when the young boy blew himself up. How do you think it affected him? And did this also change your relationship with him?'

'He was badly hurt, too. He came to see me in hospital as soon as he could, but felt guilty that he'd been unable to protect me. He's a soldier-turned-war-photographer. He's always been there for me; my blindness didn't affect our relationship at all. And now,' I lean back in my chair and smile, 'now, we've become lovers.'

Dr Roberts stops taking notes for a few moments. Then he makes a rather curious suggestion: 'With your permission – and Paul's, too, of course – I would like to involve you both in a role play in our next session.' He explains that, with the help of 'significant others' (though I'm not sure what he means by that), he'd like us to act out the trauma scene and change the outcome.

It turns out to be a heart-wrenching exercise. We are role-playing the original trauma, the entire scene: a mother and her teenage son, both actors, standing a few steps away. She flings her arms round the boy and pleads, 'No shoot, please – we get vest off him.' I turn round to the armoured vehicle, frantically waving my arms, signalling to the soldiers not to shoot. Paul is right behind me, filming. My adrenaline kicks in as if I'm right back in Haswiyeh.

'Stop right there,' Dr Roberts intervenes. 'Paul, what would you like to do now?'

Paul spontaneously rugby-tackles me to the ground, covering my body with his to protect me. There's a minute's silence as we lie motionless on the floor. I'm still in shock when we get up. My heart's pounding like mad. He wraps his arms around me and sobs.

'That's what I *should* have done, my love. And I failed. I'll never fail you again.'

The actors, Paul and I link arms, and we form a huddle.

A little later, when the actors have left, we relive our emotions, both feeling exhausted but somehow strangely relieved. We decide to carry on with joint sessions for a while.

Paul is ready to move in with me. He and Sylvie need to decide whether to put their house on the market. I visit Mum a couple of times over the next few weeks. The house seems so lifeless now. There're no welcoming barks from Angus and Roy any more; they died soon after Dad did. As expected, Mum's not in a good place. The only time she smiles is when she walks past the sea of condolence cards, displayed on every available surface: sideboards, windowsills, bookshelves, other nooks and crannies. Reading the odd one from a close friend out loud – with expression, as though she's talking to a child – brings her great solace.

'I can't cope with being on my own, Hannah. There's all this financial stuff … Shares, insurance, bills. Dad always used to look after that side of things.'

She can't even remember whether the four-by-four takes petrol or diesel. Has she never tanked the car up? Hard to believe that, for them, life's chores got divided up into pink and blue. How sexist is that? I help her with the urgent paperwork – will, grant of probate, pension … But she'll have to learn some of the basic tasks someday soon. *Thanks, Dad.*

'And I don't want to stay in this house. It's full of memories of a past life,' she carries on. 'Just shove me into an old people's home, and then either you or your sister can live here.' She shuffles off into the kitchen to make herself a hot milky drink for the night, not expecting a response.

When Mum has gone to bed, I find myself walking through the house, imagining what it would be like to live here with Paul. I allocate my bedroom and Jen's to 'our' children, make plans for an en-suite bathroom and construct an imaginary conservatory. Instead of Dad's scramble track, we would have a couple of horses in the empty fields. But what about Mum? We could easily convert the large outbuilding into a self-contained flat. She'd be happy to potter around in the garden, and would love spending time with little Freya. Later on, she might even have another grandchild to look after. But, most importantly, she'd still feel part of the family. I'm excited. I need to talk to Paul. I grab a chocolate bar and dial his number.

'Hi. Can you talk? You on your own?'

'Yes to both, but it would be easier to chat once you've finished your mouthful,' he laughs. 'Well, in the meantime, I can tell you *my* news. The house is on the market and we've already had a few offers. Sylvie's moved in with her mum while she's flat-hunting, and Freya is with me this week. Sadly, little one is the only woman in my life at the moment. I miss you.'

'Me too. Sorry, bad habit – I've finished eating now. That's great news about the house, though. How about buying another one with me?'

'It sounds like you're making plans for us. Are you house-hunting already? Well, as long as I'm involved, I'm happy to check anything out. Have you got any pictures?'

'I'm sending some through right now.'

'Wow! That's a bit grand. I think even half of it would be out of my price range, I'm afraid.'

'But do you like it? Can you see yourself living there – I mean, us living there?'

'Yes, of course. But, as I said—'

'Well, it's my parents' house, Paul, and half of it already belongs to me and Jen. Dad left it to us in his will. Mum doesn't want to live in the house any more, but we could move her into the outbuilding, refurbish it for her … if you don't mind.'

'Sounds amazing. And, if it's a case of like mother, like daughter, I have no objections. What about Jen?'

'She'll need to stay in London anyway. It would be too far for her to commute. She can stay in my London flat. Do you think you could come down to Chalfont pronto, to see the house, help me with engagement party preparations?

Sunday 21 July. Celebration time! By midday the sun is beating down strongly from a clear blue sky. Little Freya, balloon in hand, is dashing in and out of the marquee's arched doors. She is being chased by Paul, who seems slightly out of puff.

'Chase me, chase me, Daddy! More!' she shouts, seeking refuge in my arms each time he gets too close to her. I'm so happy she's warmed to me so quickly in the short time she and Paul have been staying here. She's such a little sweetie. Mum and Jen are busy preparing canapés, salads, dessert, and various other bits and pieces, while the hog roast people are setting up their equipment on the patio under strings of garlands and colourful lanterns. I'm decorating the trestle tables with pretty runners, a fruit bowl on each filled with pineapple, papayas, mangoes and pomegranates, topped with a bunch of grapes.

Eric and a couple of friends from work arrive early, having volunteered to run the bar and prepare a range of exotic-sounding cocktails. He's apparently quite a connoisseur of alcoholic beverages. I always thought he had a bit of a drinker's nose!

Family and friends arrive in dribs and drabs throughout the afternoon and mill around in the garden. I drag Mum away from the kitchen in order to introduce her to our guests.

'Hi everybody, and welcome. Can I quickly go round and introduce you. This is my mum, who's been helping us tirelessly with all the preparations. Thank you, Mum. On my left is my boss and cocktail expert, Eric. And next to him are Susan and Ron, friends and colleagues from work. You all know Jen over there, chatting away to her friends Cathy and Emily, and the guy with our little Freya on his shoulders is my fiancé, Paul. Thank you all so much for coming. Oh, and do ask Eric to make you one of his awesome concoctions. Enjoy!'

Two more arrivals are strolling down the garden path. Jen spots them first and, with a huge smile on her face, rushes to greet them. Heads are turning. It's Hamish and …? Jen flings her arms around him.

'Hello you!'

'How *are* you?' He gives her a squeeze, kissing her on both cheeks. The young woman next to him, 20-ish, blonde curly hair and a doll-like face with an upturned nose, steps forward.

'Jenny! I have heard so much about you. So lovely to meet you at last.' She holds out her hand. 'I'm Lorrie, Hamish's fiancée. I've been—'

Jen freezes.

'I'm sorry. I meant to tell—' Hamish interjects.

'Well, she beat you to it,' Jen snaps and, turning to Lorrie, 'One piece of advice, dear. Be careful with your phone. He can delve into all your secrets.'

'Let's get you all a drink.' Paul diffuses the embarrassing situation. 'Come along to the bar with me.' I link arms with him. 'Who are they?' he whispers. 'By the way, you look stunning.'

'Thanks, you don't look too bad yourself. That's Hamish, my sister's ex, who now works in Washington. I had no idea about his companion, absolutely none.'

Jen edges closer to us.

'No new love on the horizon, you told me,' she says accusingly.

'Honestly, I had no idea, Jen. And I can't imagine why he wanted to bring her here.'

'To spite me. What other motive is there?'

'You'll need to talk to him on your own, tell him about the baby.'

It's late afternoon and the party is in full swing. More guests arrive with young children, who try their hand at croquet on the lawn. The adults are chatting away in small groups, cocktail glasses in hand. A delicious hog roast smell wafts towards us. Adele's 'Turning Tables' is playing in the background. *Did Jen put this on?*

Seeing that Freya can't quite manage the croquet mallet – she pushes the ball through the hoops with her hand – I suggest a different game entirely.

'Who wants to play blind man's buff?'

'Me', 'Me', 'Me.' Several hands go up at the same time. Hamish and Lorrie watch me blindfold one of the boys. I explain the rules to the children and point out to little Freya that she can briefly touch the blindfolded boy, but mustn't get caught by him.

There's raucous laughter and screaming. The kids buzz around and tease the blindfolded boy, who eventually catches one of the others. Lorrie seems to be amused by the whole spectacle.

'Would you like to have a go, Lorrie?' I ask.

'Yeah. It's a such a cute game.'

I hand Hamish the scarf to blindfold her. As soon as the game begins, I take him to one side.

'Jen would like a word with you in private. She's over there in the marquee.'

Lorrie eventually manages to catch one of the children. I ask one of the parents to take over from me to supervise the game while I chat to her.

'So, how long have you known Hamish?'

'We've been together for nearly two months now. We met on a dating app. Well, everybody does these days, don't they? There's so much more choice. I fell in love with his profile. He's so clever, all this tech stuff. And I love his cute Scottish accent. It *is* Scottish, isn't it?'

'Wow. Two months already. And when's the big day?'

'Early next year. We haven't fixed a date yet, but we're getting married on the beach in the Bahamas, in Great Exuma.'

'That's nice. I can see you're getting on very well.'

'We are, but do you know what scares me most? How much he talks about your sister. I have absolutely no idea how I can ever live up to her.'

'Well, let's drink to that. I mean, to your future with Hamish.'

I walk her quickly to the bar, to lose her. At a distance, I spot Jen and Hamish sitting next to each other under one of the weeping willows. How is he reacting to her news? I imagine there'll be conflicting sensations of warmth and coolness. He removes his hand from hers when he sees me walking past. I follow my ears and find Paul with Eric, Susan and Ron, who are all erupting into loud laughter – laughter with an hysterical edge – which continues as I approach them.

'That's newsworthy indeed, a real tourist attraction!' Eric tells me, still holding his belly. 'Lorrie has told everybody about her wedding plans in the Bahamas. Paul's been there, and says its biggest attraction is that you can swim with pigs in the sea!' He creases up again. 'She'll be amongst friends, then!'

'Ssh! She might hear you,' I say, but I do find it difficult to stifle my laughter.

Jen brings round a selection of canapés on a silver tray. They look delicious. I pick one with aubergine and goat's cheese.

'Have you told him yet?' I ask. She nods, and wells up immediately. I take her to one side.

'When I said I had proof that it's his and definitely not John's, he said, "I'll be the best father I can possibly be. There's so much more I want to talk to you about."'

'And *do* you have proof now?'

'Yes, Mark texted me that it can't possibly be his – he's had the snip.'

'I had a brief chat with Lorrie. Apparently, he talks about you all the time. She's dead scared she can't live up to you. So, don't give up on him. Come on – let's go grab a hog roast. I'm starving.'

The fading evening sun casts a warm rosy tint across the sky. In the shadow of the marquee, there's lively dinner chatter, the clinking of glasses and the occasional 'Speech, speech' request from one of the guests, which go unanswered. The lanterns dance in the light breeze to the slow rhythm of jazz music.

Freya gets down from the dinner table to take a closer look at the little fairy lights decorating the surrounding tree trunks. Paul calls out to her.

'Would you like to help Daddy fetch a present for Hannah?'

As she rushes back to him, he whispers something in her ear. He stands up with her on his shoulders and calls for attention.

'Hannah sometimes refers to me as a man of few words, and I certainly don't wish to prove her wrong, tonight of all nights. I admit that, compared to a woman who can talk and write at the same time at breakneck speed, I'm a rather poor wordsmith. I tend to get my message across better in picture form. That's why we complement each other so well. I'd like to say this, though. Not many people get a second chance at love in their life. We both did. Neither of us wanted to settle for second best, and I have no intention of letting you slip away, Hannah. So I'd like to propose a toast to the one I love with all my heart. To Hannah!'

'To Hannah!' Everyone raises their glass.

'Can we get the present now, Daddy?'

A few minutes later, Paul and Freya return, each holding an adorable black Labrador puppy in their arms.

'Hannah, I'll have this one and you can play with Daddy's.'

I don't know whether to laugh at her innocent words or cry with joy.

'They are beautiful! Thank you so much. I really don't know what to say. For once, I am speechless.'

The rest of the evening descends into utter joyful chaos, with the puppies predictably stealing the show. When we've finally taken Freya to bed and the puppies into Dad's snug, Paul and I join the others on the terrace for a slow dance to Ella Fitzgerald's 'Summertime' and plenty more great songs.

I wake up early on Monday morning to the ping of Eric's text: 'Yanukovych's government has suspended trade with the EU, opting for closer ties with Moscow, triggering mass anti-government rallies in Kyiv. Can you both go?'

Should we go? The answer is lying right next to me. The two of them – Paul with one arm around little Freya, me tucked in snugly under the other – both breathing in deep, regular, peaceful breaths.

About the Author

Reinhard Tenberg is the author of *My Parents' Darkroom – Developing the Past*, which was shortlisted at the 2021 Next Generation Indie Book Awards for Historical Fiction.

Other works include:
Taking Time Out (2015), a novel

Poetry Soup – A Collection of Personal Poetry, illustrated by John Tordoff (2018)

What the Country Needs – Personal and Political Poems, illustrated by John Tordoff (2021)

Reinhard is a volunteer at Cam Sight, an independent charity supporting people of all ages living with low vision and blindness across Cambridgeshire.